A WOMAN COMPLETE

TB MARKINSON

Published by T. B. Markinson

Visit T. B. Markinson's official website at lesbianromancesbytbm.com for the latest news, book details, and other information.

Copyright © T. B. Markinson, 2020

Cover Design by Erin Dameron-Hill / EDHGraphics

Edited by Kelly Hashway

This book is copyrighted and licensed for your personal enjoyment only. All rights reserved. No part of this publication may be reproduced, stored in a retrieval system, or transmitted in any forms or by any means without the prior permission of the copyright owner. The moral rights of the author have been asserted.

This book is a work of fiction. Names, characters, businesses, places, events, and incidents are the product of the author's imagination or are used fictitiously. Any resemblance to actual persons, living or dead, events, or locales is entirely coincidental.

CHAPTER ONE

A WOMAN POINTED A GUN AT ME, BUT I COULDN'T SEE who it was. I shook my head, trying to clear my vision. After blinking several times, my mom became vivid in the fog. But that couldn't be. She was dead. Wasn't she? I remembered the funeral, but other details blurred and bounced back and forth in my brain.

I looked back to where my mom stood. But she wasn't there. In her place stood Tie, my deceased sister-in-law, in a jolly pink dress.

And, she was gripping a knife, not a gun.

I'd seen Tie in that dress before. Yes, when I met her for the first time. She wore pink to visit my mother in the hospital. Wait, that memory dislodged another. Mother didn't like Tie. Why were they working together? To threaten me or worse?

Again, I shook my head, trying to make sense of everything.

When the fog cleared some, Mcg, my ex, wielded the knife. Her green eyes darkening with evil delight. I didn't want to stare into them, but I couldn't redirect my gaze.

Behind me were voices, at least two different ones, but I couldn't move my body to turn to the source. I couldn't do anything. I wanted to scream for help, but my mouth refused to open, my vocal cords thick in my throat, completely silenced.

Something covered my face, and I couldn't breathe.

The chatter grew louder, and now I made out the three distinct voices of my mom, Tie, and Meg. Something poked me. It hurt. Was it the knife? Fingers? I reached for the spot where the pain emanated from, and a warm liquid soaked my fingers. Without looking, I knew it was blood.

"W-why?" I stammered.

They burst into laughter.

There was a loud noise, and something slammed into my gut—

I jerked awake, and the typical panic after these dreams started with rapid but useless breaths. My heart thudded loudly in my ears. *Thump. Thump. Thump.*

My skin went cold. Then hot. Then cold. Tears formed in the corners of my eyes.

I wiped them away on my pillow, stifling my sobs, curling into the fetal position.

Sucking in a deep breath, I thought, *Hold it the fuck together, Lizzie. Everyone needs you to be the adult right now. So, fucking adult.* A woman with four kids didn't have the time to give into a private pity party because of a nightmare. That was all it was. Nothing to fear. I had real concerns.

My brother was in prison.

My wife was recovering from a C-section.

My father was fighting to save his company.

This was how I woke most mornings at 3:00 a.m., nearly on the dot. Jesus, even my nightmares were just as anal as I was about keeping to a schedule. This almost made me laugh, but I still struggled to breathe, as if feeling… whatever they used to cover my head. A pillow? No, it was something else in the dream because it wrapped around my head, tightening… Was it a plastic bag? Did I really want to know?

To get my brain to settle, I tried to pinpoint the first episode. Weeks? Months? Would this be my new normal?

Clearly, all of the above factors played into my fragile state of mind, but I was slowly realizing they weren't the sole reason. Forcing myself to stay awake in the predawn hours, because I was afraid to sleep, gave me much time to ponder the shitstorm some would call my life. As much as I hated admitting it, the thought of failing roused the panic inside like a witch stirring her cauldron, adding eye of this, toe of that, to curse me with every possible obstacle to bring me, Lizzie Petrie, down.

I was in the crosshairs of fate, and the bitch had my number.

I was fucking terrified.

And alone.

During my three decades on this planet, I'd battled so much. An uncaring and abusive mother. An alcoholic and blackmailing ex. A vindictive sister-in-law. Graves' disease. A self-destructive streak.

I foolishly believed all of these obstacles I'd conquered had prepared me for anything that would come my way. That I had character oozing from every pore. I'd stared into the darkness and survived.

Now, though, staring into yet another pitfall, I felt defenseless and weak and was taking hits from all sides.

God, it was exhausting constantly fighting to keep my head above water.

The nightmares, panic attacks, and feeling like the weakest individual walking the planet was happening at the worst possible time because now I needed to dig deep for a fight that would determine not solely my future but that of my four children and wife.

It didn't help that one thought rolled around in my head: my mother would be tickled pink seeing me fall apart. Why had she hated me so much? More importantly, why did I let her get to me even though she'd died many years ago?

I was nearing middle age and still had gargantuan mommy issues. How could a person with a PhD in history be so fucking irrational? A lot of people had terrible mothers. Did they all fall apart? Even if they did, I was supposed to be better. While many called me clueless, that was far from reality. At least, that was what I thought. Yeah, common sense wasn't my strength, and it wasn't advisable to ask me for directions or to calculate a tip.

Taking those two black marks into account, I still believed I had a superpower. Simply put, I was a determined son of a bitch when it came to success. I thrived from pushing myself to the brink. It was a game I played. Dancing on the line many would believe to be too much pressure and permanently break me. Too many duties. An insane workload. Not enough time in the day.

Straddling the line had never broken me before. Sure, it wasn't always pleasant, but I continually beat the odds because I lived for checking boxes on my path to success and a happy life. Tenured professor: affirmative! TV commentator: yep! Most liked history professor: two-years running! Married: fuck yeah. Beautiful kids: tick, tick, tick, and tick.

Each year, I mapped out my goals, adding more here and there. If I published two peer-reviewed journal articles, I'd set the following year's goal at three. I liked to increase my speaking events at universities across the country. Now that I published opinion pieces on *Matthews Daily Dish*, I wanted to increase that output from two a month to four.

There was always something more I wanted to do. To accomplish what many would deem as way too ambitious. And when I did, I didn't scream from the rooftops. No, I played it down, knowing full well I could do more. Wanted to do more. I couldn't be stopped.

Until...

I rolled onto my side, facing my sound-asleep wife. She'd want me to open up to her. After almost losing her before we got married by not letting her in, I had tried to be more transparent. But how could I tell her, "Honey, I think I'm about to crash and burn in every aspect in my life? Sorry about that. Do I need to pick up diapers on my way home?"

A sound on one of the baby monitors nabbed my attention, and I did what I do best. I went into action.

* * *

A HANDFUL OF HOURS LATER, IN THE KITCHEN, I PUT the kettle on. If I needed to plot my very survival, I needed another cup of Earl Grey. Strong. Was there a way to insert the liquid straight into my veins?

My youngest son, in his bouncy chair, made a grunting type of sound. I smiled at Calvin. "Hey there, Cal. You want a cuddle? I sure could use one." Scooping him up into my arms, I held him close to my torso, his tiny body fitting perfectly. He settled in his determined way. His older brother had a quiet but serious air about him. Calvin was also quiet, but I sensed a scheming mind behind his silence. He was such a Petrie, even though we'd used Sarah's egg. "You're going to cause your mommies many headaches, aren't you?"

He seemed to sigh, as if saying he didn't have time to explain to me how I wasn't his match. It made me laugh and squirm. Two weeks old and he already knew how to play me, albeit his powers ebbed and flowed. He yawned and closed his little eyes. Not wanting to wake him, I bobbed, while turning the pages of *The New York Times*.

The kettle started to whistle, so I killed the flame and made myself the much-needed tea. While the steam billowed from the cup, I continued to peruse the paper spread out on the granite island, still bouncing on my feet for Calvin.

An article about a Jewish woman, whose father was killed in a death camp, falling in love with a Nazi perked my interest. She had worked for a company that hadn't been known to support Hitler. My eyes skimmed for the pertinent details, but I couldn't focus on the words like I used to. I had a knack for burying myself knee-deep in work to keep my mind from jumping from one thought to another like a frog hopping across lily pads. It was one of my methods for how I battled the darkness within me, but now that my walls were tottering, I struggled with staying focused on the simplest of tasks, like reading a news article.

Calvin made snuffling sounds that I'd learned meant he wasn't happy and was on the verge of a full-on meltdown. There were times when he broke his vow of silence, and they were impressive.

"You getting grumpy being held?" I asked the newest addition to the family, not expecting a verbal answer.

He wiggled about in my arms. I kissed the top of his head, carefully placed him back into his bouncy chair, and kicked on the power, immediately appeasing him. While he loved me rocking him in my arms, he much preferred the smoother movement of his chair.

"You take after your sister Ollie, wanting to be independent and pampered." I gently tweaked his tiny nose.

Calvin regarded me with deep chocolate brown eyes, much like my wife's color.

"Yeah, it's Ollie he takes after, not you."

I glanced up at Maddie, the self-proclaimed best aunt on the planet, who'd just entered the kitchen via the dining room door.

"Why am I the reason for everyone's bad faults?" I placed a hand over my chest.

Maddie shook what looked to be a newly purchased stuffed sloth for Calvin's entertainment, which he ignored in his Cal-like way. "It's the Petrie curse."

"Tell me about it." My mind wandered back to the article and the feelings it stirred, but I pushed them aside. The stain of connections. "What brings you by so early?" I glanced at the clock on the microwave. "Oh, it's after ten." How had seven hours flown by since the nightmare? Not to mention, I'd barely accomplished anything for the day.

"Still early in some circles." Maddie gave up trying to engage Calvin with the stuffed animal. The only thing he ever seemed interested in was the rocking motion of the chair.

"The ones without kids. Would you like some coffee?" Without waiting for an answer, I wheeled about in search of the coffee to start the process. I'd been on hosting duties as of late, and my organizational skills in the kitchen were seriously lacking.

"You okay? You seem a bit off." Maddie added, "For you."

I forced a chuckle. "You try not sleeping for two weeks and see how on task you are."

"Are you keeping your mommies up all night?" Maddie addressed Calvin, who remained silent. "He's even more serious than Fred. Is that worrisome?"

"I think it's way too early to ascribe traits to a newborn." I didn't blab I'd been doing the same.

"You just said he's like Ollie." Maddie didn't wait for an explanation and started using baby talk to get Calvin to engage.

"Aha!" I found the coffee grounds behind the toaster, scooped heaping spoonfuls into the reusable filter, and filled the water reservoir to the ten-cup line, knowing it'd only really make six decent cups. Rose and Troy were expected at the house any minute, and that would get me through two rounds before having to brew a new pot. Or I hoped so.

"Where's Sarah?" Maddie asked.

"Hopefully getting some rest on the couch in the library after feeding Calvin around seven. She didn't sleep well, and she's not a fan of the stairs these days. Luckily, the twins and Demi stayed with Rose and Troy last night." I sipped my double-bagged Earl Grey with a generous amount of raw honey from my *Got History* mug.

"How's she feeling?" Maddie sat on one of the barstools.

"I think the soreness from the cesarean is subsiding."

Calvin fussed and balled up both fists, gnawing on one.

"I think the youngest Petrie is hungry. Do we have to wake Sarah?" Maddie looked to me somewhat perplexed, knowing Sarah was struggling after giving birth for the third time.

"No. She pumps so we always have breast milk in the refrigerator if needed." I busied myself getting the breast milk ready by placing the bottle in warm water.

"How are you handling everything?" Maddie's blue eyes softened.

I wobbled my head side to side. "Taking everything one day at a time."

"You look exhausted."

That was the least of my worries. "I am, but I'm in better shape than Sarah. While we planned for the C-section, she's not as young as she used to be. I think it's taking a greater toll than she's willing to admit." I turned my attention to Cal. "You ready for second breakfast? Or is this the third? I honestly can't remember."

Maddie took the bottle from me. "I'll feed him. Why don't you take a moment for yourself?"

"Are you sure?" I said and then yawned.

"Make another cup of tea. Read the paper, or shut your eyes. I'm a pro with babies now. I'm the—"

"Best aunt on the planet, I know. Thank you." I rubbed my left eye with the heel of my hand, extricating a crumb of sleep and trying to remember the last time I'd actually gotten more than an hour of peaceful slumber.

Maddie took Calvin to the leather chair in the family room, positioning him semi-upright, cradling his head.

After refilling my mug, I took a seat in the matching green chair in front of the fireplace, not wanting to risk falling asleep. I wasn't the type who could nap and wake feeling rested. Instead, I'd feel a hundred times worse. I'd also learned the nightmares happened when I didn't have enough time for a really deep sleep. Another reason I hated drifting off to sleep after waking with a panic attack. The second round of tortured slumber turned out to be much worse than the initial. Could a person die from too many nightmares in a row?

I read the article that had grabbed my attention earlier, learning more about the German company coming to terms with its Nazi past seventy-something years after the end of World War II. "What type of coffee did I make you?"

Maddie shrugged. "Why?"

I lay the paper down in my lap. "This company had kept their connections to Hitler secret all these years, but it's all coming out now. The truth has a way of doing that." Which was one of the issues plaguing me. The Petries and the truth didn't go hand in hand, but the family was coming to a reckoning. What hidden things were about to rear their ugly heads? I'd barely adjusted to my father's secret family when my older brother was arrested. How much more could one person take?

"Isn't that the issue with many of the older German companies?" Maddie kissed the top of Calvin's bald head as he continued to feed.

"Yes, it is. But it's still hard to swallow even today."

"Even more so these days."

Not wanting to get into another discussion of warning signs I'd been noticing about increasingly authoritarian moves by governments around the world, I simply snorted in agreement.

This wasn't the morning to open that line of discussion, not with the tranquility in the house. "It's an interesting article, though. It's about a Jewish woman, whose father was murdered at one of the camps, falling in love with her German employer, who was a diehard Nazi."

"True love, I guess." Maddie shrugged.

"Does it truly conquer all obstacles?" I dragged a hand through my newly cut hair, still unused to having it so short. "Or was it simply a way for her to survive being half Jewish?"

Maddie seemed to mull this over. "That's an interesting take. Not romantic at all. More depressing, really."

I silently laughed. "It's hard to equate romance with someone who penned a letter to Hitler, pretty much saying, *Hey, I'm all in with your treatment of Jews.*" I thought it over. "It'd be an intriguing premise for a novel. Told through alternating points of view."

Maddie eyed me with curiosity. "Have you started the second book yet?"

I shook my head. "No. My agent has put the novel on hold, waiting for a more opportune time to pitch... it." I'd been told selling anything with the name of Petrie on it was harder than getting milk from a rattler. Or had the reference been the king cobra? Either way, I took it to mean my dream of having a number one historical fiction book on *The New York Times* list had been killed. A box I wouldn't be able to check, which felt like a sucker punch to the gut. Besides, I'd published non-fiction under the Petrie name, even if it was an entirely different market, and the thought of using a penname seemed like cheating to me. Or cowardly.

Her gaze bored into mine. "I thought you had a deal."

"It fell through." I dropped my stare, picked up the paper, and turned the page, hoping she'd let it slide.

This didn't deter Maddie one bit. "Why?"

"My agent says these things happen. But..." I didn't want to admit the truth, fearing it'd give it more power than I could handle with everything going on. Ignorance was my goal. Just keep pumping my legs furiously below the water's surface like a duck. *Nothing to see here, folks. Everything is just fine.*

"Spill, Lizzie," Maddie prodded with sympathy in her tone.

"Come on. It's not that hard to figure out. I'm Peter Petrie's sister. The recent so-called exposé on television about his career and the questionable death of his wife hasn't done much to improve the Petrie image in the world."

Maddie remained silent, not her typical tactic during these moments.

"Please don't mention the book-deal situation to Sarah."

"She doesn't know?" Maddie arched one thin eyebrow.

"I found out the day after Calvin was born. I'm absorbing the news, and well… does Sarah really need to take that on right now given everything else? It's hard enough raising four kids. Dealing with the Petrie scandal fallout won't help her body heal." While I had a history of keeping things from Sarah, I was convinced this was the best method of handling the situation right now.

Maddie started to speak, stopped, and then settled on, "I do see your point, but don't keep it from her for too long. Lying isn't good for any relationship. No matter the good intention."

"I'm not lying." *Am I?* "Protecting. It's my job." I stared at my son. "I'd do anything for any of them."

"Just don't do what you usually do."

"What's that?"

"Keep everything bottled up until you explode."

Sometimes I hated how on point Maddie could be, but I fluffed it off. "Dramatic much?"

CHAPTER TWO

Sarah staggered into the room, yawning and looking more asleep than awake.

I discarded the paper and jumped to my feet. "What can I get you?"

She smiled, but it didn't ease the discomfort in her expression. "Nothing. It was quiet. Too quiet."

"Everything is under control," I assured her.

"It's like none of you need me anymore," Sarah joked.

"Oh, trust me; you're the linchpin of this family." Maddie set the bottle aside and patted Calvin's back to get him to burp.

Sarah yawned again. "I hate feeling like dead weight."

"Don't," I said in my serious but supportive way. "Your body needs to heal. We all don't mind pitching in to give you the time to recover."

"What? I'm not getting paid for this?" Maddie flashed a smarmy smile.

"Name your price," I prompted with a flick of my hand, relieved she was using her snark to distract Sarah from my weirdness. Sarah had a way of sensing when I was falling apart.

I'd need help to get her off my scent to keep up my *everything's fine* routine.

"I'm not sure you can afford me."

Sarah settled on the couch, putting her hands out for Calvin. "I need some love."

Maddie rose to hand off Calvin, who immediately settled into Sarah's arms.

"You see? We need you. Cal most of all." I smiled at my wife and son.

"What were you two talking about?" Sarah kissed the top of Calvin's head, which was a common occurrence no matter who cuddled him. There was something special about the baldness of a newborn's head.

"Uh…?" I turned to Maddie, unable to come up with something other than the topic I didn't want Sarah to know anything about. Not yet. Would I ever want to tell her I was afraid to sleep? How could she respect me if she knew everything?

"Lizzie was discussing the Nazis, per usual. Does she ever shut up about them?" Maddie gestured with her hand, acting out incessant chatter.

Sarah looked at me lovingly, which twisted the imaginary knife in my side a bit more. "She does like to go on about them."

"What can I say? It's how I pay the bills around here."

Sarah scrunched her face. "It's ghoulish when you put it that way."

"It did come across more sinister than I intended," I confessed with a whoopsie shrug.

"These days, we have to prescreen those allowed in the library in case they get the wrong idea from all the swastikas on book covers." Sarah's eyes glimmered with humor.

"Do you want herbal tea?" I asked, a shiver overtaking me. "There's a chill in the air."

"Please."

"Maddie, would you like a fresh cup?" I swept her empty mug into my hand, surprised she'd drained it without my noticing until now. My hosting skills were severely lacking.

"Nah, or I'll be bouncing off the walls."

In the kitchen, I filled the teakettle and flicked on the gas burner.

There was commotion, and soon enough, the air was filled with children laughing. Rose spoke, followed by Troy and Sarah. Then Olivia burst into tears. Everything was back to normal, much to my relief, allowing me to drown out the nagging thoughts in my brain.

I placed Sarah's herbal tea, another strong cup of Earl Grey for me, mugs for Rose and Troy, and a carafe of coffee, along with milk and sugar on a tray. Setting it down on the table in the family room, I said, "How were the kids?"

"Perfect angels." Troy poured a cup of coffee.

"Now, now. We don't lie in this family," Sarah admonished.

Maddie's gaze briefly landed on mine, and I braced for one of her ill-timed comments, but it failed to surface.

With my tea in hand, I retook the seat next to the fireplace. "Is it Saturday or Sunday?"

Rose laughed heartily. "It's funny that you're a historian but never seem to know what the date is lately."

"I'm much better with dates way in the past. Present and future ones cause me nothing but trouble." I blew into my mug, the steam causing my cheeks to feel the heat.

"It's Saturday. Isn't it?" Sarah turned to her mom.

Rose shook her head. "It's Sunday."

"It is?" Sarah sounded defeated.

"Don't worry. I'll be over tomorrow to help when Lizzie heads to campus," Rose reassured in her motherly way.

"Does that mean it's two weeks until Thanksgiving?"

"Eighteen days to be exact." Troy drummed a tune on his

thigh, and I was willing to bet it was "Twinkle, Twinkle Little Star," his nervous habit.

"Your passion for national turkey day is commendable." Maddie wore a shit-eating grin.

"I always have a countdown for Thanksgiving. Once it hits, the rest of the school days 'til winter break are smooth sailing." He followed this with a hand motion in the air.

"Speaking of Thanksgiving, what's the plan this year?" Maddie asked.

"We'll have it here like normal," Sarah stated as if there was no reason to question it.

"We will?" I asked in a shaky voice, showcasing I lacked Sarah's confidence.

"Of course. There's no reason to break family tradition."

I surveyed the room, mentally counting each child, which was unnecessary since it was hard to forget we were raising four kids. I, the commitment-phobe, had a wife and four bambinos. I zipped up my hoodie.

My eyes rested on Demi, my brother Peter's daughter. Peter had signed over his parental rights before heading to prison earlier this year, and we had expedited adopting her. Demi grinned at me, and I returned it, seeing Peter's crooked smile in hers. Fred waddled over to me and put his arms in the air, indicating he wanted to sit on my lap. Setting my mug on the side table, I swept him up and tickled his stomach, causing him to laugh and squirm.

"Maddie and I will help with the cooking." Rose didn't seem willing to take on Sarah's stubbornness. Or, perhaps, she didn't want everyone under her roof. The family had developed quite a holiday reputation.

"I can pitch in." I continued tickling Freddie.

Sarah gave me a supportive smile but said, "We had to replace the oven after your last attempt at cooking."

"Are you saying prepping a turkey is harder than baking a cake from a box?" I did my best to sound sincere.

"Not at all." Sarah rolled her eyes. "I'm not helpless, and I'll be back to normal by then."

"The doctor said it could take up to eight weeks. Please don't rush things." I leveled my gaze on her resolute eyes.

Sarah's upper body stiffened. "I'm resilient."

"You are, but you don't have to be superhuman. Look around you. We're all willing to help." I waved to the full room.

"Lizzie's right, and you know I hate admitting that." Maddie's wink was meant to soften the blow. "We'll watch her like a hawk and won't let her burn down the kitchen." She added with emphasis, "*Again.*"

"I didn't burn it down. Just the oven," I defended.

"You aren't helping your cause." Maddie made a *keep your trap shut* motion with her hand.

I gnashed my teeth but turned my attention to Freddie, who wanted more tickling. "It's funny. I hated when Peter would pin me down and tickle me until I peed my pants."

"Why is it whenever you share a Peter story, I like him less?" Sarah asked in seriousness.

I hefted a shoulder. "I had a difficult childhood."

"Understatement of the year," Maddie said.

"It made me who I am today. That helps ease it some." Lately, though, the strong parts of me were drifting out to sea, leaving a washed-up heap of leftovers on the shore. *Nope, don't let your brain go there.* "What about those turkey fryers? They're stacked up in the front of every store it seems. I'm pretty sure I can manage tossing a turkey into one, and the fryers have to be outside, meaning no chance I'll burn down the kitchen."

The eyebrows on all the women's faces spiked to their hairlines, but it was Sarah who said, "Hard no. Even if there was a blizzard, I wouldn't put it past you to burn down the entire neighborhood."

"You make it sound like I'm a walking disaster."

"Only when it comes to culinary skills." Sarah smiled.

"Or when giving directions," Maddie chipped in.

"My offer of hiring a chef is still on the table, and who needs directions now with GPS on every phone?" I lifted Fred up in the air. "Right, Freddie Weddie?"

"Geeeps," he said, giggling.

"G.P.S." I added, "Global Positioning System."

"Geeeps!"

"Yes, geeeps," I conceded.

"Finally, someone Lizzie will listen to," Maddie cracked.

I stuck my tongue out at her, and Freddie copied me.

"Really, honey, can you not teach our children bad manners?" Sarah's eyes blazed with humor over Freddie's antics.

"Manners," I said to Freddie. "The definition is—"

Maddie groaned. "That's my cue to leave the room."

"If only I'd known all along it was that easy to get rid of you," I shouted as she hid in the kitchen.

CHAPTER THREE

On Thursday morning, a day I didn't have to be on campus, I volunteered along with Maddie, to take Fred, Ollie, and Demi to music class while Sarah stayed home with Calvin.

"Why don't you hop in the shower?" Sarah, feeding Demi, said in a way that suggested it wasn't an option.

"Do I smell?" I sniffed my armpit while I held a spoon to Fred's closed lips.

"No, but it might wipe away some of the tiredness that's oozing from your skin. The other moms in the class will smell it miles away."

"Being moms, themselves, won't they have sympathy for me?" I gave up on getting Fred to eat more.

"Some will. Others will see it as a weakness. It's kind of a cutthroat atmosphere, since the majority have stepped away from high-powered Denver jobs and are raising their children in the burbs. They treat these events as a way of keeping their killer corporate skills alive and well." Sarah spooned another bite of oatmeal into Demi's mouth.

"I wasn't aware Fort Collins was a suburb of Denver. I

remember the days when there weren't many houses in between the cities." I suppressed a groan. "Why are the kids in this class? I hate pretentiousness." More so lately.

"I do, too, but I love our kids and want to give them every leg up whenever possible. Besides, Freddie loves playing the drums."

As if on cue, Fred started to bang his hand on his high chair, saying "Dums," silencing any attempt of me getting out of music class duties.

"I fear my black circles are a permanent fixture on my face." I finished wiping down Ollie's high chair with a wet rag and got to work on Fred's now that he was roaming free in the family room on his way to the toddler play section, where Ollie sat with Maddie, working on some type of craft.

"Go on. Take a long, hot shower. You deserve it." Sarah placed a hand on each of my shoulders and pushed me in her *get moving* fashion. "Mom and I can finish the breakfast duties."

Rose, who just arrived, set her purse down on the kitchen counter and gave me her *do as Sarah says or suffer the consequences* look.

It wasn't that I didn't want a shower. I did. But I hated letting Sarah out of my sight these days. But Rose, who was almost as protective, would keep an eye on her daughter. And God knew Sarah didn't like being questioned. Not in her weakened state. She was like a cornered animal these days.

In the master bathroom, I flipped the shower water as hot as it would go. I'd never been the type to take a lukewarm one. If the water wasn't *rip the first layer off* temperature, what was the point? Sarah referred to this as my *all or nothing* personality type. She wasn't far off the mark. It was another Petrie trait that haunted me.

After letting the water pound the knots in between my shoulder blades. I tried squeezing the lavender body wash onto the bath sponge, resulting with the all-too familiar farting sound of a nearly-empty bottle. I'd meant to replace it before my next shower but had forgotten to grab it. Not wanting to towel off, traipse naked to the walk-in closet, and then get back in, I squeezed the bottle much harder. It torpedoed out of my hand and struck my lip, the taste of blood immediately following as the bottle crashed down on my big toe. Even though it was empty, it still smarted.

"Mother fucker!" I rinsed my lip, cringing from the scalding water hitting the cut.

Foregoing the body-wash portion of the shower, I rinsed the conditioner from my hair and got out. "So much for a relaxing shower," I muttered as I toweled dry. Nothing in my life seemed to be going right, and I wasn't sure how much longer I could hold it together. *Come on, Lizzie. As Peter would say, don't be a wuss.* Maybe it wasn't best to take any advice from my incarcerated brother.

Dressed and back downstairs, I said, "All right, kiddos, who's ready for music class?"

Maddie gawked at me. "What in the f—fudge happened to your lip?"

Ollie, Demi, and Fred chanted *fudge.*

"I showered."

"With who? Mike Tyson?" Maddie slanted her head to get a better look.

"Very funny," I said with a smidge more bitterness than necessary.

"Let me take a look at it." Sarah, with a hand on my chin and one on the top of my hair, tilted my head to inspect the damage. "Does it hurt?"

"Which part? My pride or lip?"

Sarah didn't seem to appreciate my attempt at humor.

"It's fine." I attempted not to recoil when Sarah ran a finger over the swelling.

"Translation, both." Sarah's shoulders relaxed as she

regarded me in a way that conveyed she loved my idiocy but didn't quite comprehend how I could complicate the heck out of simple tasks. "How in the world did you give yourself a fat lip while in the shower?"

"The first rule of showers is don't talk about showers."

"I love you, but you can be such a dork sometimes." Sarah let go of my chin.

"I gotta be me. Shall we assemble the troops?" I asked Maddie.

She saluted me with her middle finger.

"I guess you gotta be you as well." I started to laugh but regretted it instantly, my lip smarting.

"Careful or I'll give you a black eye to match your lip." Maddie socked a fist into her open palm.

"No more injuries. You hear me?" Sarah addressed both of us with a severe mom-like waggle of a finger.

Maddie and I bowed our heads in shame, but I'm pretty sure I spied Maddie sticking her tongue out at me. It should have riled me, but I found it calming instead. A nice Maddie made it too apparent she thought me overly delicate. I hated feeling that way, and it seemed to be happening more and more these days.

"Okay, Lizzie, be on your A-game around the moms," Sarah said in a tone that couldn't be ignored.

"Keri is the one to watch out for," Rose cautioned.

"Yes. Almost everything she says is a dig. Don't engage. It won't end well." Sarah tried to bolster my confidence with an encouraging smile.

It didn't work.

In the car, I asked Maddie about Keri.

"I don't like her, but she's the queen bee of the music group." Maddie made a whoop-dee-doo hand gesture.

"Queen bee makes me think she's more like a bully." I came to a stop at a red light.

"She is."

"This is the part of parenting I wasn't expecting. I'd thought my days of being bullied ended when I eighty-sixed Meg from my life."

"And when your mom died and Peter went to jail. Oh, there was also Tie. You've had your fair share of bullies." Maddie started to count on her fingers. "Am I missing any?"

* * *

"Wow! That's gotta hurt." Claire tugged on her own lip.

"It stings a bit." I had to fight the instinct to touch it.

The kids were in their circle, being guided by the music teacher and some helpers. The parents, from a cursory look, gathered in cliques in the spacious room.

A smartly dressed woman I'd never met joined the three of us. "I'm Keri."

"Lizzie." I put my hand out to shake the woman's. Her smile didn't reassure me at all. So, this was the scary queen bee I had to be wary of. If her size was a measure of her might, she wasn't all that much to fear.

"Ah, you're the famous Lizzie." Her slender fingers curled around mine, snake-like, the rings on her hand nearly cutting into my flesh. I'd never liked women who had to wear one too many sparkling gems on their fingers as if screaming, *Look at me!*

"I think you have Lizzie Borden in mind. I'm not famous at all." I extricated my hand, foregoing the urge to wipe it clean on my jeans.

Maddie and Claire laughed heartily, bolstering my nerve. My humor had helped me in these types of situations, and I still wasn't sure Keri was the stuff of nightmares. I'd been reared by the Scotch-lady, so the overly made-up bronzed Oompa

Loompa in front of me didn't register all that high on my *stay alert* meter.

Keri didn't even crack a smile, but I wasn't sure if that was due to a Botox incident, given the lack of movement in her expression. "Would you rather be associated with an axe murderer over a Wall Street crook who had his wife killed?" Keri's sharp tone implied she'd gotten the better of me.

"Tie's death was a terrible accident. Nothing more." My upper body stiffened. So much for staying calm.

"Not according to the TV show—"

Claire inserted herself between us and said, "Jason's really getting the hang of the xylophone."

"He prefers the bongos, but some kids don't share well." Keri's stare dug into mine.

Bring it, bitch.

I glanced at Freddie pounding away on the bongos, smiling inwardly. No reason to poke the bear.

"Mia loves the maracas." Claire beamed at her daughter.

"Is it a cultural thing?" Keri asked with what seemed like forced sincerity.

"I'm not an expert, but I think maracas are more Latin American," Claire said without losing her shit.

Maddie and Sarah hadn't been wrong about the back-stabbing music class moms. Were they all like Keri? So far, she'd called out my tainted last name, which was easy pickings these days, but bringing attention to Claire's adopted Asian daughter seemed so classless. Who attacks an innocent child? One word came to mind: viper. Whom would she strike next? Recently, I stumbled upon a fact that people in the US were more likely to die from a lightning strike than a snakebite. I listened carefully but didn't hear any thunder rumblings overhead. Damn. Some people needed to learn a lesson.

"What happened to your lip?" Keri asked me.

Already time for round two? "An unfortunate shower incident."

Keri's brow crumpled. "What does that mean?"

"That's Lizzie's nickname for Sarah," Maddie joked.

Again, everyone laughed but Keri. I tried to imagine what her husband was like, because for the life of me, I couldn't see anyone finding her attractive enough to fuck, let alone have a meal with every day. Maybe they weren't the family who sat down for meals. Was that why she had to cut everyone else down?

Feeling like I should clear the air to avoid unnecessary gossip, I detailed what actually happened so no one could misrepresent it.

When I finished, Maddie placed a hand on my shoulder. "Assaulted by an empty bottle. That's a first."

"What can I say? I'm gifted." I gazed at Keri, who seemed to take the truth on board.

"Would you excuse me? I need to speak to Melissa." Keri left without another word.

I whistled under my breath.

"She's such a bitch," Maddie whispered to Claire.

Claire nodded.

I couldn't wrap my head around the situation. We all were in our thirties or forties. Why in the fuck did anyone care about Keri and her digs? Given the terrified expression on the woman I assumed was Melissa, I seemed to be the only rational adult in the room. This was new territory for me, the Clueless One. And, I simply didn't have the bandwidth to deal with idiocy.

CHAPTER FOUR

Later that afternoon, I camped out in my office to catch up on work.

Maddie waltzed in. "You're up!"

I glanced at my fitbit. "It's after three, and I was with you this morning with the kids." Since my attention was on the watch, I peeked to see how many more steps I needed before the end of the hour. Fifty-seven. A lap or two around the library.

"No, I didn't mean awake. You're going to the salon with me to get a pedi." She did a little dance move.

I pushed my chair back from the desk. "Um, isn't that your thing with Sarah."

"It is, but she's not up for it today. I don't want to go alone."

"Can't you take Rose? This seems like a girl thing, not a Lizzie thing."

"You're a girl, right?" Maddie's smile was teasing.

"I am but not the girly type."

"Trust me, Lizzie. You need to start. Everyone's feet need love."

I wiggled my toes in my house slippers. "My feet like to be left alone, like me. Besides, I'm drowning here." I pointed to the stack of blue books that needed grading.

"The best way to recharge is by taking care of yourself. I know everything has been landing on your shoulders. Let me help you relax." She placed a hand on her chest, martyr-like.

I sighed. "Gabe is more in touch with his feminine side. Take him."

"Nope. I'd rather spend time with you."

That wasn't a good thing for so many reasons.

"Sarah *suggested* I take you." Maddie emphasized *suggested*.

"That's not fair. Both of you know I won't say no. Did I do something wrong, and this is my punishment?"

"Maybe I did, and this is mine. When's the last time your feet received any kind of treatment?"

"I trim my nails every other Tuesday."

Maddie's eyes darted heavenward. "Give me strength, Lord." She snapped her fingers in a menacing fashion. "Up. We need to leave in five."

I followed her directions for two reasons. I liked completing my hourly step count before the fitbit squawked at me. Also, I liked being on Sarah's good side.

While Maddie bounded upstairs, I went into the front room with my shoes. "Why do you hate me?" I asked Sarah, taking a seat on the ottoman in front of her chair. Slipping on my right sneaker, I said, "A pedi? Really?"

"I'm too tired for Maddie, and I thought it would be something you'd like."

"Yeah, right."

She gave me her sarcastic *poor you* face, and gingerly leaned forward in her chair. "I think Maddie needs to talk. This is when we usually have our heart to hearts, but I just can't do it today."

I gave Sarah's hand a quick squeeze and put on my other shoe. "You owe me."

"You can't cash in for another month or so."

Judging by the heat in my cheeks, my face was on fire. Avoiding looking in Rose's direction, I called out. "Are you ready?"

* * *

"NO SARAH TODAY?" A WOMAN IN HER TWENTIES asked Maddie, giving me the once-over, and I was fairly certain I didn't pass muster.

"She's tired. This is her wife, Lizzie." Maddie did a ta-da motion as if I was some kind of oddity, like a monkey playing a musical instrument.

The woman shook my hand, her gaze taking in my fat lip, but she didn't make a comment, much to my relief. She led us to two massive black chairs. Out of the corner of my eye, I followed Maddie's lead, removing my shoes and socks and shoving my jeans up to my knees.

A different woman perched on the stool in front of my chair, holding a bottle of lilac polish. She motioned for me to put my feet in the water.

Dear God! The water was effing hot.

"Is the temperature okay?" she asked.

"Perfect," I said, trying not to grimace.

Step one of the pedi and I was already firmly in the *do not like* box.

"How are things, Maddie?" I asked, relieved the water was cooling off a smidge, or my body was adjusting. I was a fan of hot showers, but it wasn't until today that I realized my definition of scalding was different than others'. Was I wimpier than I thought?

"Did Sarah tell you to ask?" Maddie gave me side-eye.

"Absolutely. I'm doing everything I can these days to follow orders."

Maddie grinned. "How are things with you?"

"Overwhelming. Grading exams for one class and research papers for another. The Wednesday before Thanksgiving, my night class is scheduled for a test. Every time I pass one stage, there are three more waiting."

The woman took my right foot out of the water and used tweezers or something to yank skin off. It was unpleasant, and I was seriously starting to question why people do this.

"Now that I've shared, what's going on with you these days?" It seemed best to stay focused on Maddie to avoid screaming at the woman to stop torturing my feet.

She let out an anguished breath.

"That bad?" I turned in my seat to face her.

"Why didn't you tell me couples therapy was hard?"

"I'm pretty sure I did, and even if I didn't, it's not like that's a big secret. You watch enough chick flicks to know that." It wasn't like she informed me pedis were a modern-form of foot persecution. "What's the issue, really?"

"It's hard."

"You said that. What exactly is hard?" I waved for her to fill in the gaps.

"Finding out my true feelings."

The woman placed my right foot back into the water and reached for the left. I said a silent prayer for the appendage to survive. "Feelings are slippery little suckers. When you think you understand, they shift." Again, I had to stifle the urge to shout at the foot lady, "Why do you hate my feet?" But that didn't seem like the right way to handle the situation. Instead, I focused back on Maddie.

"Why do you let me hang out with you and the kids so much?"

"I like to suffer." I waved to my feet for case in point.

Her eyes darkened. "No, seriously. I can be a pain in the ass."

"Oh, I'm aware, but you're family. It's part of the package." I shrugged.

She gripped the armrest nearest me. "Would I still be considered family if I wasn't with Gabe?"

"You were family well before you started dating my stepbrother."

"But I was engaged to your other brother."

I glanced down at the women working on our toes, but neither flinched. "Being with one of my siblings isn't a requirement to be included in the family. Ethan's family, and he hasn't been with any blood relations. For some reason, Sarah enjoys your company and the kids adore you." I tried to reach for her arm to give it an *I'm kidding* pat, but she was too far away. "Are you really concerned you'll be banished if you aren't involved with one of my brothers?"

"It's just with everything that's happened over the past year, I'm really taking a hard look at my life and my relationships." She stared at the fake tree off to the side.

"And you want to make changes," I supplied.

"I think it's best. I can't give Gabe what he deserves and…" She didn't complete the thought.

"Peter."

She met my gaze. "I guess it's not much of a secret."

"You visit him more than Dad and I combined."

"He's alone in there, and I know what it's like to feel that way."

Her sad eyes broke my heart. "You aren't alone, Maddie. Maybe on the… intimate level, but there's someone out there for you. I feel it in my bones."

"I know it's not Peter, but I don't know how to walk away for good."

"Baby steps. I think you need to talk to Gabe. Does he have an inkling?"

She nodded. "He's constantly harping on the Peter issue in therapy."

"That sounds fun." The woman put some type of exfoliating cream on my right calf and massaged it, her fingers digging in, causing more pain. Strike three on the odds of me ever coming back to this establishment. I'd rather my feet fall off.

"It's not all Gabe's fault."

"It never is. The opposite is true as well. It's not all your fault."

Her eyes started to pool. "I feel so guilty."

"Letting go of someone isn't easy."

"It's awful."

I wondered if she was referring to Peter, Gabe, or both?

"It is." Especially when someone was always around, which was Gabe's case, or at their rock bottom like Peter. "What can I do to help?"

She laughed. "Can you even take on more? I see how exhausted you are all of the time."

"I'll dig deep." I patted my chest, Tarzan-like.

Maddie didn't speak, but her eyes were on mine, as if trying to see past my barriers. "You need to learn you don't have to control everything. When things go wrong, it's not on you to put the pieces back together."

I gaped at her, trying to speak but unable.

"I know it's difficult given Peter being in jail, Sarah's condition, and you're the adult everyone looks to because you have this remarkable ability to say what no one wants to hear but should. Just don't let everything break you. That's the last thing the Petries need."

I burst into a fit of giggles, and Maddie's face drained of blood. Her gawking made it pretty clear she thought I'd lost my mind. It wasn't until she noticed the woman using a pumice stone on the bottom of my foot that the concern started to drain from her face. The fact that she had thought I'd lost my mind was unsettling, but I really didn't have the time or energy to contemplate everything.

CHAPTER FIVE

Friday afternoon, around two, my desk line rang, causing my heart to leap into my throat, nearly strangling me.

Swallowing a couple of times, I raised the receiver and forced out, "Dr. Petrie," trying to sound confident, not like a terrified child.

"Dean Spencer would like to see you in his office." The woman's cold, commanding voice could sink the Titanic all over again.

"Sure. When?" There was still a pang of remorse that Dr. Marcel, my mentor, no longer worked at the university. While I'd hated admitting it at the time, I had been his favorite and received special attention. In my mind, I saw my bearded high school political science teacher scrawl *TANSTAAFL* on the chalkboard. *There ain't no such thing as a free lunch.* Was I about to pay dues I'd been shirking my entire time as a professor?

"Would now suit you?" Her authoritarian tone implied *it better or tough noogies.*

I didn't enjoy being bossed around by an admin who was a

decade younger than I was, but what could I do or say? "Yes, of course."

There was dead air.

Guess I got my marching orders. I placed the receiver on the base, my mind swirling. I hadn't assumed the department's transition from Dr. Marcel's kind reign to a braggart would be turbulent free, but I hadn't expected to grapple with the attitude of Dean Spencer's admin. From day one, she'd made it clear she didn't like me. Was she simply too young to know how to deal with people, or was there something else under the surface that I hadn't put my finger on quite yet? As a millennial, I didn't peg her as homophobic, but could that be the root cause? Oftentimes, the simplest answer was the right one; however, I couldn't bank on this, either.

In the hallway, I noticed another professor and started to say hello, but he turned on his heel and ducked into the mailroom, which he'd just exited. There was a reason professors earned the stereotype of being absentminded.

"Good afternoon, Brittany," I said, silently wishing the next time the young snot was in the gym, because there was no way someone with toned arms like hers didn't live in a gym, she'd get crushed by one of the weight machines.

"He's waiting for you." Brittany motioned for me to enter the room, all the while keeping her eyes on her computer screen.

Nothing like the personal touch.

I knocked on the door once before turning the knob.

Dean Spencer glanced up from a book in his hands, his smile tightening on his face as if the muscles were being tugged against their will. "Dr. Petrie."

"Lizzie, please."

He waved for me to take a seat.

I did.

He stared at me.

I returned it.

Dean Spencer cleared his throat and laid the book down on his desk, still open face up, a finger marking his place as if my intrusion would be short-lived. "We've been going over the fall schedule."

Who was we? I had been under the impression it was set in stone, and I was slated to teach three classes.

"Given the climate as of late, we think it wise to pare down some of the European offerings."

"The climate," I parroted, taken aback by this pronouncement. What climate? The actual *climate* climate? Did this yahoo have it in his pea brain that rising seas were going to wipe out the European continent? Scientific evidence wasn't great, but I didn't think the end of times was imminent.

"I know you're the Nazi expert on staff, and they're still cool, but we want to switch the focus of this department to American West studies."

Did the dean of the history department really just say Nazis were cool? He was supposed to be an esteemed historian who would raise the profile of the department, which had been struggling with draconian budget cuts. While I believed wholeheartedly history was super-duper cool, I would never use the word to describe the Nazis. And, I had dedicated my adult life to studying them.

I gulped.

"We'll still need to offer Western Civilization courses, and I've heard you've taught them before."

"Yes." When I was a grad student and didn't have much sway in the department.

"Good. It's settled then."

I shifted in my seat. Did he mean I'd be teaching four classes in the fall? There was no way I could take that on. Not with four kids at home. I shifted in my seat, causing the leather to creak. "I'm not following."

"Next fall you'll be teaching Western Civilization."

I'd gotten that much, asshole. "On top of my other classes?"

"No. Instead of your other classes."

The air whooshed out of me like Dean Spencer had just sucker punched me in the gut.

"Only one Western Civ course?" I had to force the question from my mouth.

"Unless you don't want to teach at all. Take some time to get your home life in order. That would be perfectly understandable given…" He folded his hands on the book, his gaze narrowing in on my lip, which still looked bad.

I needed to get out of the room before I gave him a piece of my mind, and I wasn't liking his not-so-veiled hint. Did he really think my home life was in such a disarray, or was he simply using the so-called evidence of my fat lip to twist things to suit his purpose? As a historian, if he watched the Peter *documentary*, he would have been able to spy all the dubious facts and sources.

Hoping my true feelings didn't lace my words, I finally answered, "Of course, I want to teach." A trained monkey probably could handle the Western Civ class, which more than likely would be a bigger draw for the likes of the Nazi-loving dean. I guessed a monkey probably had more street cred than I did these days. Would that hold true if the animal flung his poo at students? Was I seriously comparing my abilities to an imaginary shit-flinging primate? I did enjoy the image of my new invisible friend tossing a particularly steaming pile at the dean and his admin, their mouths wide open.

He picked up the book.

I took that as the sign he was done with me.

I rose, my legs trembling. "Have a good weekend."

As I walked through the door, I made a silent prayer while touching the wood frame: *I fucking hope you get struck by lightning.*

Back in my office, my phone rang again.

A chill went through me.

"Yes?" I said in a weak voice.

"Dr. Petrie?"

"Yes." It was as if I couldn't say any other words.

"This is Rick from the TV studio. There's a scheduling conflict, and…" He cleared his throat.

"Yes?" I said yet again.

"We won't be able to accommodate your TV appearances anymore."

"I see." I should have been bolstered by my ability to say something other than yes, but the news had drained all hope out of me. For the past several months, I'd used the TV studio for my appearances on JJ Cavendish's show, which originally aired only on Sundays but quickly morphed into more. Who knew the political climate would be a boon for academics who loved to argue? I was under the impression the university was supportive since the screen behind me had the university seal. All press was good press. Wasn't that the adage?

Not anymore, apparently.

I hung up the phone, my gaze bouncing around the four walls of my office, feeling like Alice in Wonderland after drinking the wrong potion, getting trapped with no chance for escape.

* * *

Before turning the SUV onto my street, I pulled over to think. Only one class in the fall? And an entry-level course, which wouldn't be challenging. Now I couldn't fulfill my TV show obligations without the school's studio, which would put another dent into my income, not to mention letting down JJ, whom I'd come to think of as a good friend. I wasn't a regular on the show, but I appeared often enough in a month that the additional money in the account was noticeable. Both of these struck after my book deal had been scrapped. It wasn't like Sarah and I were hurting for money since we both had trust funds, but neither of us wanted to tap into them unless the shit had really hit the fan. Was this the definition of that? Would it get worse?

Dropping all this news on Sarah wasn't an option until I had a plan, but what would that even look like? I'd always kept myself busy with teaching, writing, and now punditry. The rug wasn't simply being pulled out from under me. The floor was, too.

Should I call Dr. Marcel for advice? Dad? Neither option was appealing. Dr. Marcel had recently retired. Did I really want to yank him back into the intrigues of academia so soon after putting the job in the rearview mirror? Dad had his hands full steering his company through turbulent times due to Peter's shenanigans and that goddamn exposé.

There was Helen, my stepmom, but then the news would get back to my father. I'd consulted Courtney in the past, but she was close with Jorie, one of our part-time nannies, and besties with Maddie, so it might be asking too much for her to keep everything private.

Who did that leave? Maddie wouldn't be able to contain herself much longer and not spill her guts to Sarah. Maybe not outright, but she'd act abnormal. Ethan's marriage was crumbling. Was everyone in my life falling apart?

One name came to mind, and I texted asking for a meeting whenever it'd suit her. We arranged to meet on Monday morning. Feeling somewhat at ease or at least able to get through the weekend, I steered the vehicle home, but before I turned into the driveway, I got a 911 text from Sarah saying we needed diapers, yesterday. Nothing like stay-at-home-mom-flair when it came to guilt.

I U-turned, heading for the closest store. After a brief call home, I asked for all the other possible items we'd need for the weekend. It didn't take long to load up the cart to nearly overflowing, and I was willing to bet there'd still be another trip to a store for something before Saturday night. That seemed to be the new norm.

Loading the items into the back of the SUV, I heard a woman's voice mutter my name. Before I could stop myself, I turned toward the source, and the woman spat on my shoes, the globule sliding off the side into the frozen slush under foot. I froze.

"You're a murderer!"

I blinked.

"Murderer!"

Glancing about to see how many people witnessed this, I hurriedly emptied the rest of the cart and then shoved it to the side, not bothering to return it to the proper place.

The woman shoved her phone into my face, and a quick glance showed there was a Facebook group dedicated to Peter and me killing Tie. Who did this woman think she was? And who was the founder of this group? Surely, this wasn't legal. But who did I go to? The Facebook police? Not that I wanted to hit the pause button in front of this deranged woman who apparently had too much free time to give me, a total stranger, a piece of her mind. I added this to the list of bullshit to discuss with JJ, who had much more experience with internet freaks.

I got behind the wheel, and as calmly as possible, I drove out of the parking lot, the woman standing in my abandoned parking space with her fist in the air, still shouting, "Murderer!"

When safely in my garage, with the door closing, I steadied my breathing and heart rate. *Pull it together, Lizzie. Pull it the fuck together.*

Entering the kitchen via the door from the garage, I found Sarah cradling Calvin to her chest, her brow slightly damp from the effort.

"Cal, my man, give your mom some love." I eased Calvin from Sarah's arms and kissed her cheek.

"Did you tell Keri I gave you a fat lip?" Sarah perched on the edge of the barstool, her grimace making it clear she was in pain.

I had to downshift my brain to remember who in the fuck Keri was and why she mattered. "Oh, that. Maddie made a crack."

"Maddie said I gave you a fat lip?"

I nodded. "She was teasing." I pretended to gobble one of Calvin's tiny hands, his expression not changing much, making me worry. Up until Cal's birth, Freddie was our serious child, but Calvin was making it seem like Fred was the loosey-goosey child.

"I could kill her."

I gawked at Sarah. This was the bridge too far? Maddie, while a supportive friend, hadn't always been an angel. Not that I wanted to delve too deeply into the past these days. A really bad sign for a historian. "What's wrong?"

"Keri's telling everyone I hit you."

I cocked my head, puppy-like. "Who's everyone?"

"All the moms."

I rolled my eyes. "I sincerely doubt anyone is taking Keri seriously. It only takes a minute of speaking to her to discover she has ulterior motives."

"It doesn't matter if anyone believes her or not," she explained in the way she does when I'm being naïve.

Too tired to puzzle out what I was missing on my own, I said, "Can you connect the dots for me, please?"

She let out a puff of air. "If Keri directs everyone to stop associating with us, they will."

"If that's true, so be it. Do we really need people like Keri or cowardly moms in our lives?"

"You don't understand." She wiggled one of Cal's feet.

"This is about the kids, not us. They won't be invited to parties. Nor will anyone come to their parties."

"We have four kids. Do we really need to add more to the mix? Besides, I sincerely doubt Claire and JJ will follow suit, so Mia will still be Freddie's bandmate."

Sarah conceded with a nod but said, "I wish that was enough."

"What's really bugging you?"

Her eyes avoided mine. "I don't like being blacklisted. This is all new territory for me."

I wish I could say the same. While the scene in the parking lot had been a new experience, I hadn't always been the type to fit in. "You aren't," I said with as much conviction as I could manage, and given the rotten hand I'd been dealt earlier at work and with the crazy person, it wasn't convincing at all. "Have you ever thought of moving? Starting over? Give us and the kids a chance to make a mark without all this baggage?"

"Where?" she asked, floored.

"Back East. There are a ton of universities. Massachusetts comes to mind. I have some ins at Harvard."

"We can't move so far!" she screeched.

Calvin startled, and I cuddled him closer. Speaking with a calm voice for both Sarah and Calvin, I said, "It was just an idea. I didn't mean to upset you."

Sarah plowed on. "All of our friends and family are here. What would we do without them?"

My brain started to calculate how much it would cost me to uproot all the key players in our circle. Before I got too far, I realized I couldn't expect the likes of Ethan to ditch Colorado because of the Petrie stink. Nor Maddie, who was in the process of breaking up with my stepbrother Gabe, but she was too attached to Peter to leave the state, even if that would be best for her to get a fresh start and possibly find someone not related to me to date.

Would Rose and Troy consider moving? How could I start putting out feelers without alerting Sarah that I wanted a break from Colorado? Rose had moved to Colorado when Sarah started college in Boulder. Would she follow to be close to the grandkids?

"Have you received an offer?" Sarah asked.

I'd been trapped in my head and wasn't entirely sure what Sarah meant. Surely, she didn't know about the Western Civ situation.

She must have guessed from my expression I hadn't been listening and clarified, "A job offer?"

"Oh, no, I haven't." But if I wanted to continue teaching, I'd better start looking because I was certain I was being pushed out of my current position since the grounds for getting a tenured professor fired were non-existent. Was it solely Dean Spencer who was coordinating a one-two blow to my academic career? Were there forces hidden deeper in the trenches? The detestable Facebook freaks?

"Are you okay?"

"Me? Yes, I'm fine. Just a long week." I raised Calvin in the air. "But the weekend is here, isn't it, Calvin? And there's no place I'd rather be."

CHAPTER SIX

Monday morning, I found JJ sitting at the back table in the diner in Laporte, just north of Fort Collins. It was closer to JJ's home, and I wanted to meet someplace that wasn't near the university to avoid unwanted ears.

JJ hunched over a tablet, not looking up.

"Hey there," I said in a soft voice so I wouldn't startle the crap out of her. Despite the fact I had the height advantage, I suspected if it came down to it, JJ could pummel my ass, and I'd rather not find out by surprising her. Something about her demeanor gave me the impression she was used to protecting her flank, which was one of the reasons I'd reached out to her. For tips.

She glanced up, grinning, completely at ease. "Hey back at you."

I slid into the booth opposite JJ, wondering how she'd shifted from studious to carefree in under a second.

"You look like the school bully stole your favorite toy at recess." JJ slanted her head.

How had she pegged my mood so quickly? "Whatcha reading?"

"A fascinating article about a lizard cult and how social media has helped it grow."

"The lizard or cult?"

JJ laughed. "The cult. There's no lizard involved." She shifted in her seat and folded her hands on the tabletop. "Well, that's not entirely true since the cult believes lizards from space—"

"Alien lizards?" I scoffed, hugging my chest.

"Yes, exactly!" She raised a hand in a *your guess is as good as mine* motion but continued to explain. "The leader claims these lizards from space have subverted segments of the human race, and their end game is world-wide totalitarian government." JJ tapped the screen of her tablet. "It's fascinating stuff in the way you can't look away from a car crash."

"How exactly have they subverted people?" I tried catching the waitress's eye but failed. If I was going to start off my day discussing lizards from space, I needed another strong dose of caffeine.

"Body snatching and mind control, obviously," JJ stated with conviction. "I mean, how else would they do it?"

I dipped my head to the right, my ear nearly touching my shoulder, the tendons in my neck making it known they didn't appreciate the strain. Had I misjudged her tone when she'd said *obviously*? "Are you, um, a believer in this... religion?"

"If I said yes, would you lose all respect for me?" She splayed her fingers on the tabletop as if readying for battle.

While I wasn't wanting an ass-kicking, I couldn't fib. Not about something so completely inane. The historian in me wouldn't allow it. "Yes. Without a doubt."

She let out a bark of laughter. "I do love your frankness. Fear not. I'm not a devotee of the lizard cult or any cult. I just find it mesmerizing that these nutjobs are able to rile up hundreds if not thousands to believe something so absurd. Yet, I can't get half the country to believe facts are synonymous with truth in the news articles we publish on *Matthews Daily Dish*."

"Oh, I'm not sure it's that hard to believe. People like to put their faith in external things. Especially if it allows them to point a finger at someone or something else for all the wrongs in their life or the world instead of peering inward."

JJ opened her mouth, closed it, and then looked toward the ceiling. "That's a pretty simplistic view, but it does get to the heart of things. How many years?"

"I'm sorry?" Why was the waitress not looking in our direction? This never happened on Sunday mornings when Ada was running the show.

"Of therapy?"

"Oh, that. A few." I waved a dismissive hand in the air. Why I didn't know, but it was something I couldn't stop myself from doing when therapy was mentioned.

"Did your therapist talk about taking things one day at a time?"

"Yep."

JJ's eyeroll was impressive, like her eyeballs actually spun in their sockets. Maybe she was part alien. "So, what's the problem? Or do you want to continue discussing lizards taking over the world? Wasn't there a sci-fi show about that in the eighties?" She tapped a finger to her chin.

Not ready to switch gears quite yet, I finally flagged down the waitress to request a cup of tea.

JJ appeared to have tossed in the towel, trying to conjure up the TV show and had checked back into the conversation. Her *hit me with it* expression indicated she was done with the small talk portion of the meeting, and I should get to the point.

"I'm not sure I can continue being on the show." I opted for the *rip off the Band-Aid* method.

She straightened. "Why's that?"

"The university won't allow me to use their studio anymore."

JJ slumped in her seat. "Really?"

"The studio manager delivered the message on Friday after the dean of the history department informed me I'd only be teaching one class next fall."

JJ puffed air into her left cheek, switched the mass to her right, and then let it seep out of her mouth. "Wow."

"My thoughts exactly."

"What does it mean?" She spoke more in the way that suggested she was consulting the universe, not me.

I answered anyway. "Clearly, I'm not wanted, but I have tenure, so they can't fire me outright, but they can do everything to push me out."

"Do you know why?"

"I have a theory. Or two."

JJ waved for me to share.

"First, I'm a Petrie." I stabbed the air with a finger.

Her head bob indicated she agreed on that front. "What's the other reason?"

"This one has been swimming in my head since Friday, and I'm only eighty-five point two percent positive—"

"Love the point two part." JJ waggled her brows. "Go on."

"I don't think they, and by that, I mean Dean Spencer or his admin, like having a lesbian in the history department. From the moment I met both of them last summer, I feel like they've been gunning for me."

JJ's forehead crumpled. "Fort Collins, in general, is pretty liberal. Not to mention Colorado is purple on election maps."

"True on both counts, which is why I'm fourteen point eight percent uncertain. It's not like the dean is going to say, *You're a dyke, so I don't want you*. I could sue or at least make things difficult for him."

The waitress set down my tea. "Anything else?"

"Two cinnamon rolls, please," JJ answered. After the woman left, she said, "Okay, the studio issue won't be a big deal. You can use the one at Claire's office."

"She won't mind?"

"Are you kidding me? She's loving the internship you've started." JJ leaned back so the waitress could top off her coffee. The woman dashed away, and JJ lifted the mug to her lips but didn't take a sip. "You chair the history club as well, right?"

I nodded.

"In the past year, you took over the history club and started an internship for students. Now the new dean is trying to push you out, and the university is saying you can't use the studio. Most universities love the exposure." She tapped the side of her head. "Even if the professor is a pompous prick."

"Thanks."

"I'm not placing you in that category. Just stating many universities put up with big personalities that bring any type of publicity."

"I don't think it's the university calling these shots. There's been a seismic shift in how the other professors in my department treat me. Most avoid me like I'm Himmler. Hey, maybe Dean Spencer is a lizard person, and he's doing that mind-control thing!"

"*V*! That was the name of the show."

"Just *V*?" Even though I never did so under the watchful eye of Sarah, I added two packets of real sugar to my tea.

"Yep. It was a great show about an alien invasion."

"You really like aliens." I sipped my drink, holding in a moan of pure delight. Sugar, while terrible for me, tasted so fucking good sometimes, especially when stressed.

"I don't think so. At least, not that I'm aware of." She rubbed her chin. "I know the Peter issue is uncomfortable, but…"

"I should have taken Sarah's last name. Now, our children are forever cursed," I blurted.

"Why didn't you?"

"Sarah saw it as a way of me proclaiming no matter what, I was stronger than what my mother thought. Grabbing the bull by the horns." I acted this out and then released a massive groan. "This Peter business would have killed my mom."

"Because he was the favorite?"

"Because she thought I'd be the one who'd destroy the family. Lizzie the Lezzie and all that."

The waitress delivered the cinnamon rolls, allowing JJ to absorb the news. Or was she still pondering the eventuality of an alien invasion?

"I don't get parents like that." JJ cut off a portion of the roll, blowing on it before placing it in her mouth.

"Me neither. I can't imagine rooting against any of my kids." I sipped my tea. Would it be wrong to add two more packets?

"How are the munchkins?"

"Running me ragged," I said, sounding happy for the first time.

"And Sarah?"

My eyes fell to the tabletop. "She's having a hard time recovering from the C-section."

"Have you told her about any of the work stuff?"

I shook my head, slow-mo style.

"Yeah, I wouldn't either if I were in your shoes."

"It makes me feel terrible." I blew out a breath and hunched over the table to whisper, "She's going to be pissed when she finds out I didn't turn to her right from the start."

"I bet. Claire would be the same way."

I tossed my hands in the air to convey I didn't know what to do.

"Before you say anything, let me do some digging on this

dean. If there are clues this is about family values or whatever, we can come up with an action plan."

"I can't ask you to do that."

"You didn't."

"But—"

"But nothing." She raised her hand to stop me right there. "I know what it's like to feel like everyone is against you. It's not great. Shitty, actually. Besides, not only are you one of my employees, you're a friend."

"Does that mean you'll still let your kids play with mine?"

JJ flinched as if I'd tossed my tea in her face. Like I'd waste the sugar.

She asked, "Do you honestly think I wouldn't?"

"Sarah's worried that Keri is spreading rumors about us, and none of the moms will let their kids come to any of our birthday parties and vice versa." I cradled my head with both hands. "It really is like I'm getting hit from all sides."

JJ snorted. "I haven't met Keri yet, but Claire hates her, which means I won't get along with her."

"I met her briefly last week, and count me as not a fan."

"What's the rumor?"

"That Sarah split my lip."

JJ propped up her chin with an open palm. "It amazes me that some people never mature past the junior high level."

"I didn't have many friends, so I'm not prepared for this mean-mom bullshit." Was that why Sarah was overly concerned? She didn't want our children to turn out like me, the Petrie pariah?

"I had lots of friends, and I don't know how to handle the likes of Keri either. Mom bullies. It's just odd."

"I was bullied by my own mother," I confessed.

"How'd you handle that?"

"Not well, if you ask Sarah or my therapist. It's much better now that she's dead. Which I probably shouldn't say out loud."

If Sarah were here, she'd be kicking me under the table, even if she agreed.

"I don't think that route is one we can bank on with your current situation."

"Oh geez, the Petrie name wouldn't survive, and then my mom would have been right. She'll probably haunt me the rest of my life, chanting, *Lizzie the Lesbian destroyed all.*" I tried to cackle like a witch but failed miserably, sounding more like a cat puking.

JJ ignored my antics and asked, "Did she really say things like that?"

"She was a difficult woman to be around growing up," I conceded.

"I grew up with parents who were the exact opposite. Loving and caring. And yet, I'm the recovering addict and you're the esteemed historian."

"Not so esteemed these days. Before Dr. Marcel retired, I thought I was doing all the right things to become dean someday. Now, I have no idea if I'll have a job in a year. How can things unravel so quickly?" I sighed. "And, I still haven't told you everything."

JJ's eyes widened, but she gave me a supportive smile to tease the rest out of me, so I told her about the Facebook group dedicated to theorizing how Peter and I got away with murder.

As she scanned the group on her tablet, she whistled. "You really are getting hit from all sides."

CHAPTER SEVEN

After finishing my Wednesday night lecture, I switched my phone back on to see Ethan had sent an SOS message. He knew my schedule, meaning he texted with the understanding I wouldn't get it until well after nine. But he still wanted me to see it. To say I was alarmed would be an understatement. Of course, that had been my current mood twenty-four seven for weeks now.

I replied with: *You still up?*

It was only a quarter to ten, but Ethan's school day started at fifteen past seven in the morning, so I suspected he'd be in bed.

He wasn't. *Can you talk? In person?*

I texted Sarah to see if it'd be too much trouble for me to meet Ethan. Of course, she said to go ahead, wanting me to fill her in when I could.

Ethan said he'd meet me at Denny's because it was open all day and night. Did mentioning that fact mean he expected our talk would go into the wee hours of the morning? What in the world was going on?

Since he was traveling from Loveland, I arrived first. There was something about the restaurant at this time of night. A foreboding atmosphere and even the dead-on-their-feet staff seemed to believe the end of times were near. Or was I projecting? Fearful of whatever bomb Ethan was about to drop in my lap? Why had he requested to talk to me, not someone more capable of dealing with human things? Frankly, I was at my max for human interactions, and the only thing I wanted to do that night was crawl under the bed covers and sleep like the dead. Meaning no dreams, even ones with puppies, kittens, or puffy white clouds. I bent the bill of my new baseball hat, still getting used to wearing it whenever in public, not simply on bad hair days.

Blinking Christmas lights hung in the window. Part of me was relieved the Thanksgiving decorations were down. It was creepy to see happy turkeys plastered everywhere, knowing they'd end up on dinner plates. Not the cartoon versions, but it was still disconcerting to me. I wasn't ready for the Petrie Christmas madness.

While nursing a black tea, I pulled out a printed copy of a journal article I was in the midst of. Something about it was giving me trouble, but I'd been unable to detect the issue on my own. Dr. Marcel had read it and provided his thoughts, although I hadn't had time to digest them yet. I shoved down the whimper threatening to escape over the fact Dr. Marcel was no longer my boss. He would have done everything he could to insulate me from the Petrie fallout. More than likely, he still would. The guilt of not confiding in him festered, but at what point did I have to stand on my own two feet, no matter the depth of the threats and consequences?

"Hey." Ethan's lanky frame collapsed into the booth.

"This place doesn't sell booze, does it? Because you look like you need whiskey shots or something."

"I don't think having whiskey at Denny's would solve

anyone's problems. It'd only add to them." He asked the waitress for black coffee.

"Did you miss me? Is this why we're meeting in one of Fort Collins's top establishments at ten at night?"

"Terribly. I couldn't go another second without seeing your ugly mug." He pressed his palms together and batted his eyelashes.

I removed my hat and ran a hand over my head. "Remind me again why I rushed to meet you."

"Because you're my only friend who would. I'm really digging the new haircut." He flicked a hand at the do.

I ran a hand over my hair once more before replacing the cap. "I have to get it trimmed every three weeks now. It's still an adjustment when I shower. I don't have much hair left, and I keep applying way too much shampoo and conditioner."

"You've always been slow on the uptake." He made a drumming motion with his hands, seemingly pleased with his slam. "At least, it's not in a shapeless ponytail anymore."

"Keep giving it to me straight."

One side of his lips curled into an odd smile that wasn't comforting.

"Are you going to tell me what's going on?"

He sighed, removing his thick glasses and cleaning them with the hem of his sweater.

"Maybe we should get pancakes. This seems like a pancake conversation." I swooped up the menu to peruse the options. "Oh, they have cinnamon roll pancakes. Perfect!"

He rapped his perfectly cut fingernails on the Formica tabletop as he scanned the options. "I'm going to get steak and eggs."

"That's very manly."

His eyes started to water. "I'll be right back."

"Take your time."

Ethan fled to the restroom.

I shot Maddie a text for reinforcements. I simply said: *At Denny's with Ethan. Help!*

Be right there.

That eased the roiling feeling in my stomach. Some. Was Ethan about to tell me he was getting divorced? That news wouldn't be too shocking, but still... Would he and Casey need to move in? Or would it just be Ethan? How did custody work with straight couples these days?

When the waitress set down our drinks, I placed the food order for both of us, not sure what to get Maddie, so I didn't try. Before kids, Sarah and Maddie had been on a quest to seek out all the nice restaurants in Fort Collins. Now, I'd summoned her to a Denny's of all places.

Ethan lumbered back doing his best impression of a zombie facing a town with double-barrel shotguns.

"I hope you were serious about steak and eggs, because I ordered it."

"Yeah." His shoulders sagged.

"Should I start guessing so you don't actually have to say it?"

"Maybe." His eyes dropped to his hands on the table.

"Casey's been accepted to Harvard?"

"Not yet, but she has her sights on that in the near future."

"She's told me the same. I have to admire her gumption considering she's not even in her double digits." I really hated myself for playing the *Casey distraction* card, but I was so tired. I hoped Maddie would arrive in the nick of time. She loved butting into things, so why not let her?

"I don't think Casey cares for simple rules or thinks they apply to her. I've always said she's too smart for her own good. What's your next diversionary tactic?" He crossed his arms, but it seemed more like an effort to hold his shit together and not a defensive measure.

How much longer until Maddie arrives? Was she coming from my home or hers? "You joined a lizard cult?"

He stared at me as if I had spoken a bizarre language. Or in tongues. It seemed religious zealots who believed in alien lizards taking over the world would speak in tongues. I had to suppress the urge to break out into giggles, knowing that would be wrong. Once again, I wondered why everyone in my circle came to me with their problems when I was swimming in my own. I had no idea how to solve anything these days. Couldn't they see that even if I hadn't let anyone in all that much?

But I needed to buck up and be there for Ethan.

"What did Lisa say?" I dove into it.

His bottom lip quivered.

"Separation or...?"

"You don't seem surprised it's come to..." He looked out the window, where car headlights were traveling north and south on College Avenue.

I remained silent, giving him all the time he needed to speak. Or to have a good cry. How many people had come to Denny's late at night to have conversations like this?

"C-Co-parenting," he stuttered.

Weren't they already doing that? It wasn't like Ethan and Lisa had sex due to his issues with fluids. So what exactly was changing about the relationship? "What does that mean?"

"It means Lisa and I will take turns living in the house with Casey so she doesn't have to go back and forth."

"Take turns? Meaning you'll need a second place to live part-time?" I'd recently read an article about these arrangements and only thought rich couples in LA or New York City actually did this.

"Yes."

"Can you afford that?" I instantly regretted asking that question.

"No."

"You can stay with us, but I should proffer full disclosure; you might have to bunk with Maddie on occasion." I laughed, but it died quickly when Ethan burst into tears.

"I see you're handling this with your typical Lizzie panache." Maddie gestured for me to scoot over.

Funny, at the salon she'd said I handled these conversations well. My guess was she was using snark to help siphon the sadness from Ethan. If that was the case, I didn't mind all that much. Only a little.

"Lisa's in love with someone else." Ethan dabbed his eyes with a paper napkin.

I honestly didn't see that twist coming, and I blurted, "Holy fucking Christ, that's gotta hurt!"

Maddie must have been in shock as well since she didn't kick or hit me under the table, her usual reaction whenever I was an idiot.

"With a coworker."

"Mothers who work full-time have affairs?" I stupidly asked, trying to imagine sneaking dates into my schedule. Not that I wanted to be with anyone else. In all likelihood, Lisa probably had needs, and maybe she craved a *non-battery gadget* release.

"Apparently," he snorted.

"I… You… Wow." I leaned back and wrapped my head with my arms as if I needed to prevent it from exploding.

Maddie nodded in agreement.

"Does Casey know?" I asked. The kid was smarter than the three of us put together, but did that involve real world experiences, or was it more along the lines of having the ability to sequence DNA code?

Ethan wiped his nose on his shoulder. "I don't think so. I knew Lisa was unhappy, but I didn't suspect… this."

"Do you know the guy?" Maddie asked.

"It's a woman."

Lisa was a dyke now? The bombshells just kept on coming. I pictured the three of us in a World War One foxhole, German bombs lighting up the sky, the ground flying every which way, smoke strangling us, with nowhere to run because of barbed wire.

No, Lizzie. Don't retreat into your mind.

I peeked at Maddie, praying she'd say the right thing to make all of this better, but she remained quiet. This was bad. Ethan and Lisa had been together their entire adult lives. And they'd adopted Casey together. How was this happening? They had money problems, which destroyed many couples. Also, there was the issue they never had sex. Was that the clue Lisa was actually a dyke? Marrying a man who didn't want to have sex? Ever?

The waitress set down our plates and asked if Maddie wanted anything. She requested French toast and a chocolate peanut butter shake. I dittoed for the shake. Ethan asked for a strawberry shake. Ice cream—the ultimate comfort food in times like this.

"The thing is I knew Lisa was spending more time with Delores—"

"Her name is Delores?" I chimed in.

He nodded.

"Is she a hundred years old?" I did every type of mental ninja skill to block out images of old dyke pussy but was unable to. A shudder whooshed through me, which I tried not to show outwardly and probably looked like I was constipated.

"Twenty-five. And she prefers being called Lola."

"More like Lolita," I said.

This time, Maddie did kick me under the table. Really fucking hard in the right shin. I shot her a look, but her focus was on Ethan.

"How can she do this to me? To us?" Ethan sucked in a

deep breath in what seemed like an effort not to burst into tears again. "An affair. She's sleeping with someone else."

I'd always wondered if Lisa had a free pass to have sex with others given Ethan's no-sex rule, but I guess not. Not officially, which, as it turned out, didn't stop her.

"You know, monogamy is quite rare," Maddie said in all seriousness.

My head whipped to face her. "That's your way of making Ethan feel better?"

"It's just a fact of life." Maddie shrugged.

"Are you saying given enough time, everyone will cheat? No matter what?" I pressed.

"It's possible."

"You have a terrible opinion about relationships."

"Maybe. Or I'm just realistic." She tossed her hands up in a helpless manner.

"Why'd I call you and not Sarah?" I shook my head. I knew Peter had cheated on her, which she evidently hadn't gotten over. Or was she trying to make herself feel better for sleeping with Peter when he was married to Tie? Did it dull her guilt to believe it would have happened eventually because that was what humans did? No exception?

"She has four kids at home, leaving me as your only option."

"Can you two please stop?" Ethan asked, his pained expression deepening.

"I'm sorry. I am." I covered my heart. "When did you find out?"

"A week ago. Or not quite. It was the day after Thanksgiving, giving a whole new meaning to Black Friday."

And he was just telling me? "Oh, Ethan."

"This is my first night on my own." He held up his palms, sarcastically implying he was living the dream at Denny's.

"Wait." I repositioned. "This co-parenting situation is already in effect?" Who did that right before Christmas?

He nodded.

"Shit. Lisa doesn't fuck around."

"*Au contraire,* she does." Ethan wasn't using humor as a way of dealing with the situation. His words came out harshly. Probably the harshest I'd ever heard him speak.

Maddie gave me her *way to go* glare.

I wanted to raise a white flag to life. Enough with all the hard knocks. Could at least one aspect go swimmingly? Not that I hadn't seen the demise of Ethan's marriage on the horizon. It seemed inevitable, although slow coming. It was like being trapped on a one-way road behind a blue-hat driver going thirty under the speed limit with her blinker on, wavering from side to side for miles and miles, making it impossible to safely pass.

"I blame you two." Ethan held his knife, the sharp point aimed at my chest.

"Us?" I motioned to Maddie and then me.

"No. You and Sarah. Being the perfect lesbian couple. Sticking together no matter what. Weathering one impossibility after another." Considering the statements, he spoke the words with venom. "No wonder Lisa jumped ship."

"From your marriage?"

"To women!" Ethan pounded a fist on the table, causing his plate to rattle.

After the plate came to a rest, I placed a hand over my heart. "You're blaming my marriage for Lisa having an affair with a woman?" I simply couldn't understand his logic. I was floored. Beyond floored.

"I sure am. You and Sarah are always so happy." He pressed his palms together, fluttering his lashes and making kissing sounds. When he'd done this earlier, it was funny. Now, it was mean as hell.

I thought back to my conversation with JJ, about the need for people to believe anything to avoid looking inward. Ethan was a shining example, but it didn't seem the time to carefully explain to him why he was grasping at straws to explain the collapse of his marriage.

"Ethan..." Maddie entered the fray.

"And you." He wielded his knife again in her direction. "Having an affair with Peter after he was married." He shook the knife at her. "Do you have any idea how much it fucking hurts?"

"Yes, I do. Peter cheated on me," Maddie's voice stayed neutral.

"And you still inflicted that pain on Tie. She..."

Wherever he was going with that, he couldn't seem to finish it. No one in our circles truly thought of Tie as a victim. However, it didn't stop Ethan from practically foaming at the mouth. I'd seen him pissed before. Hell, I'd seen him completely irrational. But this was the first time I worried for his sanity. Seriously.

"Look. I know you're hurt—"

"Oh, shut up, Lizzie. I don't want to hear any platitudes. Why don't you go home to your perfect wife, perfect kids, perfect life? Let the rest of us—"

"Yeah, my life is so perfect!" I sucked in a deep breath. "That's why I'm on the verge of having my career explode. My book deal has gone up in smoke. My kids will have to carry the Petrie stain their entire lives. And, I haven't told my wife, who just had a C-section for the second time, any of this because I simply don't know how to tell Sarah that we may have to uproot our lives to start all over. Put some distance between us and my brother, hoping that the Petrie name has only become toxic in this state. Which given the number of conspiracy nuts with too much free time on the internet is a Hail Mary, but it may be all I got. I know Peter wasn't a saint when it came to business, but the wild and unfounded accusations that he killed Tie are bringing my family and me down. Not to mention the quacks who think I was somehow involved." I patted my hat. "I have to hide my identity now. So, yeah, my life is soooooo perfect. I'm living the fucking dream!"

Several heads reeled around to gawk at us.

Ethan's knife-wielding hand fell to the tabletop.

Maddie blinked several times.

Stupidly, maybe feeling emboldened by my tantrum, I stared at the unwanted eyeballs until they turned away, and I angrily slurped my shake. After several moments, I said, "I'm so tired of everyone dumping their problems into my lap as if I don't have to deal with my own clusterfuck of a life. I came here to listen. Not to be accused of things I'm not fucking responsible for." I pressed my finger onto the tabletop. "Your wife cheated, and I'm sure that fucking hurts. I can't imagine living through that. But don't you dare sit there and blame me for luring her to the dyke side. This may not make sense to you as a white male, but there actually isn't a lesbian plot to get wives to leave their husbands. Most of us only care about our own lives. Not worldwide dyke domination." I took another drink from the shake. "Why don't you go ahead and lay the blame at alien lizard overlords for wrecking your life? That makes more sense than saying my marriage wrecked yours."

Ethan supported his chin, an index finger rubbing back and forth along the lower lip.

Maddie stared at me with an expression that said, *Are you done?*

I wasn't. "Denial. That's the greatest drug throughout history, leading to scapegoating and persecuting millions of people throughout time. It's disgusting! People just need to grow up and stop blaming others for the mess they've made of their lives."

None of us spoke.

I dug into my pancakes, shoving a much-too-large bite into my mouth, and I chased it down with lukewarm tea.

Finally, Maddie said, "Worldwide dyke domination?"

"Alien lizard overlords?" Ethan added. "Who believes in that?"

I shrugged, my anger starting to dissipate, but I still spoke with gravity in my voice. "More than you think."

Maddie and Ethan exchanged a look that suggested they thought I'd lost my shit.

That made me break out into hysterical laughter. Yeah, I was the one losing my mind. In a Denny's. For speaking the truth.

"Uh... do you folks need anything?" the waitress, with a coffeepot in hand, asked.

"Do you think aliens are taking over the world?" I quizzed her.

The woman took a step backward and then beelined for safety in the kitchen.

Ethan hunched his shoulders and looked into my eyes. "Are you okay?"

Maddie turned my head with her left hand and held her right in the air. "How many fingers am I holding up?"

I jerked free from her grasp. "I don't have a head injury."

Again, the two of them exchanged worried looks.

"Are you really going to lose your job?" Ethan asked.

I hefted a shoulder. "They can't fire me, but they can make me miserable by only allowing me to teach Western Civ for the rest of my life. Unless Dean Spencer can do away with that university requirement. Do you know, recently, a woman spat on my shoes and called me a murderer? Now, every time I make a run to the store, I have to worry about how many will recognize me. I've never wanted fame. Especially not this way. It's freaking me out." I cradled my forehead. "I can survive not teaching. But how can I let my wife and kids bear this... curse?"

"You can't move," Ethan said. "You keep me together."

I laughed bitterly. "You just said I was at fault for your marriage falling apart."

"I—" He looked away. "I don't want to lose her. I don't want to be alone. I'm scared."

"You aren't alone. You have Casey. And us." Maddie reached across the table and held his hand. "We'll always be here for you, no matter what you say."

He gripped her hand tightly.

She turned to me. "Lizard alien overlords? Where do you come up with this stuff?"

"The news."

"Maybe you should stop reading it. It's warping your mind. Stick with Stephen King. At least his monsters are usually defeated in the end," Maddie helpfully explained.

Ethan nodded in agreement.

"Where are you staying tonight?" I asked Ethan.

"My car."

I sat up straighter. "No, you aren't. Shall we pay and go home? Before the waitress calls the cops or something?"

"I'm sure they've seen much worse here." Maddie surveyed the place, the faux wood booths, with red seats, lining the perimeter, circular yellow lamps overhead in the main section, tables of four clustered in the roomier space, chairs at the counter, and red lamps dangling from the kitchen area. While the interior had vastly improved over the years, I bet the designer in her was dying a slow, painful death.

"I don't want to bother you and Sarah." Ethan slumped.

"You can be annoying as shit, but you're family. One thing Petries do, these days, is stick together. No matter what."

"Do I have to take the last name? It's really not that popular at the moment." There was a wisp of a smile on his lips, proving to me he still had some fight in him.

"Maybe that'll be my first order of business. Change our names to Cavanaugh. Then move."

"I don't want you to move," he said.

"I—" I slapped what I hoped was enough cash down on the table to provide a decent tip, not wanting to get into that conversation. Not now. After paying the bill at the register, I flicked my fingers for them not to doddle. "Let's get going. We all could use some sleep, and then we'll come up with action plans for everything."

CHAPTER EIGHT

SARAH STIRRED IN BED, AND I LURCHED TO A SITTING position. "What's wrong?"

"I think Calvin is up." She peered at the monitor.

"I got it. You need rest." I'd been awake for a couple of hours, so I quickly went into action, tossing the covers off me.

"You got home late last night. I'm not helpless."

I yanked my arms through my bathrobe. "I'd never describe you that way. Please, just rest. You look exhausted. Sometimes, you have to let others help. I know it's hard for the mom in you to admit that."

Sarah settled back under the covers. "There's milk in the fridge."

"Thanks, love." I exited the bedroom and entered Cal's room, which he shared with Demi, who miraculously stayed asleep. "Good morning, Calvin," I whispered.

After getting him changed, we headed to the kitchen.

Ethan sat on a barstool at the counter, a cup of coffee in front of him.

"You're up early," I said.

"I kept having nightmares about aliens."

I chuckled. "I'm sorry about that."

"Do you need help?" He motioned to Calvin, whom I hugged to my chest with one arm, while I searched the fridge door for the milk.

"Cal, let Uncle Ethan cuddle you while I get your grub ready."

Calvin settled into Ethan's arms.

After locating the breast milk, I heated up water for it. "You going to work today?"

Ethan sighed. "I guess so. What else would I do?"

"I like to go to the zoo when my life is falling apart."

"Is that why you live in one?"

To prove his point, Gandhi, our demented Yorkie, arrived in the kitchen, wanting to go outside. I'd worked all summer training him not to wander too far from the yard. Now that the temperatures were plummeting to freezing levels, he didn't mess around in the morning. He zipped out, hoisted his leg on a planter box on the deck, much to my annoyance, and then zipped back inside. I'd have to take him for a walk later before... I tried to remember what day it was, unsure if I had to venture to campus or not.

"Good morning, Ethan." Sarah smiled. "Before you lecture me, I couldn't fall back asleep." She kissed my cheek.

I was relieved Sarah didn't ask Ethan why he was sitting in our kitchen before the sun rose, but she'd probably put two and two together to arrive at the fact Ethan needed a divorce lawyer. Did the Petries have one on retainer? None of us had actually been divorced, but it seemed like something some members would have on hand just in case. Peter had been heading down that path before getting arrested in my home, since he'd screamed at his wife he was going to screw her in the legal battle. The one-year anniversary of that fight, along with his arrest, was drawing closer and closer. It seemed unreal that it hadn't even been three hundred and sixty-five days yet considering the epic fallout.

Gandhi danced around my feet, wanting breakfast. Hank, our cat, jumped onto the counter, making it known he should be fed before the canine. I scratched his arched back, eliciting a purr.

Sarah took Calvin from Ethan. "How about fresh milk?" The two of them made their way to the family room.

I returned the milk to the fridge, went about making tea for me, spooned out wet food for Hank, and filled Gandhi's bowl with kibble. The terrier scarfed it as if we'd starved him for weeks.

"What about you? Hungry?" I asked Ethan.

He shook his head.

I peered into his eyes, ringed with black circles. "Did you get any sleep last night?"

"Do you think she'll change her mind?" His fingers curled around his mug.

It was way too early in the day for me to discuss the Lisa situation, but how could I say that. "I honestly don't know. Could you forgive her?"

He tucked his hands into his armpits. "I don't know. It's all just so much to take in."

"It is."

Maddie staggered into the kitchen with Demi on her hip. "Coffee. Stat."

I poured her a cup from the batch Ethan had made.

"You're a godsend," she said.

"Ethan should get the credit."

She repeated it to Ethan.

A chill came over me. Was this what my mornings would be like for the foreseeable future? Except some mornings would Lisa be staying with us? Or would she be shacking up with Delores? Or whatever name she preferred?

Hank, done with breakfast, jumped back onto the counter, rubbing his head into Ethan's arm. Many think cats are heartless, but I was certain Hank understood Ethan needed love. Ethan, his shoulders relaxing some, petted Hank. My loveable cat meowed.

There was movement on Freddie's monitor. "Time to get the twins, otherwise known as round two."

* * *

AFTER ETHAN AND MADDIE LEFT FOR WORK, SARAH asked me, "How bad is it?"

Not wanting to divulge the wrong information, I clarified, "How bad is what?"

"The Ethan situation."

"Lisa's having an affair. They're sharing the house so Casey doesn't have to go back and forth. He's our new part-time roomie." I closed one eye, determining if I hit all the important points.

Sarah didn't seem too fazed by the news. "I'm not surprised."

"Really? I didn't see the affair coming at all."

"How did you not? Lisa's been so unhappy for as long as we've known her."

"So has Ethan, but he's not screwing another woman."

"It'd be a miracle if he did."

I snorted. "You really thought Lisa would sleep with a woman."

Sarah elevated a *stop right there* hand. "Lisa's with a woman?"

I nodded.

"That's interesting."

"You know, when Jorie came to the twinks' birthday party, I did notice Lisa checking her out."

"Who wasn't that day? Besides, she's not with Jorie, is she?" Sarah usually was the one with all the info, and she seemed on her back heels by the turn of events.

"No. Delores."

"Who in the fudgsicles is Delores?"

"The one fudging Lisa." I waved a hand for Sarah to roll with my way to avoid saying *fuck* in front of the children.

"What's going to happen next?" Sarah stared above the kids' heads at the breakfast nook table out the window.

Not wanting to think about the future, I steered the conversation to somewhat safer waters. "How's the planning for Christmas?" We'd struck a deal. Sarah wouldn't go all out for Thanksgiving, but I'd let her have her way for Christmas, when hopefully she'd be stronger. I understood how important it was for her to surround herself with family for special occasions.

"Good." Her *good* didn't sound all that great.

"What aren't you telling me?"

"The guest list has grown some."

"Define some."

"Somewhere in the range between a few to one hundred."

I motioned for her to stop stalling.

"I may have overdone it… again."

"I thought you just wanted to fill Peter's and Tie's empty chairs."

"And George's."

"Just three more?"

"It started out that way." She avoided my gaze.

"And?"

"Don't you need to shower before heading to campus or whatever?"

That seemed the safest way to end the conversation without fighting.

CHAPTER NINE

"Lizzie! Wait up!"

I wheeled about, locating Jorie in the onslaught of professors and teachers, all bundled up in jackets and scarves, heading to the Student Union at noon on a chilly Friday in December.

"Hey there," I said when she stopped in front of me, huffing and puffing.

"I'm out of shape. I've been following you from the chemistry building, and I never caught up." Snowflakes whirled around her, and her nose was bright red.

"If you're stalking me, I don't think you're supposed to tell me outright that you are and imply I should slow down to allow you to sufficiently follow me." I blew into my gloveless hands.

She gripped the strap of her bag. "Very funny. May I buy you lunch?"

"A stalker with manners. That's refreshing. But I think I should be the one buying given all the extra hours you've been helping out with the kiddos. I was going to grab a sub. That work?"

"I could murder a footlong meatball."

I waved for us to enter the building and to head to the stairwell leading to the basement. The line was long, but I'd expected that considering the time of day. Besides, my next class wasn't for a couple of hours, and given my new persona non grata status, it wasn't like I had to rush finishing any journal articles to advance in the department. My dream of being the history dean at the university was on life support, only waiting for someone to pull the plug. If I wanted to find another teaching gig, publishing would behoove me.

"What's new?" she asked, moving a step forward as one customer placed his order and was now instructing the sandwich maker (what was the fancy name they gave them?) what he wanted on his sub.

"Geez, don't get me going. Let's talk about you. Please tell me your life isn't falling apart." Sandwich professional? No, that wasn't right.

She eyed me but didn't push me on the first. "Just the usual is going on with me. Work. School. And…" Her cheeks pinkened.

"And?" I pressed, knowing the answer but not wanting to step into any social quagmires.

"Dating."

"Oh, really? That's exciting. Who's the lucky… person?" I caught myself in time in case she wasn't really comfortable discussing dating women in public.

"Like you don't know." She chewed on a nail.

Jorie was a knockout, and I imagined her options were wide open. I also knew she was in my life, so she was probably dating the one person I would warn her off of. "Please don't make me guess. I'm too tired. Can I play the *I have a newborn at home* card?" Not to mention my entire life was crashing and burning.

"Yes, I'll take pity on you. Courtney." It was her turn to

place her order, and she requested a meatball sub on Italian bread.

I dittoed, not wanting to put any thought into the different bread options. I longed for the days when all options were limited.

After getting our subs and filling our drinks, we located a recently deserted table that would probably get a failing grade from the health department, but on a Friday afternoon, it was the best it was going to get.

Using a napkin, I wiped the round table and took a seat on a chair that listed to the right, which seemed perfect since the table leaned to the left. "Tell me about Courtney."

"What do you want to know?" Jorie sucked on her straw, her eyes shimmering with new relationship excitement.

Not a whole hell of a lot. "Does she treat you right?"

"She does. Even opens doors for me. She's old-school that way. Women of your generation are adorably old-fashioned."

I wasn't sure how to take that, so I decided to just store that piece away in the *do not pursue* file in my head. "Do you see each other much? Given her work schedule and yours?"

"Not as much as I'd like, but I think it might be better that way. Keeps things fresh. We're both looking forward to Christmas."

I finished chewing and patted my mouth with a paper napkin to get rid of marinara sauce. "Are you doing something special?"

She cocked her head, showcasing that smile of hers that probably drew many people to her. "You don't know, do you?"

"Know what?" It wasn't unusual for me to miss the obvious.

"I'm not sure I want to be the one to tell you." Her eyes darted to the left and right, never landing on mine.

"Please don't tell me you're getting married or something." *Geez, Lizzie. Way to be a wet blanket.*

She laughed, reminding me why I liked spending time with her. It was nice being around those who understood me and didn't take my grumpiness to heart.

"Nothing like that," she said. "We're just going to your house for the holiday extravaganza."

I stared at her, slurping my iced tea. "Did Sarah use that word specifically? *Extravaganza?*"

"Yes." Jorie put a hand on my arm. "It's going to be okay."

"Parties and the Petries don't really mix." I spoke like a child afraid of the monster in the closet.

"I—"

There was a scuffle as a student dropped her backpack, the contents spilling out. While her friend helped, I noticed two professors from the history department walking by, one speaking quietly to the other while both pairs of eyes were on me. If Jorie noticed, she didn't mention it.

Instead, she said, "I'll be over to help with the cooking. I've heard you aren't allowed near the oven. Something about a cake fire. And, how did you destroy a microwave?"

"Hey, it could happen to anyone!" I chomped into my sub, splattering red sauce all over my shirt. "Great. I have to teach one more class today."

Jorie assessed the damage. "It's… not that bad."

I glanced down. "It looks like someone plunged a dagger into my chest."

She burst into laughter. "It really does. Luckily for you, they sell T-shirts in the bookstore upstairs."

I groaned, but it was my only option at the moment. "I should keep spare clothes in my office."

The two professors walked by again like guards patrolling prison grounds. Had Dean Spencer tasked them to keep an eye on me? I didn't break eye contact with them.

"What's that about?" Jorie asked once the pair started to ascend the stairs.

"Just the typical Petrie treatment these days."

"Courtney has some thoughts on that."

I opened my Baked Lays bag. "Does she?"

"Yes. She thinks you should start a charity."

"For?" I munched on a chip.

"She's still working on that part."

Had Sarah hired her without saying anything? "Oh."

"It's going to be okay. The Peter mess is just one of a million scandals. Before you know it, someone else will run into trouble, drawing all the heat off you."

"Can this person hurry the fuck up? I've never liked attention." Was it wrong to hope Betty, the neighbor who hated my guts, was a serial killer and the authorities were hot on her trail? She was simply too nice to everyone—but me. And this was before the Peter mess.

"Maybe you shouldn't wear your lunch." She laughed, and it was hard to get upset by it.

CHAPTER TEN

"Since when do you teach while wearing a T-shirt?" Sarah squinted. "Aggies?"

I glanced down at the heather gray shirt under my black blazer. "The school used to be known as an agricultural and mechanical college, and Aggies was the nickname for the athletic teams."

"Are you saying you wore the shirt to teach your students about a nickname only nerds like you would know?" Her smile was alluring.

"I had to buy a shirt before teaching my last class, and buying one that had a connection to history made me feel slightly less pathetic."

Sarah crossed her arms. "You had to buy a T-shirt? You hate shopping."

"There was an unfortunate meatball sub incident." I swiped a hand over my forehead, brushing off an errant hair or something before it could get into my eye.

"Do I even want to know?"

"Do I want to know about your Christmas plans?"

"How was the rest of your day, dear?" She smiled sweetly, doing her best *I'm innocent* flutter of her lashes.

"Why does that make me even more nervous?" I circled a finger in the air in front of her face.

Sarah appraised my shirt again. "Did the new dean see you in your T-shirt? Is he the type to hold something silly like that against you?"

There was my opening for saying, "Yeah, about that. I think he hates me and wants me to quit. Are you sure you don't want to move?"

But I couldn't force myself to say any of that aloud. Instead, I made a pffft sound. "Please. You should see the American West prof. He hasn't washed his beard since the last century."

"Who's that?"

"I—I can't remember his name." Probably since I just conjured him up in my mind. Lying was a slippery slope, apparently. "Give me the lowdown here. What's new with the kids?"

"Ollie's joined PayPal's board, and Fred has decided to build an airplane in the backyard. Demi and Cal are moving to Hollywood."

"What?"

Her eyes darted toward the ceiling. "What do you think is new here? We have four kids under the age of three. Lots of giggles. Crying. Feedings. Dirty diapers. All on repeat."

"When you put it like that, I really have to question our sanity." I kissed her cheek. "Shall I make dinner?"

"Chinese again?"

"I'm thinking pizza. Are your mom and Troy expected for our new Friday night bash tradition? Last week we all stayed up past ten, a new record."

"Mom is. Troy has a boys' night out."

"Since when has Troy done that."

"It's a new thing. Mom doesn't think he has enough friends his own age."

I laughed. "She sounds like someone else I know. Speaking of, is Ethan here tonight?"

"Yes. Every other night for the foreseeable future." She didn't sound upset about that, only worried, probably for Ethan's mental health. "Should we set him up in the basement? Give him some privacy?"

I shook my head, once again unsure how to broach the we may have to move topic. I was in need of another diversion. "Please don't ever leave me."

"Don't bring it upon us," she stated in a clear voice.

"Why do you think I'd be the one responsible for wrecking our marriage?" Was she picking up on signs that I wasn't being entirely truthful? How could I ask about my tells without getting busted?

She gave me her *you can't be serious* look.

I really needed to work up the nerve to tell her everything that was going on, because living like Ethan didn't seem appealing at all. But neither did telling Sarah the shitty hand I'd been dealt because of the Peter fallout. My brother, along with my mother, made my childhood hell. Now, he was wrecking my adult life. And it wasn't like I could go to him and say, "Thanks a lot, Bro." The man was sitting in a prison cell. I was pretty sure his life was a whole helluva lot worse than mine at the moment.

* * *

THE FOLLOWING MORNING, AT THE BREAKFAST TABLE, Sarah looked at her phone. "Weren't you at Denny's Wednesday night?"

I stretched my arms overhead, yawning. "Yeah. Why?"

"Someone left a waitress a five-hundred-dollar tip."

It seemed like my breathing, pulse, and all the other functions my body did without my noticing came to a screeching halt.

"Lizzie?" Sarah snapped her fingers in front of my face. "Lizzie. Use your words. What's wrong?"

"W-where's my wallet."

Sarah's eyes scouted the kitchen. "Is it in your bag?"

"Where's my wallet?" I repeated, unable to find my words, which was something that happened to me when I was shutting down.

At the desk, she fished in my bag, pulling out my wallet.

"Do I have any hundred-dollar bills?"

Sarah yanked out the cash and rifled through. "No. Why would you have hundreds anyway?"

"I've been paying with cash lately. I'm tired of companies tracking my every movement. I'm not a fan of Big Brother." It also lessened the chance of people spying my name on the credit card, giving them the urge to spit on me.

She conceded my point with a shrug. "That doesn't explain why you just panicked."

"Because I think I'm the person who left the tip."

"Why would you do that? I mean, you're generous, but five hundred clams?"

"I didn't mean it. I had a minor meltdown and asked the waitress if she believed in aliens—" Sarah started to interrupt, but I shut her down with, "It's a long story. How'd you hear about the tip?"

"An article in Claire's paper."

"Did it mention I was the one who tipped the waitress?"

"No." It seemed like she tried to tamp down her *duh* expression, but failed.

"Jesus, I'm pretty sure everyone in town knows who I am given all the bad press, but when I warrant some good press, all of a sudden no one knows who I am."

"But you left the money by accident."

"The waitress didn't know that." I flicked up a hand, my

other holding a spoon for Demi. "She wanted her minutes in the sun, but didn't want to be associated with me. Unbelievable. I just can't catch a fu-fudging break."

"I prefer to think she honest to God didn't know you. Not everyone pays attention to the news."

"My name trended on Twitter as hashtag PeterPetrieAccomplice along with some very unflattering photos."

"Again, not everyone follows social media. Many people are too busy surviving to give two fiddlesticks about anything else."

"I really hope that's true!" After a moment's thought, I added, "Not that I hope her life is miserable."

Sarah wore her knowing smile. "Well, you'll be happy to hear your tip helped her make her mortgage payment after her car broke down last month. She says it was like her Guardian Angel swooped in and saved her family."

"Oh, in that case I'm glad it helped." I wiped Freddie's face and fingers and let him toddle off to join the rest of the kids in the front room.

Sarah wrapped her arms around my neck. "Even when you don't know it, you're being the kind and loving person I adore."

"Don't get used to this."

"Which part? Kindness? Loving? Me adoring you?"

"Very funny, wise guy. I think I need a better system for the cash in my wallet so I don't keep handing out hundreds instead of ones."

Maddie entered the kitchen. "Did you hear about the person who tipped a waitress five hundred bucks?"

"Nope." I sipped my Earl Grey.

Sarah winked at me and then said, "While the kids are being entertained by Mom and Ethan, I think I'm going to indulge in a shower that's longer than two minutes."

"Enjoy." I kissed her cheek.

Maddie poured herself a cup of coffee. "What would you do if Sarah left you?"

Again, my body started to power down in shock. "Wh-what?"

"Sarah. Leaving you. What would you do?"

"Why are you asking?" I whispered, glancing over my shoulder to determine if Ethan could overhear us, but the kids were loud enough to drown out Maddie's words.

"Hypothetically."

"That's a terrible thing to do to a person!" I waggled a finger at her.

"Ask a hypothetical?"

"Scare the crapola out of me!" I pounded my chest to jump-start my heart.

"I didn't mean to. Sarah would never leave you. How would you feel if she died?"

I stared into Maddie's blue eyes. "You're sick. Demented."

She sat heavily on one of the barstools. "I'm trying to open up to you."

"About what?"

"I've been asking myself those questions about Gabe. To ensure I want to end things completely with him."

That actually made sense. "And?"

"And, what?"

"What thoughts go through your head when you think of not being with him?"

She stared into her coffee. "Honestly?"

"No, lie to me. That'll help you the most."

"Sometimes I hate you."

"Ditto." I sipped my tea. "Seriously, talk to me."

"It doesn't upset me. The opposite actually."

"Okay..." I leaned my forearms on the counter. "Explain that to me like I'm an idiot. Slowly and carefully."

"A sense of calm comes over me..." She glanced out the window.

I wondered if she asked the same questions concerning Peter.

"I keep thinking about what you said. That you believed I could find my Sarah." She clutched the front of her sweater. "I want what you two have."

"Can you define what we have?"

"True love. Not comfort but the deep connection." She wiped a tear away. "You didn't lie to me, did you? I'll find it?"

"I never thought I would, but I did."

"What does that mean?"

"Trust the universe, Maddie." I patted her hand.

"That's a little woo-woo for you."

"It is." I straightened. "Have you brought this up with Gabe at all?"

"Sorta."

"Ah, that means no."

"It's almost Christmas," she defended weakly.

"I know. It's the time of year the Petries fall the fuck apart." I reached across the island and squeezed her hand. "Don't keep it bottled up from Gabe for too long. He should know. Like you, he also deserves his Sarah."

"I'm wondering if he's found someone else. He doesn't call or text as much as he used to."

"Really?"

"Do you know many men who would be cool if their girlfriend spent all her time with you guys and the kids?"

"Have you been using us as some kind of litmus test for his love?"

"No!" she said with too much vehemence, which meant she had been.

"Does thinking of him with someone else upset you?"

She shook her head.

"End it, Maddie, and soon."

"Get the twins and Demi dressed for a hike," Sarah barked after reentering the kitchen from the dining room side.

"Feeling energized after your shower?" Maddie asked, but I sensed from her relaxed demeanor Maddie had an inkling this had been planned. Further proof was Maddie's hiking boots.

This was the first I was hearing about a family hike. I didn't particularly like how Sarah spoke the command in a military way. Not that I was going to argue that point. When Sarah was in these moods, it was best to go along. Otherwise, we'd argue about it and then end up doing exactly what she wanted to anyway. This wasn't the hill to die on. Before kids, I'd always made time for bike rides and hiking. Growing up in Colorado instilled a love of outdoor activities no matter the weather. My philosophy was there was no such thing as bad weather, only inappropriate outfits.

Since having kids, I'd stopped my daily rides and packed on fifteen pounds. Was this Sarah's way of saying I needed to lose weight? I couldn't believe that because she wasn't the type to think that way about me, but she'd been struggling with body image issues since the twins were born.

After getting the kids prepped for a chilly hike, I asked Sarah the next step of the plan.

"First, exercise. Second, if we can find any decent ones, since it's a tad late in the season, acorns."

I glanced at the remaining ones scattered throughout our backyard. "Those don't count?"

She heaved a heavy sigh. "No. Not for this activity."

The acorns had seen better days, but where in the hell did Sarah think she'd find ones that hadn't been crunched or damaged in any way? Again, I swallowed that question. "Okay, kids, let's get loaded up in the car."

Ethan swooped Fred into his arms. "Stick with me, little man. We dudes have to look out for each other."

Freddie giggled, causing Ethan to break out into a grin. For a full second. It warmed my heart to see the two of them together.

Maddie held onto Ollie's hand. Our eldest daughter wasn't the type who liked to be lugged around unless asleep.

"You coming?" I asked Sarah.

"Of course. This is a family-bonding exercise."

I walked behind Rose and Sarah, who was holding Demi's hand, and I carried Calvin in his car seat. Amazingly, carting kids around all day hadn't helped me fight the battle of the bulge. I'd be a formidable arm-wrestling contender, though.

In the car, Sarah in the passenger seat, directed me to drive to City Park, much to my relief. I'd been envisioning Sarah wanting to hike around Horsetooth or Rocky Mountain Park, and given the fresh dusting of snow on the grass, I was picturing many tantrums from the adults and crying kids.

Maddie, who drove Ethan and Rose, tailed me.

"How are you feeling?" I asked Sarah.

"When are you going to stop treating me like an invalid?"

"I wasn't aware I'd been doing that. I will never ask how you are again." I wasn't able to keep the hurt from my tone.

"I'm sorry. I am. But, it's been over a month. I think I can manage a stroll." Her voice didn't sound as confident.

"In my defense, you said hike earlier." I patted her thigh, my way of saying everything was okay between the two of us. "And, Maddie is wearing boots worthy of climbing Everest."

Sarah laughed about the last part. Even Maddie, who'd been living in Colorado for years, couldn't curtail dressing the way those outside of the Rocky Mountain state envisioned hardy outdoor types dressed.

"Hike. Stroll. When we have four little ones, does it really matter?" She grinned, returning to her carefree self. I wondered how long hormonal Sarah would be around but then felt rotten for that thought given she'd carried three of our kids.

Also, there was the fact that word choice did matter to me, but I didn't see the point of parsing out the difference between the words given her roller-coaster emotions. I had to remember not everyone was the same. Something my therapist repeatedly brought up until the thought came naturally to me.

City Park in Fort Collins was a gem for families. In the summer, there were lots of picnic areas, a trolley, and a swimming pool with slides. In the winter, you could ice skate on Sheldon Lake. December was an interesting time since it was before winter had truly set in, but the path around the lake was a perfect activity for the twins. None of the snow from the previous night remained on the sidewalk, and the path was mostly dry. Demi and Cal were loaded into the stroller we'd gotten when we first had twins.

Sarah, Maddie, Rose, and Ollie led the way on the sidewalk around the lake.

While I pushed the stroller, Ethan held Freddie's hand.

"Do you remember them fishing a body out of the water a year or two ago?" Ethan jerked his chin toward the lake as if I was unaware of its existence on my left.

"I'd forgotten about that." I glanced at the water's surface, which had a serene feel on this particularly sunny but cold day.

"I never understood people who could kill another person," Ethan said. "When I heard about Delores, though, I wanted to punch her in the face."

I made a mental note to keep a close eye on Ethan. Should I add a Google alert for random bodies floating in Sheldon Lake? "I'm thinking getting arrested is the last thing you need in your life. Might complicate the divorce and custody case."

"Have you ever thought yourself capable of murder?" He turned to me.

My instinct was to tell him to let go of my son's hand right that second, but when I examined his eyes, I knew Ethan couldn't hurt anyone. Then, I remembered the story of Ethan beating the crap out of someone who had treated Lisa poorly back in college. If I'd been in his shoes, what would I have done if someone hurt Sarah? Or one of my kids?

"Is it ever possible to know what someone is truly capable of?" I asked. "You probably shouldn't pursue this line of questioning with a historian who focuses on the Nazis. We really aren't the most uplifting when analyzing human nature."

He grunted. "Sometimes Casey scares me."

This was an entirely new plot thread I hadn't expected. "In what way?"

"She can be so clinical about things. The other day, there was a dead bird in our yard, and she wanted to dissect it and use the microscope you got her." His tone was accusatory.

"Are you saying my microscope purchase has led Casey down a dangerous path where she might become a serial bird killer?" The thought was ludicrous, and I had to zip my lips shut so I wouldn't laugh.

"No, but is it weird that she didn't cry or...? What would you have done as a young girl?"

"I would have cried." And my mother would have teased me for showing any emotion for something so inconsequential as a bird. "You?"

He shook his head. "But I'm a boy."

"Wait a minute. Are you saying Casey should be more sensitive because she's a girl?"

"Of course not."

"Uh, I think you are. I'm betting in a few years, if the twins saw a dead bird—"

Freddie made a cheerful chirping sound, completely unfazed by the tone of the conversation.

I continued, "Fred would be torn up and Ollie fascinated. I know Casey is smart, but she's still a kid. She's inquisitive about the world. This bird hadn't been a part of her life, so it was merely a curiosity. That's all. I wouldn't stress too much over her morbid curiosity."

"Are you saying I shouldn't use this as proof to Lisa that we should stay together or Casey will become America's most prolific female serial killer?"

I laughed.

His shoulders folded inward.

"Seriously? Were you really considering that?" My brow furrowed.

"Not seriously," he said in a way that suggested he really had been.

I took a deep breath, my eyes on Ollie hunching down to look at something in the grass. Sarah joined her. Ollie picked up a battered red leaf that had seen better days, but Sarah praised the find.

Then Sarah dropped something on the ground, and Ollie swooped up a perfect acorn, ditching the yucky leaf.

"I know you can't see this now, but everything is going to work out for you and your family. It may not be what you envisioned on your wedding day, but you and Lisa are good people. You have an amazing daughter, who'll probably find a cure for cancer. Don't let the anger you feel now spoil everything—"

"It sucks, though." He blew out a long breath.

"Yes, I bet it does. It will for some time. When you have these dark thoughts, come to me. Not Lisa. I can handle them. But if you even suggest anything like that to your—to Lisa, it won't go over well." I tried to imagine telling Sarah something like that, and I had to stop because imaginary Sarah was just as intimidating.

"Are you going to tell me to man up?"

"Nope. Human up. Being an adult is not fun the majority of the time. It doesn't change the fact that you are one."

"I hate when you say things like that." He shook his head as if not wanting my words to sink in.

"Like what?"

"Like I don't have a choice."

"You don't. As soon as you adopted Casey, you decided to put her needs ahead of your own. You can't go back on that. Not ever." My eyes swept over my children, and I vowed to tell Sarah the news about Dean Spencer before the day was over. "And tonight, when you go home to spend the rest of the weekend with her, you have to act as normal as possible."

"You don't think I know that?" he growled.

"Yes, I do. But it doesn't hurt to remind you since one of the solutions you came up with was saying, *Let's stick together so Casey doesn't start tossing bodies into Sheldon Lake*."

"I hate Delores. How can I be civil around her?"

"Hating her is fine for the moment. Hate her guts. Don't kill her. That's a statement I never thought I would ever have to say to anyone in my life." A thought crossed my mind. "Wait, when do you have to be civil around her?" Had Sarah invited Lisa and Delores to Christmas?

"I don't know. If they stay together, it's possible I'll have to interact with her at some point."

That relieved my mind some. Sarah hadn't lost her mind completely. "Do you know how long they've been…?" My voice drifted off, allowing him to fill in the blank.

He shrugged.

Freddie wiggled free and ran on his wobbly legs to join Ollie. The two of them joined hands, giggling. Once again, I spied Sarah drop an acorn, which Freddie scooped up and held above his head, Maddie, Rose, and Sarah acting like he'd found buried treasure. I suppressed a laugh. Sarah wanted the kids to find acorns for what I assumed would be that afternoon's craft project, but she knew there wouldn't be acceptable ones this close to Christmas. My love for her grew exponentially considering how much effort she put in for our kids. Sarah glanced over her shoulder and met my eye. I mouthed *I love you*. She smiled. Maddie must have cracked a joke, because Sarah and Rose burst into laughter.

I checked Ethan's mood, but his gaze was on the water, with his hands dug into the pockets of his jacket.

"You know what used to make me feel good when I was a kid?" I said to Ethan.

"What?"

"The swings. I bet I can get higher than you."

He gave me some serious side-eye, but I detected a faint smile. "I bet you can't."

I made a megaphone with my hands and shouted, "Let's go to the playground so Ethan and I can settle a bet."

Sarah craned her neck over her shoulder, giving me that look of hers that implied I was being an idiot, but she was curious to see how it'd turn out. This was becoming the theme in my life. Seeing how it would all work out in the long run.

*   *   *

THAT NIGHT, GETTING READY FOR WHAT I HOPED would be a peaceful slumber, I stood at the foot of the bed, flossing my teeth. While switching the floss from the top of my mouth to bottom, I said around my fingers, "How do you know when someone is about to snap?"

Sarah yanked the covers back and climbed in. "Can you be a bit more specific?"

I moved closer to Sarah's side of the bed and whispered, even though the door was closed and it was his night with Casey, "Ethan."

Sarah nodded her head thoughtfully. "I don't think it's time to worry just yet. He's reacting to his entire life being turned upside down. People often don't react well when that happens."

I parked my butt on the edge of the bed. "He was considering telling Lisa their separation will force Casey into becoming a serial killer or something nefarious like that."

Sarah chuckled. "That's an interesting argument to present to Lisa as a last-ditch effort to save the marriage."

"You think that's all it is?"

"I hope so." Sarah placed a hand on my thigh. "Don't go all Lizzie thinking you need to hire PIs to follow Ethan or Casey every second of the day to prevent them from going on a killing spree. Neither has it in them."

"I hadn't thought of that avenue." I glanced at the ceiling, trying to factor the cost. Maddie had hired a PI to tail Peter years before to find out if he was cheating. Would he give me a discount if Maddie referred me?

"Damn. I shouldn't have mentioned it. Can you pretend I didn't?"

"I'll try, but I am worried he won't dig himself out of this funk. I know it's early days in the separation, but it seemed inevitable, didn't it?" I continued flossing, giving up the idea of a PI for the moment.

"It did, but even when it does, it's still a lot to process. I'm also worried. You and I will be there for him every step of the way."

I finished flossing, trying to buck up the nerve for the other conversation. "Would you ever consider leaving me?"

Sarah bowed her head, peering into my face. "Again, I feel like I need more details before committing to an answer."

I laughed, but it came out more as pathetic choking. "Let's say I hadn't been all that forthcoming with information in order to protect you."

"Ah, you do love being protective."

I remained silent, waiting for the *but*... She didn't offer it up right away, so I gestured for her to get to it.

"Do I need to point out it usually ends up biting you in the ass?"

My gaze dropped to my lap as I fiddled with the dental floss until it snapped into two. "Some things have been happening since that so-called documentary on Peter."

"Go on," she said with trepidation in her voice.

"My book deal is on the back burner at the moment. My agent said it's probably best to not approach a new publisher right now."

"Oh, Lizzie. I'm so sorry."

I looked her in the eye. "There's more."

"I figured. You usually start off small."

I sighed. "It's possible I'm being pushed out of my teaching position."

Sarah's eyebrows arched as this nugget washed over her. "Okay. I wasn't expecting that."

"The dean is cutting back my classes next fall."

"To how many?"

"One."

"From your tone, there's another shoe about to drop."

I licked my lips. "He's only offering me Western Civ."

She inhaled through her nostrils. "That's—" She glanced away. "Not what you want at all."

"Not really. It's an entry-level course for freshmen. While all history is worthwhile, it really wouldn't let me dig into the subjects that intrigue me. And I have to wonder what it would do to my research."

"I understand." She reached for my hand. "Is there more?"

"The school won't let me record in their studio, but JJ is helping out on that front. I think the other professors in the department know I'm toxic and are going out of their way not to allow me to taint their reputations. It's going to get very lonely or lonelier."

"You, the self-described loner, are worried about getting even lonelier." Her smile was sad. Squeezing my thigh, she said, "How long has this been going on?"

"I found out about the book the day after Calvin's birth. A week after the Peter Petrie exposé," I said in my exaggerated gotcha TV journalist voice. "A woman actually spat at me and called me a murderer in a parking lot. There's a Facebook group that claims I helped Peter."

"That's why you've started paying for things with cash. I thought that was odd."

"I'm trying to get a handle on all of this. I don't want you going to the store. Ever!"

Sarah released a gut-wrenching sigh. "While I feel terrible you've been dealing with this all alone, I do understand why you kept it to yourself."

I leaned over to kiss her, but Sarah laid a finger on my lips. "But that stops right here, right now. Don't continue to keep things from me."

"Is this the time to mention I'm thinking of reaching out to professors I know in Massachusetts to see if there's an opening?"

"Ma-Massachusetts," she said with a tremble. "That's all the way across the country."

"Technically, it's only two thousand miles away, not three. If we lived in San Francisco, you could say that."

She started to speak but zipped her lips shut while she seemed to mull over how best to deal with the topic. "We should go to bed."

"Does that mean Massachusetts is dead?"

"No. It means I need to sleep and let all this news sink in."

"Sink in? You sound like me."

"I know. Some of the things you do make sense. A very small percentage." She held her fingers in the air with the tiniest bit of space between them. "Do you really think I'm so unreasonable I wouldn't consider moving given the situation?"

I let out a huff of air. "I hate when you set me up like this. It's not nice."

Sarah's stern expression gave way to such a sexy smile. Our eyes locked. I questioned with a raised brow if I'd be rebuffed again. She beckoned me with a finger. Our lips met. Soft. Inviting. I let the dental floss fall from my fingers onto the carpet. I climbed on top of Sarah, still kissing.

"I've missed you," I said between kisses.

"Me too."

"Are you—?" I glanced down at her midsection.

"Yes. Just be gentle."

I kissed the tip of her nose, her lips, the hollow of her neck.

Sarah released a moan, signaling she was content and excited. It'd been a long time since we made love. I couldn't even remember our last roll in the hay. Way before Halloween.

My hand slid under her shirt. Sarah lifted off the mattress to allow me to remove it completely. My gaze traveled up and down her torso. Creamy skin. Pillowy tits. I wanted to suckle her nipples but knew they were off-limits. Sarah gazed down at them, her expression claiming she wished I could as well.

"I love you, Sarah. So very much."

She cupped my cheeks. "I can see it in your eyes."

I softly kissed the swell of each breast before arriving at her mouth again. Our tongues danced, the heat level at the sweet stage. But the eagerness ticked up a notch with each passing second.

Sarah's hip ground into my pussy.

"Naked. Need. Now," I said in between kisses.

Not wanting to struggle getting stripped down while on top of Sarah, I hopped off the bed, removed my shirt, and let my PJ bottoms billow to the ground. Sarah easily dispatched her remaining articles.

Once again, our eyes locked on each other.

"Sometimes, when I see you like this..." I swallowed. "It's overwhelming."

"What is?" she asked in a soft voice.

"You loving me no matter what."

"I do."

"But why?"

Her expression turned even more tender, which I didn't think possible. "Only you would ask that right now."

"Still waiting." I pushed my ear out with my palm.

She crooked a finger. "I won't answer until I feel your skin on mine."

I would never say no to that request.

Sarah ran her hands up and down my back. "Because I do."

I started to prod for more, but her smile, which communicated love, sadness, fear, happiness, and every other emotion a human could feel all blended together, knocked the words out of my brain.

"Some things can't be explained, Lizzie. They can only be felt." She gently brought my head to her chest. "Can you feel it?"

My ear was pressed against her, allowing me to detect her heartbeat. But it wasn't as simple as that. Nothing ever was when it came to Sarah. It was the connection between the two of us on every level: physical, spiritual, emotional, and levels the simpleton in me couldn't fathom. I sincerely doubted anyone would be able to expound on it. Only couples like us experienced simpatico like this.

I ran a finger down her side, enjoying her writhing underneath me. Switching gears, I started to explore her body with my mouth. I could never get enough of tasting her. Or leaving my mark, not in a possessive way, but to show I didn't take any part of Sarah for granted. Including her C-section scar.

"It's hard to believe." I peppered the line with soft kisses.

"What?"

"Our little ones came out of here."

"Technically, only two."

"They owe you big time." I placed another soft kiss on the scar.

"That they do. So do you."

"I'm aware. I'll try to pay you back every single day."

"With sex? I appreciate your drive, but we're not in our twenties anymore."

"Not solely sex, smart-ass."

"Good to know. Not that you're off the hook for now. Hup, hup!"

My tongue traveled past her scar, over her pubic hair, and farther. Her need hung in the air. I'd always cherished her musky scent. But it didn't match the extraordinary experience of that first taste every single time. My tongue was right there. I didn't want to make my move yet.

With a finger, I eased between her wet lips, sliding inside.

Sarah closed her eyes, her head pressing into the pillow. "Oh..."

There may have been more words that should have followed that *oh*. I suspected it was a similar situation to being unable to explain her love with words. Because this moment was the same. We didn't fuck to fuck. We did so to connect. In one of the most primal fashions that belonged to the two of us. Nothing could get between us when making love. Not a thing.

My mouth moved closer to her pulsing clit, another finger going inside.

Sarah's back arched in anticipation.

Her scent filled my insides with love.

The first taste sent my body into a tizzy, like it always did. How could this keep happening? The perfection that was us making love?

I lapped her bud, increasing my finger thrusting as I went in deeper.

Her hips moved in concert with the emotions.

Her fingers raked my short hair, her nails scoring my scalp.

Why hadn't I lopped off my ponytail sooner? The sensation of her tousling my pixie haircut in every direction was euphoric. As if knowing the effect she was having on me, perhaps possibly by me ramping up my efforts, Sarah went to town on my head.

The closer she came, the more I wanted to get her there.

"I'm so—"

Her orgasm hit.

Hard.

I continued, not wanting the feeling to end.

CHAPTER ELEVEN

My eyes popped open way too early on Christmas Eve morning. I had hoped to sleep through the day, but my body betrayed me. It wasn't that I didn't want to spend the day with Sarah and the kids. It was all the other people expected that made me feel like Sisyphus. Rolling the rock up the hill, only to have it crash back down, repeating the process over and over for all of eternity. That was the definition of insanity. It also nailed what it was like being a Petrie. Constantly pushing the boulder uphill against the odds.

"That's not a good face to wake to." Sarah rested her hand on my cheek.

"Terrible news for me, or you rather, since this is the face I was born with."

She chuckled quietly, probably not wanting to wreck the silence of the house so far. "I'm trying to picture you as a newborn with a furrowed brow. It's not that hard, actually."

"Very funny." I rolled onto my side. "Not all of us can be beautiful and smart. Some of us have to be the worker bees."

"Are you saying I'm the queen bee?"

"Absolutely."

"Where does everyone else fit in?"

"Good question." I mulled it over. "Let's see. You're the queen. We've already discussed Freddie is the thinker and Ollie the enforcer. Demi is the sweet one, which is shocking given her parentage. And Calvin is the grumpy one. That used to be my place." I held five fingers in the air, studying them. "Maybe I don't fit in anymore. If I ever really did."

Sarah forced my fingers into a ball, holding the fist in her palm. "You're the glue that holds us all together."

"I really hope you're right, because these days I feel like I'm the one tearing us apart." I pantomimed a bomb exploding.

Sarah's gaze bored into mine. "Don't ever think that."

"We may have to uproot our entire family because of my last name." I didn't want to cry, so I focused on the naked lady lamp on the side table. I'd used this trick since I was a kid. Zero in on something, and only think of that. Shut down all emotion. *Stare. Focus. Don't feel.*

"It's not your name that's toxic, Lizzie. It's Peter—no, that's not entirely true. He was an asshole, but should his entire life be judged by who he was and not how he'll turn out after this stage? Even before his arrest, he was taking a hard look at who he was becoming, and he started to make changes. Getting arrested doesn't change that. Hell, he put Demi before himself. I have to admire any father who can do that."

Since my staring at the lamp hadn't worked, I swallowed in an attempt to stave off the emotions but failed again. Getting older was making me soft.

Sarah flicked a tear off my face. "You need to stop being the tough one all of the time."

"You just said I was the glue."

"Even glue needs to be reapplied."

I closed one eye. "I don't understand."

She kissed me on the lips. "It's early."

"Do you mean early in the morning? Or early in analyzing the theory?"

"Yes."

I wagged a finger in her face. "You're making up shit."

"Prove me wrong."

"I don't know how."

"The real question is why would you want to." She cradled my face in her palm.

"I really hate when you do that."

"What, exactly?"

"Confuse me with logic that isn't really logical. Not for the black and white battle raging inside me."

Her smile was the type that stilled all thoughts in my head. "Why do you think I do it?"

"Is this a confession? You're intentionally trying to drive me insane. Too late, lady. My family will more than likely finish me off before the first toast tonight."

"At least you think we'll last that long. That's a good sign. Not as negative as normal." She jostled my arm.

I responded by getting on top of her. "I have an idea for helping me stay positive." I spied the clock. "Got eight minutes?"

She laughed. "You're feeling ambitious."

"I like a challenge. Shut up, and kiss me."

* * *

IN THE KITCHEN, ETHAN AND MADDIE SAT AT THE island, talking quietly. I placed Calvin, whom Sarah had just fed, in his bouncy chair. The twins and Demi were still upstairs with Sarah and Rose.

"Whenever I find you two whispering, it makes me very nervous." I grabbed the kettle from the stovetop and filled it with water.

Maddie wiggled Cal's feet. Was he already outgrowing the grumpy stage, leaving it solely to me? Things were looking up.

"You like that, baby Calf?" Maddie cooed using her goo-goo voice that brought a smile to his face.

"Calf?" I questioned.

"It just came out." Maddie elevated a shoulder and returned her attention to Calvin. "You have deep brown eyes like your mom. Soulful."

"I'm still hoping he'll get my work ethic." I pulled two mugs from the cupboard. "So, what are you two conspiring about?"

"How to avoid a Petrie meltdown."

"Hey now, don't feel left out. You two may not have my name, but both of you contribute to the meltdowns like true Petrie pros."

Ethan beamed as if I'd given him a compliment.

Maddie laughed.

"The question is what type of meltdown to prepare for. Epic to mildly annoying." I bit into an apple, still cold from being in the fridge.

"That's an interesting sliding scale for meltdowns." Maddie gazed upward. "What qualifies as *epic* in the Petrie playbook?" She made quote marks in the air.

I groaned. "Murder isn't out of the equation. Not anymore."

"Are you plotting anyone's murder in particular?"

"I'm keeping my options open." I chomped into the apple with gusto, enjoying the crunching sound.

Sarah staggered in with Demi on her hip, Ollie and Fred trailing her, and Rose bringing up the rear.

"That was fast!" I looked over the kids. "I see Mommy still loves to make you look—"

"Adorable." Sarah gave me the evil eye.

"I was going for cutest kids on the planet." I peeled a banana and sliced it onto three plates.

While Sarah and Rose got the kids ready at the table, Ethan

took Calvin out of his chair and held him close. It always took me by surprise, seeing Ethan, the fluid hater, hold one of my kids. He was a natural, and I had to wonder why he never gave in to Lisa about having a second child. Would that have saved his marriage, or were they doomed from everything else?

"What time are Lisa and Casey coming over?" I asked in an effort not to say, "Why didn't you just have another kid?"

"Two-ish." He tickled Calvin's belly, extracting a giggle.

"It's like overnight he developed a playful side." I handed the kids' plates off to Maddie. "Thanks."

"Can I assume you two will play fairly today?" I asked Ethan.

"I can't imagine why Cal and I would cheat at anything," Ethan deadpanned.

I poured water over my Earl Grey tea bag and then Sarah's herbal one. "Have you considered stand-up?"

Ethan raised Cal in the air. "What do you say, little Cal? We can go on the road together."

Calvin's eyes peered into Ethan's as if giving the question serious consideration. If the idea of making money factored into Cal's decision, he was a Petrie to the core.

"Would we get a cut?" I added honey to my tea, giving it a stir with a spoon.

"Possibly." Ethan put Cal back into his chair. "Maddie, you need another cup?"

"Does Santa do the nasty with Mrs. Claus?"

I inhaled deeply, knowing this was only the beginning of Maddie doing everything she could to get on my last nerve. She claimed it was her way to keep me sane, but I think it was her way of keeping her wits about her with the bonus of annoying the fuck out of me.

Ethan did his anti-fluid cringe but calmly said, "I don't rightly know, but I'm going to assume that means you want another cup."

"Speaking of Santa, who's dressing up this year?" Maddie asked Sarah, the party general.

Sarah looked at me with an *oh shit* expression.

"Dad, of course." I set down her tea.

"But the suit hasn't been dry cleaned." The color was seeping out of Sarah's cheeks.

He only wore it last year, but I had already anticipated this. "Actually, it has. It's hanging in the hall closet."

Sarah crossed her arms. "You're telling me that you, of your own volition, took the suit to the cleaners, and now it's hanging in the closet?"

"That's exactly what I'm saying." I vigorously nodded my head to drive home the point.

"How did you remember?"

"You made me do it last year." I pulled up the to-do list from the previous year on my phone. "Sometimes being anal comes in handy."

Sarah blinked.

"Did I do something wrong?" So much for gloating.

"Not at all. I'm shocked." She circled a finger in front of her face. "I forgot, but you didn't."

I looked at all of our children. "You've been taking care of four kids. I think that means you can forget whatever you want whenever you want, and I'll do my best to keep us on track."

"Glue. You." She kissed me on the cheek.

"I'm going to hop in the shower before I start my errands."

"Don't you need breakfast?"

"I had an apple and"—I grabbed the chocolate and peanut butter protein bar from the pocket of my robe and waggled it in the air—"this."

"It's like you don't need me anymore." She feigned pouting.

"Luckily for you, I need you for…" I whispered in her ear, "sexy times."

I started to walk away, but she grabbed the front of my robe, pulled me back down, and whispered in my ear, "Tonight. Don't let them beat you down, and you'll be greatly rewarded."

* * *

ETHAN AND I GOT OUT OF THE CAR IN THE DELI parking lot.

"How'd you convince Sarah to have dinner catered this year?" Ethan slid on a patch of ice but didn't wipe out completely.

"She jumped at the chance after the microwave incident on Thanksgiving."

He put a hand on my shoulder. "It could have happened to anyone. I've never seen flames in a microwave. To think you only tried to defrost a loaf of bread."

"I never considered there was the tiniest scrap of metal in the twist tie." I sighed, not wanting to relive the day anymore. "Replacing an oven and a microwave in less than a year is a feat I hope not to repeat."

"Sarah's not taking any chances this time. She had her mom bake all the cookies for the kids to decorate later today."

"I know!" I said with too much glee. "I didn't have to clean cookie dough from every crevice in the kitchen, and Rose let me send Miranda over to her place to tidy up. I swear, I'm this close"—I held my thumb and forefinger half an inch apart—"from getting Sarah to let me always hire people to do things."

Ethan laughed. "What will you have to do to get her to hire painters? Burn the house down?"

"Oh boy, I hope not. Besides, wouldn't that be considered arson? One Petrie in prison at a time." I opened the door to the deli and waved Ethan in with added flair. "I wouldn't want to ditch you on Christmas."

"I like it when you do everything possible to cheer me up."

"I'm glad you're noticing, but wait until you see how much food we'll have to truck out of here." I caught the owner's eye, a grad school connection who'd ditched academia, and she held a finger in the air before disappearing into the back.

Two employees started to cart everything out. After several trips, Ethan wheeled about, shaking a finger in the air. "You fooled me. You said it'd be good for me to get out. Now, I know you needed me for my guns." He flexed his arm and kissed his jacket over where I assumed his bicep was. Or should have been.

"Yes. When I ran down the list of contenders, you and your bulging muscles soared to the top." I acted this out with my hand.

"Mock all you want, but I'm much stronger than I look."

"I'm counting on that. You might want to move the car to the curb, though, while I pay an arm and a leg." I tossed him my key fob, which he dropped. "Is that a sign for the rest of the day?"

"Please. This is nothing compared to a normal Petrie disaster." He bent over to pick up the key fob. "It's not even broken." He left to get the car.

At the register, I pulled out my credit card. Surprisingly, considering how much action it'd been getting this holiday season, it wasn't smoking or anything. Reconciling the bill later would require some Dutch courage. I hated dipping into the money we'd set aside each month into our savings, but I feared not being able to avoid that this Christmas.

"Are you excited to see what Santa brought you?" Molly, the owner, asked as she rang me up.

Not wanting her to know I was turning even more into Ebenezer every passing second, I simply offered a tight-lipped smile.

She was too busy punching in the order to even notice. I imagined her day wouldn't be that enjoyable either. Did any adults truly love the holidays, or did they just drive themselves beyond their limits all for the sake of their children?

In the car, Ethan asked, "Any other stops before heading home?"

"Do you think we got enough booze earlier?"

He gave this question serious consideration given the deep groove in his brow. "It wouldn't hurt to get more just in case."

"My new motto is *better safe than sorry*." I added, "Or *stay drunk so I don't give a fuck*."

CHAPTER TWELVE

By the time we returned to the house, Sarah was in full party mode. Meaning she was bossing everyone around, even the twins who were picking up their toys in the front room. Freddie would put something away, and then Ollie would get it back out, with an evil grin on her face. Fred repeated the action without complaint. He truly was a Petrie, rolling that imaginary rock.

"Keep up the good work, you two!" I encouraged. It was better to have them confined and busy, which I suspected was Sarah's true purpose with the task. In the kitchen, I asked Maddie, "What smells so good?"

She surveyed the various Crock-Pots. "I have no fucking clue."

"Keep up the good work!" I gave her a thumbs-up.

She gave me the middle finger. "I hate when you treat me like one of the kids."

"I call a spade a spade."

"Yeah, yeah. You're Lizzie the Straight Shooter." She added her other middle finger, moving both in the air with enthusiasm, and I had to wonder what Maddie was like as a teenager. Probably not much different.

"When are the guests arriving?"

Maddie consulted her watch. "Two minutes. You cut it close."

"Why did you invite the world over for another holiday?" Sarah gave me a kiss on the cheek, wrapping both arms around my neck.

"Yep. This is all me. Every single damn time. I never learn my lesson." I threaded my arm around her waist. "Please tell me you aren't planning on caroling tonight. It's not snowing like last year, but it's *freeze your nips off* temps."

"It really is."

I whirled around to JJ, Claire, Ian, and Mia.

"Oh, hey," I said as if I hadn't just referenced my nipples in front of one of my employers, not to mention her children.

JJ held a casserole dish in her arms. "Hope you like seven-layer dip. Claire insisted we bring something that didn't require the oven or microwave."

"I'm never going to live that down, am I?"

Everyone shook their heads, doing their best to curb their laughter, given the tightening of their lips.

"Ethan told me this morning it could have happened to anyone," I defended.

"Keep believing that." Sarah took the dish from JJ and placed it on the kitchen table, which appeared to be appetizer central.

Ian placed two large bags of tortilla chips next to the dish, and Sarah complimented his sweater with a dinosaur wearing a Santa hat.

"I have one with unicorns to wear tomorrow, but Dad got me this one for the party."

"You can never have enough Christmas spirit." JJ ruffled the top of his head, and I guessed within a year or two, Ian would be taller than she was.

"We have a car to unload, right Muscles?" I nudged Ethan's side.

He scowled. "I only use them once a year. I'm an English teacher."

"There's no time like the present to develop better habits."

"I'll help." It was Darrell, Ian's father but not Claire's ex-husband, who had been way in the back of the group, so I didn't notice him right away. If I was getting the story right, he had been Claire's boss when Ian was conceived, and while Ian knew his father, no one had known Darrell was the father until JJ, Claire's wife now, fired him. Briefly, I closed my eyes to ensure I'd gotten the details right. Never mind, I just wouldn't say anything until I consulted the intricate family tree I'd been concocting. It seemed every day it became more convoluted. As a Petrie, I couldn't really say anything about JJ's family situation. Maybe that was why we hit it off.

"Ian!" Casey zipped across the kitchen to hug the boy. "Come with me! There's a puzzle Allen and I are working on." She led him to the front room.

"Take Mia," Ethan said. "She can do crafts with the kiddos."

Casey held the little girl's hand, asking, "How is Miss Mia on this beautiful day?"

Ethan beamed at his daughter, seeming relieved Casey was acting like her normal positive self.

"Where's Calvin?" I asked Sarah.

"In the garage, changing the oil in the car."

"What?"

"Kidding." She shook her head in disbelief. "I can't believe you keep falling for that. He's with Mom and Troy in the living room."

"I need a baby to hold," Claire said as if that was her mission for the day.

Part of me went cold. Would Sarah start to think that in a year or so and want another child? Was it too late for her to become a pediatric nurse? How could I get the ball rolling on that mission? Maybe I should consult Ethan and Maddie later. Given his separation, and Maddie's own relationship past and the thorny situation with Gabe, perhaps they were the worst ones to ask for marital advice.

My brain nearly slapped into the side of my skull.

I hadn't seen Lisa.

Did she drop off Casey? Or was she hiding somewhere in the house? If I didn't pursue that line of questioning, would the whole Ethan and Lisa drama stay far away from me? That didn't seem fair to Lisa. While Ethan and I had been friends first, Lisa had always been kind to me. How could I turn my back on Casey's mom? Also, this Christmas was the one-year anniversary of Lisa losing her mom.

"Shall we unload the car?" I said, not wanting to seek out Lisa quite yet, unsure how it'd go. I hadn't seen her since the separation, and I didn't want to blunder by saying something like, "Welcome to the lezzie side." Followed by a fist bump.

Gabe appeared with a floral centerpiece in his arms. "Where's this going?"

I sized up the piece and wanted to say outside, but something told me that would be the wrong decision. "My guess is the dining room."

"This is the smaller one."

"Oh. Here then, maybe." I pointed to the appetizer table in the kitchen nook that didn't have much space. "Actually, what about the side table?" I pointed to the piece under the window.

"You don't do anything by half measure, do you?" Darrell asked.

I splayed my fingers over my heart. "I do whenever I can get away with it. Sarah never does."

"I don't miss this part of marriage," he said.

I was relieved Sarah hadn't heard that because I feared she'd invite his ex and their kids over for the night. Sarah was big on healing breaches through communication. I was big on plugging my ears with my fingers. Somehow, we made it work.

After loading Ethan and Darrell up with platters from the back of my SUV, I sent them inside.

JJ, who'd tailed us, asked, "How're you hanging in?"

"Not bad."

"You see Peter today?"

I shook my head. "I went on Saturday. It's so hard. I'm running around like crazy, doing my best to ensure everyone will have a wonderful Christmas, but I can't do a thing to help him. He's alone. In prison. This is new territory for me." I pulled out some of the bags from the back of my SUV in time for Darrell, who seemed grateful to be put to work. Ethan was taking his sweet time. Or maybe he decided he'd done enough and joined Casey at the puzzle table. I couldn't blame him, really. Darrell, with a half smile, went back inside.

"It's nice of you two to include Darrell," JJ said.

"Is that weird for you?"

"Having Ian's father with us all the time? He practically lives at our house."

"Maybe he and Ethan should get an apartment together."

JJ laughed, but it subsided, and her face lit up like a lightbulb. "Do you think it'd work?"

"You should turn it into a reality show. A modern-version of *The Odd Couple*."

That spurred the fire in JJ's eyes to burn hotter. She loved a business opportunity. "That could be gold."

"Please don't tell anyone I gave you the idea. I have enough shit to manage."

"I'm more than happy to take the credit." She squeezed my shoulder.

"For what?" Ethan asked, not looking enthused to carry another load.

"Looks like someone wants his Christmas gifts this year." I pinched his cheek. "I was expecting you to let Darrell carry in the rest."

"Sarah gave me the look." He shoved his hands deep into his pockets and rolled onto his heels.

"Oh, poor guy. Having to act like an adult."

"It's not fair. My life is falling apart. You'd think she'd take it easy on me."

"Trust me, she is."

CHAPTER THIRTEEN

Back inside, I rubbed my palms together and then stuck them in my armpits to trap the heat. "Why do we live in Colorado? It's always freezing on Christmas. We should have gone to Jamaica or somewhere like we'd talked about last year."

"Palm trees don't jive with Christmas." Sarah ticked off something on one of her lists.

"So I have to freeze off my tits?"

Sarah gave me one of her *stop whining* looks before she left the room on some mission. When the coast was clear, I stuck out my tongue.

"Very brave, you are." Maddie grinned.

"I may be slightly grumpy."

"What's your definition of *slightly*?"

"Right now, I'm considering the definition of another word. It sorta rhymes with burger." I wasn't happy with the rhyme, so I added, "Or birder."

Maddie's face screwed up, but then she dismissed my threat of murder with a shake of the head. "I wish you hadn't said the first. Do you have any burgers? I could kill for one right now."

I appraised her face to see if she was fucking with me, and I had to wonder if she was a much more gifted actress than I gave her credit for or if she had no clue the word I was rhyming with was *murder*, the new word associated with being a Petrie. "No. Just deli shit."

"Deli shit. I think you need some time in the library, guzzling eggnog before Sarah finds out she's married to the Grinch." Maddie tugged one of my hands out of my armpits. "Come on. Courtney and Jorie are hiding in there."

"Are they just hiding or...?" Last Christmas, my library had become the hot zone of misbehavior, and I'd contemplated having it fumigated, but Sarah would only agree to Miranda and her team doing a deep clean. Twice.

Maddie glanced over her shoulder. "Only one way to find out." She threw the door open but caught it before it slammed into the wall.

Fortunately, Courtney and Jorie weren't canoodling but sitting on one of the couches, eggnogs in hand.

"Mads, this year's batch is superb." Courtney hoisted her glass in the air.

"Crud, I forgot to get us cups." Maddie shoved me toward the free couch. "Sit. I'll be right back." She made a show of exiting, stealth-like.

"What's she doing?" Jorie asked.

"I'm guessing her impression of a Navy Seal sneaking into an enemy's camp." Courtney laughed. "How are you, Lizzie?"

I yawned but mumbled, "Fine," through the cracks of my fingers.

"We were just talking about you," Jorie said.

I rubbed one of my ears. "Is that good or bad?"

"Depends on your definition." Courtney sipped her drink.

"Why does everyone keep saying that to me? My definition of Petrie meltdown? Slightly?" I held up three fingers, trying to recall if there were other incidents I was forgetting.

Unperturbed, Courtney responded, "Uh-oh, Bottle Rocket. Are you one step from exploding?"

My eyes darted to the ceiling. "I wish. Then all of you would leave. Unfortunately, I have to adult today. Just like every other day." I chewed on my bottom lip, nearly to the point of drawing blood. "Not that anyone around me repays the courtesy. And to add insult to injury, the president has stolen my moat idea."

Maddie had returned in time for the last part.

Courtney gave a sideways glance to Jorie and then queried Maddie with a look that was nothing short of *is she fucking serious?*

Maddie handed off my eggnog and drank heavily from her glass.

"Okay, I'll bite. What moat idea?" Courtney asked.

"Last spring, I briefly considered constructing a moat to seal me off from the Petrie curse."

"Did you have someone price it?" Jorie asked as if the conversation was perfectly normal.

"I don't have an assistant," I said in a tone that implied if I had, I would have.

Courtney bobbed her head. "Let's circle back to the Petrie curse. That's what we were discussing when you barged in."

"How can I barge into my own library?" I huffed.

"Construct a moat, and you wouldn't have to worry about people like Jorie and me." Courtney winked.

I gnashed my teeth.

The library door opened. "Oh, sorry." JJ put up an apologetic hand.

Courtney waved her in. "Actually, we could use your help. Lizzie is losing it."

"Am not!" I shouted.

JJ chuckled, but she came in and sat down in one of the wingback chairs in front of the roaring fire. "What's up?"

"I'm trying to convince Lizzie to start a charity for motherless kids."

I gazed at Courtney, unsure if the topic had actually been brought up, but I'd been too busy sulking to hear. "You are? I thought we were talking about moats."

Courtney nodded. "I'm good at multitasking."

"I'm not, clearly. Why orphans?" I chugged some eggnog.

"You have some experience with it," Court explained.

"My mom didn't die until I was an adult, and my father is still alive." Even to me, it came out like I was complaining about all of it.

"I wasn't planning to restrict it solely to orphans, but kids without moms. As you say, yours is dead, and you adopted Demi. Then there's your research about the Hitler Youth boys being taken from their mothers to support the Nazi cause."

"Oh. That makes more sense." I straightened on the couch. "I don't know how to start a charity, though." If I only taught one class per semester, I may have more free time, but that wouldn't help me pay the bills.

"That's where I come in." Courtney spread her fingers on her chest, tapping each digit to some tune. Maybe to the Christmas song playing on the speakers throughout the house.

"You want me to hire you to start a charity? Doesn't that go against being a charity?" I rubbed my eyes, trying to figure out that puzzle.

"People and organizations hire my company all the time to restore their public image. But I'm not pitching you for work. I want to help."

"Why?" My brow furrowed.

"For some reason, I find your grumpiness adorable."

"That's not the intended consequence to my acting like an asshole. I'd like to have one holiday to myself."

Courtney grinned. "I know! But this"—she circled a finger in the air—"makes me smile."

I folded my arms across my chest.

This only caused Courtney to grin even more.

"Have you considered writing your memoir?" JJ asked.

My head whipped around in her direction at bone-cracking speed. "You're suggesting I write a memoir? The first time we met, you said you wished people hadn't read yours."

"True, but I'm also the first to admit the book helped rehab my image. The public loves someone who had the cards stacked against them but still succeeded on their own."

"Oh, please. I'm a trust fund baby." I flicked a hand in the air. "I'm hardly a Horatio Alger type."

"You still worked to support yourself. If I remember correctly, you had a paper route, which involved getting up at three in the morning. You weren't like your brother, who went into the family business," JJ said.

"You make the Petries sound like gangsters." I groaned.

"They're in finance. At least, that's how the average person thinks of them. And, Peter stabbed you in the back, telling your uncle you were gay to get his grubby paws on your inheritance," Maddie added.

I stared at Maddie, openmouthed. "I can't tell the world that."

"Why not?"

"H-he's my brother," I stuttered, not understanding why I had to explain this fact to Maddie, who may have been more attached to him than me.

"I'm amazed you haven't given up on him," Courtney said in a way that was difficult to determine the tone. Was she impressed or worried?

"Everyone walking this planet has made stupid decisions. Peter wasn't always the best sibling, but before he was arrested, it seemed like he was trying to be a better man. How could I give up on someone when they need me the most?"

Maddie met my gaze. "Maybe you should ask him if he would mind. I don't think he would."

"You want me to ask my brother, who is in prison, if he'd be cool with me tossing him under the bus so people will stop spitting at me while at the grocery store?"

"Yes. Tell him exactly that. He'll want to help."

"How do you figure?"

"Because I've talked to him. He's miserable knowing you're going through this, and he's worried for Demi's sake. Let him help in the way he can. He wants to come out of this mess a better man. That'll take some sacrifice on his part."

"You've been telling him these things?" I'd been doing my best to protect Peter from the negativity surrounding the exposé.

Maddie gave me her *you're such a stubborn moron* expression.

I let out an anguished breath, turning back to JJ. "You're forgetting my book deal was axed. How can I find a publisher for my memoir?"

"I'm pretty sure I can help with that," JJ said.

"Let me see if I'm getting this right. You"—I pointed to Courtney—"want me to start a charity. And you"—I aimed my finger at JJ—"want me to pen my memoirs to repair my reputation?"

Both nodded, with Jorie and Maddie joining in.

"I still prefer my moat idea. Seems simpler."

"Let's keep that as plan Z." Courtney flashed a killer smile. "My mom has a koi pond. It's a bitch to maintain in the winter. She has to pour hot water into it when the water freezes, which can be a couple times a day on really cold days. I'm thinking a moat might take more work than you want."

"Doesn't everything?"

CHAPTER FOURTEEN

BACK AMONG THE PARTY MASSES, DAD AND HELEN cornered me at the sandwich station in the dining room.

"Lizzie, do you have a minute?" Dad asked.

I was midbite into a ham and cheese and decided to inhale a much larger mouthful than normal. Maybe if I didn't speak, this conversation would stop before it really started. Maybe I would choke to death, and all of this would be over.

Dad's eyes bored into mine.

I forcefully swallowed the half-chewed food, thumping my chest to help it go down. "Okay, but if this is about the moat, Courtney already convinced me I'd have to move to a warmer climate to enact it. I don't want to keep pouring hot water on to the ice."

Dad looked to Helen with the expression everyone ended up with when talking to me lately. The one that screamed, *Call the people in white coats!* "How are you holding up?"

I want to build a moat, so what do you think, Einstein? "Just dandy. Things couldn't be better. Have you seen the tree? I'm quite proud of the Christmas village this year." I puffed out my chest. "It's nearly double the size of last year's. How are things for you?"

"We're worried about you." Helen rubbed my back.

Get in line. "Don't be. I got... this."

Dad sighed. "I'm hearing rumors about your book deal falling through and the dean pushing you out."

My eyes surveyed the room, wondering who'd squealed to my father, but there were simply too many suspects, and I wouldn't put it past the man to have someone following me or something. I ended up nodding and taking another bite of my sandwich. Seriously, what could I say?

"Why didn't you come to me?" he asked, his eyes showing kindness.

"I assumed you have enough on your plate, steering your company through this... mess."

"It doesn't change the fact that I want to help my daughter."

He didn't refer to me that way much, and part of me liked hearing it. But it was difficult to banish the impulse to question his motives. Speaking of motives, I asked, "Can you convince Sarah the best move would be to pack up and start our lives over someplace far away from Colorado?" I had been thinking Massachusetts, where they had more universities than Taco Bells, but now with the moat complication, maybe Florida. That was where crocodiles and alligators coexisted, which would be a boon for my keeping people out. It made it tricky for the kids and pets to go in the yard. Would I need an electric fence on the right side of the moat? Was my thinking all of this through a sign my sanity was close to permanently disappearing?

"You want to leave?" he asked.

"Perhaps it's time for me to strike out on my own. I'm teaching at the school where I studied under Dr. Marcel. Dean Spencer wants me out. Does he have reason for that? I mean, am I a crappy professor, or does it simply come down to the

Peter mess? I think it's time for me to stand on my own two feet. Find out if I can cut it in the big, bad world of academia."

"I see," Dad said, looking unhappy, if his sad eyes were to be believed.

"It's nothing personal. It's just—my children have to come first." I inhaled the rest of my sandwich, while the two of them stared openmouthed. Pounding on my chest, I asked around the remaining food, "Are there more Petrie skeletons I should prepare for? I feel like we should get everything out in the open." I licked ham juice off my finger.

"What else are you expecting, dear?" Helen responded.

"With this family, who the f-fudge knows. But I need to know. As things stand, I can't go into a store without wearing a poncho. I never knew so many people's preferred method of violence was spitting."

"You're being spit on?" my father asked, shock clouding his eyes.

"In truth, it's only happened twice, but it's not something I want to keep enduring, and I never want Sarah to experience it." I made a slicing motion with my hand.

"Lizzie, please let me help you." He clutched both of my shoulders. "After the holidays, we'll sit down with my team and map out the best way to deal with all of this. You are not alone."

"Okay… that sounds good." It did. I never thought I'd be the type who'd want my daddy to rescue me, but I'd never been through anything like this.

Right then, Ollie ran through the room, completely naked.

Everyone laughed, including me.

Soon enough, Fred, also in his birthday suit, streaked through the dining room en route to the Christmas tree, both twins squealing and doing some type of dance.

"Is that a plea for help?" I asked Helen in jest, but a part of me really wondered.

"It's toddlers. They love to get naked, mostly because they can undo buttons and snaps now." Helen's smile made me try to imagine for the umpteenth time what life would have been like if Peter and I had been raised by a human instead of the Scotch-lady.

My gaze landed on Sarah, who was grinning at our twins. "Are you telling me you don't want to wear your elf costumes?"

Olivia nodded firmly. "No effies. Big girl, now."

Sarah hunched down. "What about reindeers? They're big."

"Deer poop big," Ollie said as if weighing that morsel to decide her next outfit.

"Flower!" Freddie squealed, spinning in a circle.

"Dee-vil!" squealed Ollie. "Me dee-vil!" It was like she knew saying it in a sinister way had just the right attitude for the conversation.

"You're a devil alright." Sarah tweaked Ollie's nose.

Demi, still dressed, danced with her cousins—er, siblings.

"Okay, let's get you into your Halloween outfits." Sarah took each twin by the hand. "Demi, what about you? Do you want to change?"

"Flower!"

I laughed. "I think I need to help Sarah get the kids dressed."

Dad nodded. "We'll talk more later. I promise."

I really didn't want to. Everyone wanted to help me open up more, when all I wanted was to put this whole situation in the rearview mirror. Talking all the time couldn't salvage everything. I swooped Demi into my arms. "You want to be a flower like Fred. It figures. You two are the prettiest flowers on the planet." I tickled her belly.

The party guests returned to their conversations, and I hoped the Christmas music streaming throughout the house would mute their words. I really didn't want to hear what anyone was gabbing about. I was fully embracing the *ignorance was bliss* philosophy.

Upstairs, I asked Sarah, "Would it be wrong if we slipped out of our party and checked into a hotel?"

"Tel?" Freddie asked, his head cocked to the side.

"*Ho*-tel," I emphasized for him. "Mommy wants to go to a *ho*tel."

"Mommy wants hoes," Ollie attempted.

"Don't say that to Aunt Maddie," I cautioned, pressing a finger on Ollie's nose, much to her delight. "She'll teach you other bad words."

"Mommy wants hoes!" Ollie repeated, with Freddie joining in.

"You know they can pick up on what they should never say in public, right?" Sarah rifled through the closet in search of the Halloween outfits. By the time we found them, Ollie had changed her mind and wanted to be a princess paired with a devil's tail and trident. It was disconcerting to say the least, but I doubted Olivia understood why. Or I hoped not. Fred and Demi wore the daisy outfits Rose and Maddie had made for them.

Back downstairs, Maddie took photos with her phone.

Ollie, Freddie, and Demi chanted, "Mommy wants hoes!"

"Another vocab lesson gone tragically wrong," Sarah said, smiling in my direction.

I shrugged. "Can't win them all. I would like it noted checking into a hotel is still an option."

Sarah got to their level. "Yes, Mommy wants to stay in a hotel." She looked up at me. "She needs a break."

The three of them continued their version, much to the delight of the audience, our family and friends.

I pressed my palms together. "This calls for more eggnog."

Hiding in the kitchen nook, I sipped another of Maddie's concoctions, knowing I'd regret the decision in the morning, but what the fuck? The slight boozy fog enveloping me was warm and cozy, dulling my thoughts some.

Then there was a shout from the living room.

I took another drink, refusing to be pulled into more Petrie drama. *Nope. Not going to do it.* I held a hand over my head. "I've had my fill for the year," I said to the Santa on the table. "I mean, seriously, how much can one human take in three-hundred and sixty-five days? Of course, there's still a week left."

The Santa didn't speak, but I thought, if I squinted just enough, his cheery smile morphed into supportive.

Now, there were muffled angry voices, one being my wife's. After years of marriage, I could zero in on her screech from anywhere in the world.

Would it be wrong to hide in the garage with the entire bowl of eggnog? Surely, that would be one of the last places any of them looked. Or what about under one of the beds? Maybe I should invest in some risers to make it cozier. This wouldn't be the last time I'd want to hide. I searched for options on my phone.

The bickering increased.

I looked upward, saying to no one in particular, since I was an atheist, "Please, make it stop."

I strained to hear Maddie defending herself and Sarah not taking it all that well. Good, Maddie was in the doghouse. I could live with that.

I refilled my cup, still no intention of joining the quarrel.

Instead, they charged into the kitchen, bringing it to me.

"Lizzie, honey, we seem to have a situation." Sarah employing her *don't freak out* voice wasn't comforting.

I slugged the eggnog and refilled my cup.

Maddie's face was ashen. "I'm sorry. I had no idea..."

"Question." I raised a finger in the air and turned to Sarah. "Is this something I really have to know about? I was just telling Santa I'm at my max for problems." I held my glass above my head to indicate drowning, and part of me wanted to douse myself with eggnog. Would the booze soak through my skin right into my bloodstream?

"No. Not at all." Maddie yanked on Sarah's arm, but my wife wouldn't budge.

"It involves our children, so yes, I say you have to know about it."

Based on Maddie's impression of a ghost wanting to die for a second time, I had a feeling I really wasn't going to like whatever it was.

"It's Keri," Sarah started slowly.

"The mom bully?" I asked, not at all sure why I would give two shits about her at the moment. She wasn't a Petrie. Nor a friend. Those two categories seemed to be the ones wanting to bring me to my knees. Keri could fucking die for all I cared. If I saw a falling star in the near future, that was going to be my wish. Or Dean Spencer. If I said it really fast, could I include a smorgasbord of names on one falling star?

"Yes. She's telling everyone in the mommy Facebook group that our children are possessed by Satan and you hire prostitutes."

I tried to focus on Sarah's face, but it blurred somewhat. "That makes zero sense. Do mothers of Satan also hire hookers? Is that in the bible or something?" This theory made me laugh. "I would have taken more religious history classes if I'd known it was that entertaining."

Maddie's grimace didn't relent. Fuck.

"True, it's far-fetched. That's not the point." Sarah mimed putting a pin in my theory.

"I'm so tired of living in a world where the facts don't matter." I rubbed my forehead. "As a historian, it's just not something I'm equipped to handle."

Sarah continued, "It doesn't matter what she's claiming.

The issue is she's making it clear that all children of the group shouldn't be allowed to interact with ours."

Sarah had mentioned this possibility before, but I hadn't entirely believed Keri would have this power. Given Sarah's tone and strained expression, I gathered she was sincerely worried. That sobered me some.

"What instigated this? It's Christmas Eve for fuck's sake. Shouldn't Keri, the perfect mom, be busy planning the perfect holiday?" Okay, my bitterness hadn't ebbed entirely, and luckily the kids weren't in earshot to hear my f-bomb.

"I posted some photos and videos of the kiddos on Facebook. Keri must have seen them and decided it was the best time to pounce. She'd probably been waiting for this moment." Maddie's face continued to pale.

I motioned for her to cough up the damaging dirt, and she handed me her phone. There were photos of the trio dancing in front of the tree in their Halloween costumes. The video was of Fred, Ollie, and Demi holding hands and singing "Mommy wants hoes" with childish glee.

The Satan part was a stretch, because even in her princess outfit with devil's tail and pitchfork, Ollie looked darling.

"What's this about... Gandhi?" I squinted at the comment under Keri's post, but Maddie swiped it from my hand.

"Oh, no. Betty, the neighbor who hates you, says she's always known something was wrong with our family ever since you screamed about killing Gandhi."

"Does she at least explain I was referring to George's dog and not the historical figure who's been dead as a doornail for decades?" I tried to pry the phone from Maddie, but she clung to it.

"I'm not sure clarifying that point will improve the matter." Sarah wrung her hands. "And definitely not in those words."

"Why is Betty involved in the mommy Facebook group?" I asked.

"She's Keri's aunt." Sarah said the words like I should have known this.

"Why would you post the photos in the group?" I asked Maddie.

"I didn't. And, I had no idea Keri was one of my Facebook friends." Maddie scrolled through her friends list. "She's not here. My posts can only be seen by friends."

"She probably uses a fake account to spy on us." Sarah looked longingly at my eggnog, sighing.

"I'm really starting to hate people. All people." I topped off my drink, trying to convince myself I was doing so to help Sarah, who couldn't partake since she was still breastfeeding. "It's a holiday. Why does everyone insist on piling onto my misery?" I heard the kids giggling in the living room. "You know what? Let's not worry about it right now. Let Keri do her bully thing. We'll figure it out later. Right now, we should be merry because no one can take that away from us." I set my eggnog down on the table. "Beelze! Bub! And Minnie Beelzebub. Let's sing Christmas carols."

For a moment, Sarah's pinched face showed she disagreed with my desire of pushing the Keri situation to the back burner. As the seconds ticked by, her expression eased.

I kissed her cheek. "It's going to be okay. I promise."

CHAPTER FIFTEEN

"Lizzie!" Casey ran to me, stopping before she took out the tree.

"What's up, dude?"

Ethan scrunched his face. "Dude?"

"Just roll with it." I turned back to Casey. "Do you want some lime sherbet?"

"You're giving me wine. Ian, come here!"

He did.

"You're fast." I chuckled. "But I'm afraid it was all for nothing. I'm not giving anyone wine sherbet. Lime." I spelled it out and then laughed again.

Both agreed to the sherbet sans the wine, and I ruffled the top of Ian's head. "Did anyone post that to Facebook?" I glanced around, but only Ethan was paying any attention to me.

"You seem really relaxed. What's wrong?" Ethan asked.

"I'm enjoying the day. It's a holiday. We're having a party." I waved my arms in the air. "Listen up, partygoers. This is a party. Wipe off your worried expressions. Eat the yummy food. Fill up on eggnog. Gorge on frosted sugar cookies. And let's sing Christmas carols. Troy, my man, I'm counting on you to lead us." I pointed at Rose's husband.

Everyone stared at me.

"If you don't start enjoying the day, I'm taking your gifts away!" I said in a tone that I hoped was teasing.

"Did you get hit in the head?" Helen asked.

"In a way, yes. I've just come to the decision that I'm not going to let outside forces determine whether or not I can be happy. I'm almost forty. Who gives a f-fig if the world thinks my children worship Satan? Or that I pay women for sex? Or that I helped Peter murder Tie, because I know some think that? The likes of Keri and her ilk don't have power over me." I whirled around to Troy. "Seriously, man, let's start singing."

He looked to Rose, who gave him an encouraging nod and said, "I'm in agreement with Lizzie. Let's enjoy the day, right kiddos?"

The kids, Casey and Ian included, clapped their hands, both with light-green foam on their upper lips.

Troy started singing "Santa Claus is Coming to Town."

Sarah rested her head on my shoulder. "Eggnog seems to agree with you."

"For the moment. I'm thinking tomorrow will be an entirely different matter." I laughed.

"We can't wreck Christmas morning. For the kids' sake." She handed me her cup. "Try the kiddie punch. It's not bad."

"I love you. And, I would love you boatloads more if you get me some grappa. I promise to drink two Nalgene bottles before bed."

Sarah's sigh conveyed she wasn't thrilled to contribute to my drinking, but wasn't willing to argue. She kissed my cheek before heading to the library.

JJ approached. "Bravo, Lizzie."

"For getting drunk? I would have thought you'd be against that. Since you're an alcoholic."

"I wasn't applauding your drinking. I'm pleased you didn't feed the troll."

"She is a devil." I smiled at Ollie.

JJ shook her head, chuckling. "Sometimes, I really can't tell if you're being serious or not."

I rubbed my left eye with the heel of my hand. "Me neither these days. I'm just making it up as I go now. Maybe that's the key to happiness. Believing in what Disney movies teach us."

"What's that?"

"The happily ever after no matter how unreal it seems."

Sarah returned with the grappa bottle and glasses on a tray. "Help yourselves, everyone." She placed one in my hand.

"Does Ollie look like a troll?" I asked her.

Sarah glanced to JJ as if she immediately knew I'd misunderstood something, which only made me giggle.

"I was congratulating Lizzie about not feeding the troll, aka Keri," JJ explained.

The group started to sing "Rudolf the Red-Nosed Reindeer."

I bobbed my head, realizing I didn't know any of the words. How was that possible?

"She may feel differently tomorrow," Sarah stage-whispered to JJ.

"I have a feeling she's on a different plane right now," JJ concurred.

"I can hear both of you, yet I'm choosing not to give a s-shitake about it." I waved my glass in the air to the music.

"You know, Sarah, this mom problem has got me thinking about the Astors and Vanderbilts." Claire now stood next to her much-shorter wife. "Alva Vanderbilt wanted to be accepted by the Astors, who were old money and thought the likes of new money as interlopers. Alva came up with a brilliant plan to get Caroline Astor, who had the power to block Alva from the pinnacle of society, to call on her."

"How so?" Sarah asked.

"As the story goes, Alva planned a legendary ball, and Carrie Astor wanted to attend. But Carrie couldn't get an invite without Caroline, Carrie's mother, calling on the Vanderbilts."

"Did she?"

"Yep." Claire took a sip of grappa.

"So, Caroline caved so her daughter could go to a party?" Sarah clarified.

"Exactly," Claire chirped.

"That's interesting."

I could see the cogs turning in Sarah's head, but in my inebriated state, I couldn't decide if it was good or bad. When Claire and Sarah drifted away to discuss the topic in more detail, I knew it was going to be something I'd have to deal with later. For the moment, I was still determined not to let anything wreck the jolly spirit. Even if staying merry fucking killed me.

CHAPTER SIXTEEN

THE LIVING ROOM WAS IN COMPLETE DISARRAY AFTER the masses opened presents. The only people who hadn't stayed the night with us were JJ and her family. Everyone else, including Ethan's soon to be ex-wife, had stayed. Not only was the room in complete shambles, but the volume of Christmas tunes and chatter could probably be heard on the far side of the moon.

Sarah gave me a look that conveyed I should let everything be for now. Not worry about the mess or the noise. Given the massive headache I had from imbibing eggnog the previous day like it was water to drown out my worries, I was willing to do just that. Would anyone notice if I put on my new noise-cancelling headphones? Or if I slipped upstairs and climbed back into bed? Could that be my gift to myself? Wasn't that the thing these days: be kind to oneself?

Casey sat between her parents on one of the sofas, and I had to give it to Ethan and Lisa for acting like friends, which was what they had always been. Again, my eyes landed on Sarah. She was watching our friends and their daughter, and I detected her eyes getting misty. I hoped over the next few months, while they hammered out the details of their separation, Ethan and Lisa held onto what mattered: their friendship and daughter. Because life was hard enough. Losing what mattered most would only make it miserable.

Freddie, with his stuffed monkey, climbed into my lap and ordered, "Tickle, Mommy."

I eyed his new toys on the floor but simply laughed it off. "Next Christmas, I'm just going to give you tickle coupons."

He giggled, happily squirming on my lap.

Ollie emptied Fred's LEGO DUPLO box that had a train set with numbers that was supposed to help with learning how to count. She spread all the pieces, looking for something and not seeming to find it. Fred slid off my lap like an amoeba and started to put some of the pieces together.

"Can I join?" Gabe asked, sitting cross-legged on the floor with the kids.

Fred handed him an orange block with a bright blue *two* painted on it.

Allen and Demi joined them, and Sarah gave me a jerk of the head that implied this would be the perfect opportunity for me to have some bonding time.

I guzzled more sparkling water, in hopes it'd ease the swelling of my brain, and got on the floor.

"What comes after two, Fred?" I asked.

"Tree," he said, handing me the number five block.

"Technically, five is after two." Allen found number three and handed it to Freddie.

Before Fred could attach it to the number two part of the train, Ollie swiped it and placed it on her head. "Ollie tree."

"You love to stir the pot, don't you Ollie Dollie?" Gabe tickled her side.

The three of us let the kids dictate the construction of the train.

"How was your semester, Allen?" I leaned back on my elbows.

He shrugged, not making eye contact.

Gabe met my eye and jerked his head toward the office.

I really wasn't in the mood for a chat, but Allen was the baby of the family. Aside from the actual babies, but they were too young to know much about the Peter mess. Digging down deep, I said, "Is it too early for eggnog?" I got to my feet. "Would you two like to start a new sibling tradition?"

"Which is?" Gabe asked, hopping to his feet.

"Getting snockered in the library."

"Can I crash?" Lisa asked.

Gabe put an arm around her shoulder and gave her a noogie, "Yep!"

The two of them seemed cozier than I'd ever seen them before. I'd been quite drunk last night and hadn't paid much attention when Sarah started shuffling off people to different parts of the house to crash. From what I could tell, Maddie and Gabe had agreed to ignore each other. Had Maddie taken my advice and cut Gabe free, causing Sarah to pair up Gabe and Lisa, thinking that would be safe considering Lisa had joined the lezzie side? Had they…? *Nope. Lizzie, go to your happy place.*

"I'm going to make a mimosa. That has to be healthier than eggnog." Lisa retreated to the kitchen, with Allen tailing her, who also seemed closer to Lisa than normal. Had the three of them been meeting up? It wasn't all that unlikely, but how did I not know?

I raised an eyebrow at Gabe, but his attention was on Maddie, who was across the room talking with my father and Helen. Okay, maybe he was simply friends with Lisa. His eyes clouded over. Did he also think Maddie was talking about Peter? I was starting to wonder if Maddie would ever be able to get the Peter Monkey off her back.

After everyone got their drink of choice, the four of us

slipped into the library, and as I took a seat on the couch next to Gabe, I struggled with how to get a safe conversation going. Lisa's impending divorce? Had Maddie officially dumped Gabe? My studious brother not enjoying college?

"Who's going to start?" Gabe looked at each of us. "Seems like we all have something to talk about."

"Is this group therapy?" Allen asked with relief in his voice.

"I hadn't considered that when I proposed us coming in here, but, Allen, why aren't you enjoying school? You love learning."

Allen sipped his orange juice, and I wondered if there was any booze in it. What was the law about giving an underage family member booze on Christmas Day in the privacy of one's home?

Lisa nudged Allen's leg with a knee. "It's okay. Lizzie's been dealing with the same stuff."

That was when I realized I hadn't considered that Allen, Peter's half brother, would also be experiencing the fallout. I also picked up that Lisa still was in the know about my life. Was that through chats with Ethan? Gabe? Maddie? Sarah? I shoved that out of my head and said, "Allen, I'm so sorry. I should have reached out sooner."

"It's okay." He rubbed his chin, which had the same dimple as our father's.

"No, it's not. I've been feeling sorry for myself. I'm your older sister. I should act like it." I sucked in a deep breath. "I need to adult more."

He looked up but wasn't able to say anything, opting to swill more orange juice.

"Says the woman raising four kids." Lisa patted my leg. "Not to mention letting Ethan live with you part-time and always including Casey in family outings. Don't be so hard on yourself. I don't think you realize how much you take on."

I nodded, letting her words seep past my stubbornness of

thinking I could always handle more. "I would like to know what's going on, though. With all of you."

"He's been considering transferring," Gabe offered. "Out of Colorado. The local press has been merciless."

"I'm not sure bloggers count as press," I said bitterly. "They do anything to get clicks. That's neither here nor there. What schools are you considering?"

"You don't think it's cowardly to leave?" Allen's shoulders slouched.

"Nope. You have to make decisions based on what's right for you. Not on how you think others would perceive your actions. Your mental health should always come first."

He perked up a bit, speaking with more animation. "One of the professors I like teaches at Boston University."

"Wouldn't that be something?" I sipped my eggnog.

"What?" Allen gave me a perplexed look.

"One of the last things I did before leaving campus until the start of the spring semester was to reach out to a professor I know at Harvard to discuss an open teaching position."

"You're moving to Massachusetts?" Allen grinned. "It would make it so much easier if I wouldn't be without family."

"Well, I don't know yet, but it's a possibility. Like you, my academic life in Colorado has gotten uncomfortable. It seems every part of this state has gotten to me."

"Does Ethan know?" Lisa asked, her expression showing concern.

"He knows I'm being pushed out at my current job, and I have mentioned that I may have to look elsewhere."

She exhaled a rush of air.

"Don't worry. I'll still be there for him. If need be, I'll get him a place. Sarah and I won't let Ethan suffer. Or anyone in our circle."

"He won't accept charity." She tapped her nails against the stem of her glass.

"I know. We'll have to come up with a way to get him to think he's helping us out. Like staying in our house, keeping it in shape for us to return."

"Will you return?" Gabe asked.

"Uh, I really haven't thought that far ahead. Besides, I've only put out feelers. I don't have a job offer. I haven't even applied. The next step is chatting with the gatekeeper of the history department to discuss the possibility, but still, that's just a baby step." I turned to Allen. "If we do move to Massachusetts," I was liking the sound of that more and more, "you're more than welcome to live with us."

"Are you serious?"

"Yes. We never got to bond." I turned to Gabe. "That goes for you as well."

"I won't be moving. Not with Mom retiring."

"She's *retiring* retiring? Not just taking a break?" That was what I'd heard on Thanksgiving.

"Nope. Her hands are getting bad."

I furrowed my brow.

"She has arthritis in her hands, which makes it hard for her to do arrangements and deal with the cold room. And, she never really liked the business part. So, she's handing over the reins to me officially after New Year's."

For someone about to take over the family business, he didn't seem all that jazzed. Before the Peter mess got out of hand, I knew Gabe had his sights on joining my father's finance business, but Dad had hinted at dinner the previous evening that he was considering stepping down and installing another CEO as a way of saving the company's reputation. Even with Peter in prison, there had to be a sacrificial lamb to appease the public.

Did Helen's health issues also factor in? They'd been together secretly for years, but they'd never had time to simply enjoy being a couple. I understood my father's desire to not let his company crumble, but in the end, what was more important? His business reputation or his relationship with his wife and family? He was at the age when many considered retirement.

"So many changes on the horizon," I said.

Lisa nodded.

"How are you doing, Lisa?" I shifted on the sofa. "I know Ethan and I are close, but if you ever need to talk, Sarah's a good listener."

Everyone laughed.

"All kidding aside"—had I been joking?—"I'm here for all three of you."

"I do know that. Having us here for Christmas has made everything much easier, especially for Casey. She loves spending time here with her bestie."

"Ian's pretty cool," Allen said. "He taught me a few dance moves."

Lisa smiled at him. "He is, but I was talking about you. Casey adores you, and she's loving the Russian lessons."

Allen's grin went ear to ear, and he casually swiped his left eye. "She's like another sister."

"That's what I love about this family. The way you accept everyone." Lisa put her arm around my shoulders.

"It's funny, in a really sad way, but all of this didn't happen until my mom died. She had so much control over everyone's life, and fuck, that woman didn't want anyone under her sway to experience anything other than misery. All during my childhood, she pitted Peter and me against each other. She iced out our father through threats and blackmail. How did one person have that much power? How did I not see it?"

"It's hard when it's your own mother doing that shit," Lisa said.

"I never want to be like her. Never."

"Fat chance since you have a heart." Gabe covered his own. "I wish I'd be like you if I ever have kids."

"Ditto," Allen said.

"Thanks." I dried my eyes with my sweater, but it didn't staunch the flow.

Sarah popped her head into the library, her smile slipping when she saw me. "Everything okay?"

"It will be as long as we all band together." I briefly met everyone's eyes before landing on Sarah's.

"I think this calls for a group hug." Gabe wore a million-watt smile, as he yanked me to my feet, the others, including Sarah, engulfing me in an embrace.

CHAPTER SEVENTEEN

Part of my Christmas pact with Sarah involved New Year's Eve. I wanted the night to be about us after tucking the kids in a bit earlier than usual. I think all the holiday madness had wiped them out, so even Olivia didn't kick up too much of a fuss when I started rounding all of them up for their bedtime story at seven.

At eight, Sarah and I sat in the library, snuggled on the couch, a fire roaring, making the room toasty.

"Olivia essentially told me no more early bedtimes." I reached for the Perrier bottle in the ice bucket and topped off Sarah's glass. "It's cute how she thinks she's in charge."

"You didn't say that, did you?" Sarah took her drink.

"Nope. I figure the less she knows the better."

Sarah settled back into my arms. "It is best to let her have the last word."

"She takes after someone else I know." I elbowed Sarah's side.

Ignoring my jab, she sighed. "This was such a great idea. Can you hear that?"

I craned my neck to hear better. "No. What?"

"Nothing. There isn't a sound." She yawned.

"Time for me to put you to bed?"

She nestled closer to me. "Not yet. I want to enjoy this a bit longer."

I kissed the top of her head, basking in the moment.

"Do you have any resolutions?"

"What happened to cherishing the silence?"

Sarah shook her head. "Why do you hate resolutions or anything that has to do with the future?"

"Do I need to remind you, dear, that I'm a historian?"

"Do I need to remind you that talking to me while ensconced in our warm library is a lot easier than going to couple's therapy?"

I tossed my head back and laughed. "Please. I'm not the only one who doesn't want to go back to the head shrinker."

Sarah's sheepish smile was proof her threat was hollow.

"I really haven't given the upcoming year much thought."

"Liar. I found your list of how many articles you want to write for JJ. TV appearances." She waved etcetera.

"Oh, does work shit count? I thought you meant on a more personal level. Like make three new friends, jot down daily gratifications, check out my vag with a hand mirror, or other woo-hoo stuff I hate."

"Please don't make any more friends. The ones we have are enough work." She shivered, kindly ignoring my other comments.

"Did you know Lisa, Gabe, and Allen have formed a clique of their own?"

"Do you feel left out?"

"I wondered the same thing. While I think it's good, I just feel bad. Do you think the three of them feel like they're on the outside looking in?"

"I hope not." She sat up with purpose.

I pulled her back. "Not tonight, Sarah. Can we talk about that or plan something tomorrow to ensure they feel part of the... inner family...?" I slanted my head. "That sounds terrible, doesn't it? I don't want anyone to feel like they don't matter. Because that hurts. I don't want to be the source of misery for anyone. Fuck, I didn't realize until Christmas morning that I haven't done enough for Allen these past few months."

"If it makes you feel better, I didn't do a good job of it, either."

It did and didn't, but I left that unsaid. "Tomorrow. We'll start to rectify everything tomorrow. I need to stop feeling sorry for myself. Not give these crackerjacks power over me. I didn't murder anyone. I didn't plot with Peter. I didn't harbor a murderer. The truth may not matter to everyone, but I know there isn't anything to the wild accusations. I have to be content with that."

"Content? Is that enough for you?"

"It has to be. I can't let this resentment take root. There's simply too much at stake. And not over something so inane. The people who have time for conspiracies must be terribly troubled or utterly lonely and need some type of community. I feel sorry for them. I have everything. A stunning wife. Beautiful kids. Friends. Family. What do they have?"

"Good question."

I placed my lips on Sarah's. "This. You. They don't have what we have. I wish everyone did."

"You want to share me with everyone?" she teased.

"Nope. I want to be the only one to do this." I kissed her softly. At first. It was difficult to determine which of us kicked the smooching into hardcore lip-lock, our tongues entwined. "Let's move this upstairs."

"Now you're talking."

We held hands and walked side-by-side, not speaking, but

words weren't needed. When we reached the bedroom, I hoisted Sarah's shirt over her head.

"You aren't wasting any time."

"Not on this part, no."

"Do you plan to savor other aspects?" She arched a hopeful eyebrow.

"Sleep." I unhooked her bra.

"Does that mean sex is just something you need to tick off the New Year's Eve to-do list?" Her breath hitched as I slipped my fingers under her panties.

"You're the taskmaster. I'm simply following orders." I lowered her pants and underthings.

"If I'd known all I had to do was put something on the list, I would have done that ages ago."

I ran my hand up the inside of her leg. "I'm confused. Haven't you been crafting me honey-do-lists from the beginning?"

"Apparently not specific enough."

"Can you make me one for fucking? Step one: kiss. Step two: undress. Step three: nibble on right earlobe." I did just that, causing Sarah's breath to hitch again.

"Step four: don't stop with the ear thing, because it's fucking working." Her fingers dug into my back.

My tongue went inside her ear. She moaned. I continued while my hands fastened to her ass cheeks, pulling her closer to me. "I love you," I whispered, my mouth moving down the side of her neck.

Sarah lay down on the bed. "Step five: you strip."

I did and climbed on top of her, naked. "This. Our skin. Pressed against..." I couldn't complete the thought.

"I know. I crave it like you."

We kissed again. Her hands ran up and down my back. I loved the way she touched me. Tenderly but also with ownership. No, that wasn't the right word, but I couldn't conjure up the appropriate one. I could only feel it.

I moved down her torso, my tongue exploring her skin. Her hands cradling my head. When I reached her pubic hair, I sucked in a deep breath, allowing her patch to redden my chin. Sarah's hips were moving with wanting. Her musky scent becoming stronger.

My tongue slid past her mound and separated her slick lips, her desire intensifying. I went inside her, Sarah reacting by arching her back, her hands fisting the sheets. Replacing my tongue with two fingers, I lapped her bud. Nice and slow.

This was the part I enjoyed savoring, much to her consternation. Part of her wanted me to take my time, while the other half wanted the release. I had the same battle stirring inside, but we'd done this so many times we both knew what the other needed and at what speed. Tonight was a slow burn type. So, my fingers eased in and out without frantic urgency, and my tongue kept her in the mood, while we took the time to make love. Her hips still gyrated but more in tune with my steps than *the take me there* way.

My left hand sought her right, our fingers entwining.

"I fucking love you, Lizzie."

I met her gaze, not stilling my fingers or tongue.

Neither of us broke contact for many minutes, but then her eyes had to fight to stay open. I moved my fingers in deeper, allowing her to give into the ecstasy. Her hips moved with need, and my tongue kicked into a higher gear. Our conjoined fingers tightened.

I went in deeper, and Sarah bucked off the bed briefly. My tongue knew the exact circling motion along with pressure to get Sarah to the cliff when my fingers arched up, initiating the Big O, which turned into a rolling orgasm that lasted many wonderful cycles.

Afterward, I held Sarah in my arms. "This is what life is about."

"Afterglow?"

"No, feeling complete. As cheesy as this will sound, you and the kids complete me."

Sarah regarded me with an awestruck expression. "Did you just now realize that?"

"Nope. It's happened over time. I'm a slow learner. Like the day of our wedding. The first time I heard the heartbeat of the twins. Adopting Demi. Bringing Calvin home. Every step of the way has cemented this feeling. It's why I'll fight every battle to ensure I can take care of all of you."

"Don't forget we'll all fight for you."

CHAPTER EIGHTEEN

On January third, I huddled in my library to catch up on email. One in particular from a Harvard professor I'd met many years ago when still in grad school responded warmly to my inquiry about what I should and shouldn't say when I talked to the professor with all the power in the department. We'd spoken at a handful of seminars together and had become friends over the years. She wished me a happy New Year and said, "Hopefully we'll be colleagues soon! You'll love Cambridge."

Maddie and Sarah waltzed in like they owned the place. Well, Sarah did. Part of me had always considered this room as my sanctuary.

Maddie had a tape measure. "If we remove the furniture"—she extended the tape measure several feet—"I think we can get all of them in here."

Sarah, with hands on her hips, nodded.

"All of what?" I asked.

They ignored me.

Maddie asked Sarah, "How many are you factoring in?"

"At least a dozen. Hopefully more."

A dozen what? Christmas, thank God, was over, so I knew they weren't talking about trees to decorate. It was way too early for Valentine's Day, wasn't it? Was there a January holiday other than New Year's I'd been blissfully unaware of until today? It wasn't like I'd ever been invited to a Martin Luther King Jr. shindig. Usually, there was a special talk on campus, which never necessitated people coming over for food and drinks.

I rose to my feet and stood right in front of Sarah. "A dozen what?"

"Birthday party tents," she breezily mentioned as if I should have been able to puzzle that out on my own.

The three words didn't go together for me. We'd thrown birthday parties for the kids, but none of them had one coming up. And how did tents factor in? The Petries weren't the camping type. Oh, I loved to hike and be in the great outdoors, but at the end of the day, I wanted a hot shower and cozy bed. Not to mention a meal that wasn't prepared by me, and if I could figure out a way of never doing dishes again, my life would be grand. Aside from every part of it falling apart.

"It's winter. No one camps in the winter. Well, do igloos count as camping?" I placed a finger to my chin. "I'm betting Eskimos don't put them in their libraries. It'd destroy the floor, not to mention the melting factor."

Again, they ignored me.

Something else Maddie said started to sink in. "Remove the furniture? You can't. This is my office." My gaze bounced over the two sofas, a pair of wingback chairs, my desk and chair, and other random shit.

"Your office?" Sarah boosted a teasing eyebrow. "It's our library."

"Not going to work. Explain. Now." I planted my feet, bracing for the battle.

She handed me a glossy brochure.

"Tiny Tots Tents?"

"We're throwing a party in March for two of the kids."

"Demi is the only spring baby." I raked a hand through my hair.

"It'll also be Cal's half birthday." Sarah whirled around, not allowing me to look into her eyes.

"You're renting a tent for Cal, who'll be six months? Does it come with a crib?" This wasn't adding up.

"Don't be silly. He'll be too young to sleep in the tent. We're inviting all the kids from music class."

"I'm pretty sure all of our toddlers are still too young to sleep in a tent on their own as well. Who's watching them now?"

"Jorie and Bailey are on craft duty. Cal's asleep upstairs."

"We're going to have to de-Nazify the space." Maddie took several books, with swastikas on the bindings, off a shelf, her face puckering as she examined the covers, one by one. "As a precaution, we probably should remove all the books from the bottom rows so no one gets hurt." Maddie handed me the books she'd snatched.

"It's January. Surely, you don't mean to clear out the library today?" I placed the books on the edge of my desk, aligning their spines.

"Just crafting the to-do list." Sarah tapped the side of her head with a pen.

A shudder went through me. I still hadn't recovered from Sarah's end-of-the-year to-do lists, and she was already plotting another Petrie party. Granted, I wouldn't begrudge a party for Demi, but this proposal was way more extravagant for my already over-the-top wife.

"How tall is the kangaroo?" Maddie asked.

"Come again?" I glared at my wife. "What kangaroo?"

"We're renting a kangaroo."

"A stuffed one? Why not just buy one for the nursery?"

"Not a stuffed one." Sarah avoided my gaze again.

"A dead one?"

Sarah rounded and studied me as if I had a fever. "A live one."

I held up my hands, one still clutching the brochure. "Can you please walk me through this? And, by all means, speak slowly and use small words because, for the life of me, my brain can't comprehend anything you've said so far."

"Says Ms. Vocab." Sarah kissed my cheek. "Don't you trust me to plan a party?"

"No." I slapped the brochure against my thigh. "Not when you're talking about tents, kangaroos—"

"Just one kangaroo," she cut me off.

"Still seems like one too many considering it's a wild animal."

"He's been raised by humans after his mother kicked him out of her pouch. If he wasn't adopted by the animal rescue place and bottle-fed, he would have died. You wouldn't want that, would you?"

I waggled a finger. "Don't try to twist things. I didn't imply anything that would endanger the poor creature. I'm just not seeing why you're inviting a kangaroo to an overnight party."

"Oh, the kids won't stay overnight. They're too young."

I glanced at the flyer again and demanded in a much-louder voice than normal, "Then why do we need tents?" Okay, by the end of the statement, my voice reached screeching level.

"For naptime." She took the paper from my hand. "Each kid will have their own tent, plush memory foam mattress, sleeping bag, and stuffed zoo animals. And, they'll get to take home the stuffed animals and sleeping bags."

"Oh, we should get everyone a hamster." Maddie bounced on the balls of her feet.

Sarah considered this. "I'm not sure that would go over well with the moms."

"What about goldfish?"

"I hate seeing them in plastic bags. So inhumane."

Says the woman wanting to hire a kangaroo so Keri, the queen bee, will have to come to our house. I knew on Christmas Eve, since Claire had mentioned the Astors vs Vanderbilts scenario, I'd have to deal with… this. "Wait," I said. "Can we hold a raffle, and the winner can adopt Gandhi?"

"We can't raffle off our family dog!" Sarah said with fire in her eyes.

"Especially not one named Gandhi. One hint of that on social media and the Petrie name will be ruined for good." Maddie stated matter-of-factly.

"But we can order up a kangaroo?" Should I alert PETA? Probably not since I had a feeling it'd backfire. I could see the headline: *Wife Calls PETA on Wife!* Wait. Did that imply Sarah was an animal? Both of us? Many homophobes loved to claim if you legalized gay marriage it'd lead to bestiality. No reason to give stupid people more ammo.

"It's educational. The handlers will bring him in a crate," Sarah defended.

"Not seeing the friendly angle. Wild animals should be treated with respect. Not as pets."

Sarah placed her hands on my shoulders. "I need you to trust me on this. I will not do anything that will cause you any stress."

"You talking about taking everything out of my space and cramming a dozen tents with toddlers and a zoo creature in here for an afternoon—that seems like the very definition of stress."

"What about a chocolate fountain?" Maddie tossed out.

My gaze fell to the carpet. "Hard no." My head snapped up, causing a slight twinge in my neck. "Is the kangaroo potty-trained?"

"That's a good question." Sarah wrote down a note on her pad.

"Sarah, sweetheart, I know you're worried about our children's social lives, but don't you think your plan is slightly over-the-top?" I boosted my hand to a foot over my head and then elevated it more by getting onto my tippy toes.

"I knew you'd act this way."

"Like a rational adult?" Which wasn't my specialty.

"Trust me, Lizzie." Sarah put a hand on my shoulder. "The kids will love this."

"Can we wheel and deal?" I pleaded, my palms pressed together.

"Which part?"

All of it. "Um, do you have a plan I can look at?"

"You've always stayed out of the planning stages. What's changed?" She tapped her right foot.

Where in the fuck should I start? "When you started talking about bringing a kangaroo in a crate to a party with a dozen toddlers, three of which are ours, not to mention our youngest who can't even walk yet—do I really have to point out what could possibly go wrong?"

CHAPTER NINETEEN

After our conversation, we went into the kitchen so we could have tea, which I think was meant to calm me, but it had the opposite effect. Sarah explained in excruciating detail why this elaborate party was necessary, and I spent the entire time digging my nails into my palms to avoid saying she was batshit crazy.

I managed not to utter any curse words during the tea chat, and quickly retreated into my office when my cup ran dry. She knew she had me over a barrel considering we were doing this for the sake of our toddlers' social lives. Sarah never brought up the crucial fact that most of the drama revolved around the criminal elements of my family. I was 99.876 percent certain she didn't think I was to blame.

I did.

I'd also do anything for my children, something I'd been denied most of my life. Caring and supportive parents.

After pacing my office, longingly looking over my pristine bookshelves, where my books were organized by a categorization I'd developed on my own, I resigned myself to shelling out a bucketload of money to pay for a once-in-a-lifetime nap party to celebrate Demi's second birthday and Cal's six-month birthday, even though I didn't think one of the tents was for him.

Nap party!

Okay, maybe my brain wasn't completely harmonizing to the need, but I wasn't going to get in Sarah's way. It wasn't like I could say, "Hey, Peter and I didn't have friends growing up, and look how that turned out."

Peter was in prison, and I wasn't really known for my excellent people skills. Unless you counted my ability to stick my foot in my mouth at every possible chance.

I checked out the Tents for Tots website and cringed when I started calculating the amount with the extras. I'd been meaning to see if I could get our credit limit extended. Now seemed like the best time for it.

Logging into my account, I merrily clicked on the online chat option, because the thought of speaking to someone on the phone sent shivers through me. Additional proof that our children should have more human interaction. However, when they were adults, what would the robot to human ratio really be?

The chat box appeared, and I typed in my request.

The reply was: *It'll take 10 days to receive a new card.*

I didn't want a new card. I wanted more credit.

I retyped my request.

This time the chat box informed me my next payment was due on the third of December. It was January. Then I saw a message saying something went wrong, and the box closed.

Why was it whenever I wanted to avoid all human contact, or at least have a barrier between human to human interaction, like a chat box, I had to reach out to a real live human? Fucking karma had it out for me.

Groaning, I reached for my phone and punched in the number for customer service.

The recorded greeting said it had successfully matched my

phone number with my account and asked me to type in or say the last four digits of my social security number. I entered the numbers on the keypad.

The robot voice thanked me for proving my identity. This made me laugh, because how hard was it for a hacker to obtain these details? Never mind.

Next, the voice prodded me to say why I was calling.

"Customer representative."

The voice didn't catch that.

"Customer representative," I spoke slowly but much louder.

Again, my request wasn't getting through.

I tried again, to no avail.

"Customer representative!" I screamed.

"I understand you want to speak to someone. Can you tell me what it's regarding first?"

"Credit limit."

"You need a new card?" The robot sounded helpful and friendly. I wanted to strangle its metal neck, even if it really didn't have a human form. In my mind, it did.

"Credit limit!"

"I've cancelled your card and am sending a new one. Do you need to cancel all cards with this account?"

"Customer representative!"

"I've cancelled the other card on the account. Would you like two new cards?"

"Mother fucker!"

"Thanks for calling."

There was a dial tone.

I yanked my phone from my ear, staring helplessly at the blank screen. "Why can't robots listen?"

I stormed out of my office into the kitchen, where Sarah and Maddie sat at the counter nursing more herbal tea, more than likely needing to calm themselves from having to deal with me and the nap party wet blanket.

"Don't use your credit card," I barked.

Sarah set her mug down on the granite counter. "Why?"

"The fucking robots!" I flicked my hands up in the air.

Sarah gave Maddie a furtive glance before asking me, "Can you provide more details?"

"Not really. The robots are out to ruin me. Everyone is out to ruin me. I need to go for a bike ride or something. Just don't use your card. Not until I figure out a way to get around the robot situation. There has to be a way to outsmart them." I walked through the door leading to the garage.

"It's snowing," Sarah hollered after me.

"Does that mean the weather is also against her?" Maddie asked Sarah.

"Probably," Sarah replied.

She may have said more, but I opened the garage door, which mercifully blocked out their chatter. As the door creaked upward, the pile of snow in the driveway confirmed Sarah's statement. It wasn't like I hadn't known the forecast, but a part of me had been hoping for a miracle. Couldn't one thing break in my favor?

While I couldn't hop on my bike, especially since I was wearing a new pair of jeans and a sweater, not my usual bike gear, I fired up the snowblower. Might as well use my negative energy for good. Besides, the way things were going, someone would slip on ice out front and sue me, draining me of every last penny. Clearly, Betty had it out for me, and I regretted sending her and her waste of space husband a sausage-and-crackers basket for Christmas. Maybe I could demand she give it back. Oh boy, what if she recorded me ranting and raving about wanting my wieners back. Hell, it might be worth it, and maybe people would stop shouting "Murderer" at me and opt for "Wiener thief" instead. That thought put a smile on my face. I'd rather be known for something so completely ridiculous.

CHAPTER TWENTY

That night, after getting everyone tucked in, including Gandhi who liked to have a stick that was supposed to help his breath but never seemed to, Sarah asked me if I'd like to have a nightcap in the office.

"Is that your way of saying we need to talk?" I sulked, sitting my buttocks on the couch.

"It's my way of saying you've been wound tighter than normal, and I think it'd be good to discuss why that is. I mean, you threw a fit about robots earlier and then plowed and shoveled our entire street." Sarah took a seat next to me, angling her body to face me and sitting cross-legged.

"I'm tired of everyone hating me."

"That never bothered you in the past."

I swiveled my head to look into her eyes. "Are you saying everyone has always hated me?"

"Of course not. I meant you never really cared what people thought of you until recently."

I huffed out an angry breath. "That's because I really don't care what people think. Most are effing morons."

"Yes, you've been clear about that for years. What's changed?"

"These morons have children my kids want to play with. And they can't because some bitch of a woman pulls all the other moms' strings like a demented Geppetto." I acted out an evil puppeteer.

"How exactly do robots factor in?"

I sighed. "I promise I'm not losing my mind. I was trying to up our credit limit. The chat box acted up, and the automated system refused to let me speak to a human. It somehow cancelled both of our cards. I'm not entirely sure we're getting new ones, but I did get an email apologizing for the system going haywire. Unsurprisingly, it was from an email address you can't respond to. I guess we'll know in about ten business days."

"Why do we need more credit?"

"This party. It's not like we can pay the kangaroo with peanuts. Do kangaroos even eat peanuts?"

"We can't have nuts of any type. Annie is allergic." Sarah wore her teasing smile, probably in hopes to crack my anger. Usually, it worked.

I groaned. "Naturally. Let me guess; we have to fly in special treats that have been made with the purest of ingredients and by people paid fifty bucks an hour, or we'll be tarred and feathered on Twitter. Social media is ruining this world. Ruining it!" I shook my fists in the air. "It's ironic, but I think irony is dead these days, because heaven forbid you make a joke that doesn't land well. People don't let things go anymore. All they do is tear others down. I'm being shredded by all sides, even by Keri, the queen bee of the moms. If you ask me, these moms who walk two feet behind her at all times are pussies."

"Are you including me in that category?"

"Yes!" I said without thinking. Once my brain figured out what I had affirmed, I cowered behind my palms.

Sarah laughed. Quietly at first, but then her body shook with laughter. "I think you're right. I am being a coward."

"Does that mean we can call off the kangaroo nap party?"

"Oh, no. That's happening—"

"If you aren't trying to impress Keri, why do we have to?"

"Because Freddie really wants a kangaroo in his house."

I collapsed against the back of the couch. "Are you just saying that?"

"Because secretly he's your favorite?" She arched one eyebrow.

"I've never said such a thing." I knifed the air with a finger. "I love all of our children."

"I don't doubt that, but I also see you with Fred. You have such a soft spot for him."

"Not denying or confirming anything."

She smiled.

"Who's your favorite?" I asked. "Just between us?"

"Oh no, I'm not taking the bait."

"Don't you trust me?" I flashed a hurt look coupled with a hand over my heart.

"You really are learning too much from Maddie and me."

"It's sink or swim in this family. Can I ask you a question?"

"Just did. Need another?" She slapped my thigh.

I ignored her childishness. "If it wasn't for the Petrie mess, would Keri still be gunning for us?"

"I have absolutely no idea. Why?"

"Is it me?"

"Is what you?"

"Am I so unlikeable?" I asked in a meek voice.

"Oh, Lizzie. You're very likable."

"But I have a lot of evidence to the contrary. My own mother tried to destroy me. Peter did what he could to help her. Dad let me suffer, too busy with Helen and her boys. Meg used me. Dean Spencer is ostracizing me. I'm really starting to think

I'm defective or something. That you and the kids would be better off if I... I don't know. Lived in the attic à la *Jane Eyre*. The book, not the main character because she wasn't the one in the attic."

Sarah took my hand in hers. "Please don't do this to yourself. You are not some social outcast who should be locked away from society."

A tear rolled down my cheek, and my nose started to burn. "It feels like it. I mean I can't even get a robot to listen to me."

"No one can. Those automated systems get the better of everyone."

"Every time I think I have my self-doubt under control, it morphs on me, and I have to fight like hell not to slip into its clutches. Being human is hard."

"It is, but you are so very human. It's part of what makes you lovable."

I wiped my nose with my sleeve. "Being a crying mess?"

"You're always adorable. Even when ranting about robots ruining your life. Please, Lizzie, don't let all of this get you down. Everyone is cheering you on. Lean on me."

"You're busy planning a party to win over the evil mom who has it out for the Petries."

"Just so you know, I looked into the possibility of getting an otter for you, but they didn't have one that's used to being around children."

"It still worries me that you're treating zoo animals like pets. They're not. Do we really want to teach this lesson to our children? All creatures deserve love and respect for what they are."

"That right there is you being adorable again." She circled her hand in the air. "So fucking adorable."

"Because I believe in animal rights?"

"Because you argue with me concerning things you're passionate about."

"A lot of people don't like it when I argue with them. Most just want me to shut up. Is our attic habitable?" I glanced to the ceiling. "It may not be a bad choice, considering. Maybe I can teach online classes. Will our WiFi reach?"

"Stop with the attic. It ain't happening."

Still studying the ceiling, I pondered, "I wonder if we have bats. They're cool, but don't they have rabies? Do kangaroos have rabies? Do we need to get rabies vaccines? For everyone? How much will that cost?" I tried to google the answer on my phone, but Sarah took it from me.

"Why don't we go upstairs, and I'll give you a back rub?"

I massaged my left shoulder. "I am sore from shoveling, including Betty's front stairs."

"You shoveled for her?"

"Yeah. I figured it'd seem petty or possibly hurt her feelings if I did everyone else's but not hers."

"You know, ya keep saying you hate people, but you secretly are the most caring misanthrope I've ever met."

"That's the meanest thing you've said to me. Take it back." I slapped her thigh, not too hard. "I do not like being around humans. Period."

"Yes, you do. Or you wouldn't care about hurting Betty's feelings. Did she even say thank you?"

"She actually gave me a cookie."

"Did you eat it?"

I nodded. "Why?"

"I don't trust that woman."

"If I'm lucky, the poison won't be a painful way to go, and I recently upped my life insurance. Now, what about that back rub?" I tapped my fingertips together.

CHAPTER TWENTY-ONE

Sarah directed me to strip down and lie on my stomach. The room was a bit chilly, but that wasn't going to stop me from getting a massage.

She returned from the bathroom. "Would it be dangerous to warm up massage oil in the microwave?"

"You're asking me? I'm not allowed to use our appliances anymore."

"Good point." Sarah squinted, held the bottle close, and then pulled it away, trying to read the print on the label. "I'm thinking the way things have been going, maybe I won't risk it. Do you want me to skip using it?"

"I think I can manage the initial shock of cold. Is it the one for sore muscles?"

"I'm pretty sure it is, but is it just me or is the print getting smaller on shit like this?" Again, she pulled it away to try to make out the words.

I laughed. "I'm pretty sure it's everyone in our age bracket that thinks that way."

Sarah, in her flannel pajama bottoms, straddled me. "Does this hurt?"

"Never. I'll always like you on me."

"Will you still say that when you're in your eighties?"

"Less interrogating. More massaging."

"Bossy!" she said in a tone that implied she liked it.

She squeezed the oil onto her hands and rubbed them together in an effort to warm it up before applying her palms to my bare skin. Momentarily, I flinched.

"Sorry."

"Not your fault it's winter. You have many secret powers, but controlling the seasons isn't one."

Her fingers dug into my left shoulder, and I released a grateful moan. "What's one of my secret powers?"

"Your ability to keep interrogating even after being told not to." I rested my chin on the back of my hands.

"That's called being a woman."

I moaned again when she applied more pressure to my left shoulder.

"You're really in pain."

"Not at the moment. Well, it hurts a little, but in that really good way."

"We should book you a legit massage. You really need to start taking better care of yourself. When's the last time you went for a bike ride?"

"How old are the twins?"

She swatted my back. "We need to get better."

"At having twins? I think that would break us."

"You think you're so funny."

"Funny looking or funny ha-ha?"

Sarah moved to my other shoulder, which was even stiffer. I closed my eyes tightly and fisted the sheet.

"Too much?" she asked.

"Perfect. Don't stop." I gritted my teeth.

"Usually, I like it when you say that."

"Not tonight?" I looked over my shoulder.

"Oh, I do, but how do massage therapists do this all day?" She threaded her fingers and cracked them.

"You can stop. I know you're tired."

"Pretty sure I can last a little longer. Where else needs work before my fingers fall off?"

"Lower back." I braced myself, knowing it was going to hurt, and it did, but it felt oh so fucking amazing in a really excruciating way. "Would a massage therapist be gentle with me?"

"You've had a massage before."

"Not when in this much pain."

"Oh, honey. Next time, don't shovel the entire street. Hire someone."

"You hate when I hire people for things."

"I hate it more when you break yourself."

"Now you tell me."

Sarah applied more oil. "Did you take anything for the pain?"

"No."

"Of course not. I'm surprised you even told me you're in pain." I could feel her eye roll.

"Can you not lecture me right now?"

Sarah continued to work on my back, her fingers doing their best to knead out the kinks. "You're really tight. Do we have any muscle relaxers?"

"I don't think so."

Sarah got up. "I'm going to call Mom. I think she might have some."

I couldn't take prescription pills that weren't prescribed to me. "I can't—" Sarah was already out of the room. "Isn't that illegal?" I asked the sleeping Gandhi on his bed next to the heat grate under the window. The dog, dead to the world, didn't respond. When awake, he had the cutest head tilts that always made me grin, and part of me believed he was trying his best to understand me.

Sarah returned. "Troy's bringing over a couple."

I started to speak.

"You're going to take them, so just—" She snapped her fingers together to tell me to zip it.

While taking someone else's pills wasn't something I'd usually do, the pain was bad enough for me to ignore the *law and order* part of my personality. "Fine, but if I get hooked, I'm suing."

"Who? Me, Troy, or Mom?" Sarah had her *get real* smile in place.

"I haven't decided yet." I yawned.

She sat on the edge of the bed. "Do you remember the days when a back massage led to other things?"

"Not to breaking the law."

"It really amazes me that you're a Petrie. You're such a law-abiding person, yet the world thinks you're one of the masterminds in a criminal conspiracy."

"I wouldn't even have the gumption to steal a pack of gum."

"I'd pay good money to watch you try."

"Yes, that's my true purpose. To amuse those in my life by being a fucking moron."

Sarah's phone buzzed. "Troy's here. BRB."

Sarah's use of BRB to mean *be right back* made me heave a sigh about the state of language skills. While we were both nearing middle age, Sarah was still the cooler one. However, even when I was in my youth, I was never known as being hip. How did millennials say hip? On fleek? No, that didn't seem right. If I knew about it, the fad had probably already faded. Given my inability to move my arms, I didn't bother researching the correct slang term that was popular at the moment. I shifted on the bed, regretting the movement when my back spasmed.

Sarah returned with a massive, obnoxiously pink pill in her palm and a glass of water. "The lengths you'll go to avoid having sex with me."

Gingerly, I sat up, resting on a pillow pressed against the headboard. "Yep, that's the reason I did this to myself. I can't stand sex with you. It's good to get that off my chest, after all of these years."

She climbed under the covers. "Truth be told, I don't like it much either."

I looked down into her chocolate eyes. "It's a shame, really. We're quite good at it."

"You think so?" She batted her lashes at me.

I ran a finger down the side of her face. "I do."

"Get under the covers and rest. Fingers crossed we'll be back in action by the weekend."

"That's tomorrow."

"Mom swears by those pills."

Now under the covers, the sheets still cool to the touch, I yanked the soft blanket up to my chin. "Did you give me a muscle relaxer or female Viagra?"

Sarah yawned. "Does it matter?"

"I really hope I didn't swallow any of your mom's sex pills. I may never be able to—"

Sarah pressed a finger to my lips. "Sometimes you don't know when to stop. You don't have to verbalize every wild thought that pops into your head."

CHAPTER TWENTY-TWO

The following morning, I eased myself out of bed, quite surprised how much better my back and shoulders felt. Rose had been spot-on. The pill was a miracle drug. Not surprising, given that was how vile corporations got you. Well, not me, thank you very much. The last thing I needed at the moment was an addiction issue.

By the time I arrived in the kitchen, where Ollie was pitching an epic fit, I briefly considered pretending my upper body still hurt so I could go back to bed. Instead, I hunched down and asked my daughter, "What's got you so upset, Ollie Dollie?"

With a red face, she pointed to Freddie. "Mine!"

She was referring to Freddie's stuffed monkey clutched in his right hand.

There was an identical one on the floor next to her feet, but Ollie loved to take Fred's. Not wanting to encourage that behavior, I swept her monkey into my hand, placed it before my face, and said, "Why don't you want to play with me?" in what I hoped was a semi-decent monkey voice.

Ollie stopped screaming and gazed at the monkey with curiosity.

I continued, "Let's play together," unable to think of something more tempting. I hadn't had my morning tea yet, and the hamster in my brain was refusing to rally, apparently.

Luckily, it was enough. Ollie took the monkey from me and tottered off into the family room as if nothing was wrong.

"It's got to be hard to be so frustrated but unable to really express why," I said to Sarah, who handed me a mug of tea.

"Oh, she has a way of getting her feelings across." Sarah kissed my cheek. "How's your back?"

"Muchos better. Hey, I'm bilingual today."

Sarah's eyes darted upward, but she chuckled. "An interesting side effect."

"One of these days, your eyes are going to get permanently stuck." I took a drink of the tea. "You added sugar."

"I thought you might still be in pain." She reached for it, pretending she intended to take it back.

"Off me!"

"I see where Ollie gets her temper."

I shrugged. "Whatevs. What's on the agenda today?"

"It's the last day of winter break. What would you like to do before going back to work?"

I looked out the kitchen window. "It's snowing."

Sarah waggled a finger. "No shoveling. Let the neighbors take care of their own walkways. Ethan is outside with the snowblower, taking care of the drive and our sidewalk. I think he's enjoying playing the man."

"Do you think we'll ever get rid of him?" If we didn't move, but I kept that part to myself. Sarah knew I was looking, but I hadn't told her about the promising email, not wanting to get her hopes up. Or was I worried she'd be depressed?

Sarah's brow furrowed. "I'm not sure how I'll live without him, now. He's really helpful. Even Maddie has been behaving."

She said this in a quiet voice since Mads was a few feet away, feeding Demi.

Sarah had a point. While our household wasn't what most people would consider normal, somehow, we made it work. In previous centuries, it wouldn't have been so odd to have so many generations under one roof. My historian brain started to rev, but Sarah must have noticed and said, "Maybe we should take the kiddos sledding and then get hot chocolate."

"Do we have enough adults? The kids aren't old enough to ride a sled on their own."

"There are three toddlers."

"Well, you can't sled."

Sarah crossed her arms. "Why not?"

"You're still recovering."

"It's January. I had Cal in October."

"Exactly. You can't sled, and we just got my back better." I started counting on my fingers. Maddie and Ethan.

Perhaps she understood I wouldn't budge on her sledding, because she reluctantly said, "Fine. I'll call either Troy or Gabe."

"Why not both? And Allen?" Maddie suggested. "Let the men get cold and wet and allow Lizzie to have more bonding time before school madness starts again."

Sarah nodded, seeing Maddie's logic.

I raised my mug in the air appreciatively toward Maddie, somewhat relieved she wasn't avoiding my stepbrother completely. I wasn't sure if they had the *let's be friends* talk yet, but they were staying civil, which was a refreshing change to Petrie family style.

"Oh, should we invite Casey and Lisa?" I asked.

Sarah bobbed her head side to side. "Let me chat with Ethan first before springing more Lisa time on him."

"If you end up inviting Casey, we better include Ian and Mia." Maddie turned in her chair. "This family really is getting ginormous. Oh, Darrell. He seems like the type who wouldn't mind sledding, saving us from getting wet and cold."

"Is it wrong we're thinking of every way possible to get guys to do guy things? Are we terrible feminists?" I slugged more tea, loving the sugar.

"Not at all. I'll make them do the dishes or laundry just to show them who's boss." Sarah walked in the direction of the garage to chat with Ethan.

I took a seat at the table across from Maddie. "What's going on with you and Gabe?"

"Nothing."

"As in you still haven't told him, or you two are kaput?"

"Is there another option?"

"Yes. It's where Ethan is currently residing. I don't think he's enjoying it all that much."

Maddie loaded up Demi's spoon with oatmeal. "I'm pretty sure we're kaput, but we haven't sat down to hash it out. He did drop off some of my stuff at my apartment when I wasn't home."

"Did he bring it inside?"

Maddie met my eye. "Yes. Why?"

"If he'd tossed it on your front lawn or something, I think that would be a sign he wasn't agreeable to the situation."

"He even washed and folded my clothes."

"I wish I had an ex like him."

She nodded. "Gabe's a good man."

"You're such a hypocrite, ya know."

She gave me a quizzical stare.

"You always push me to talk about my feelings and all that bull, but when it comes to your own personal sh-shitake, you avoid all the yucky aspects of relationships."

"It's so much easier to tell others what to do than to do it yourself. I wonder how many therapists end up in divorce court?"

"You're an interior designer."

"I know. Maybe I should start cold-calling therapists. See how many need my help setting up a new place. Do you think if I paid them enough, they'd provide me with deets on their clients who are too overwhelmed with their separation and would want to hire me to set up their pad? I can get everything they need, even the essentials for their pantry." She spoke with hopeful sincerity.

"Wow. That's capitalism at its best or worst."

"Where there's a need, there's someone to fill it." She shrugged. "When's your next visit with Peter?"

I glanced at Demi, who didn't seem to react to her father's name. "Soon. I want to wish him a happy New Year. Or would that be cruel considering?"

"Just see him, Lizzie. He needs us."

CHAPTER TWENTY-THREE

Gabe, in snow pants and ski jacket, walked hand in hand with Freddie after a triumphant sledding run down the tiniest of hills.

"Did you see that, Lizzie? We smoked it!" Gabe squatted down to give Fred a high five, but Freddie cocked his head to the side, giving it serious thought before committing to the gesture.

I laughed.

Gabe looked up at me, still hunching to Fred's level. "He takes after you more and more each day."

"He certainly does. Great job, little man." I put my hand out for a high five, and Fred slapped it enthusiastically without a moment's thought. "Trust," I announced to Gabe.

Freddie tottered off to Sarah and Rose, who had a thermos of hot chocolate for the kiddos.

"How are you doing?" Gabe asked in the tone I was really starting to hate.

I nodded. "Fine."

"Does that mean not fine?" Gabe put a hand on my shoulder.

I knew he was being nice, but I didn't want to focus on me while the kids were now enjoying hot chocolate after sledding with their friends, grandfather, and uncles, three of which weren't blood relations but, oddly, were more helpful when it came to pitching in with the kiddos.

Allen finished his run with Ollie, the two of them squealing.

Fortunately, my phone rang, giving me the perfect opportunity to cut the convo, as the kids liked to say these days, short. "Excuse me."

I stepped to the side to answer.

"Is this Dr. Petrie?"

Hardly anyone called me that. "Y-yes."

"This is Dr. Ruth Connors."

This was the Harvard professor who held my future in her hands. If Connors approved, I would be a shoo-in. My eyes locked on Sarah with all the people she cared about circled around her, laughing and enjoying quality family time. Guilt swirled in my gut as I hoped for a jump to Cambridge, Massachusetts.

"Good afternoon," I said, feeling sicker by the second.

"I'm sorry to call you during your school break."

"No worries." I'd been waiting for this since receiving the email, even if I'd been dreading the outcome.

"I wish I had better news, but I'm afraid the position you're interested in is no longer available."

The air whooshed out of my chest. "I understand." I didn't. Was the position filled, had it been yanked, or was I not wanted? "Thank you for letting me know."

"Again, I'm sorry." There wasn't much remorse in her enunciation.

I did my best to reassure Dr. Connors that there were no hard feelings, when all I wanted to do was crawl into a hole, never to be seen again.

Sarah met my gaze, concern appearing in the crinkles

around the corners of her eyes. I pocketed my phone and smiled. She returned the smile, but the concern still resided in her face.

Come on, Lizzie. Pull your shit together.

I approached the group, shoving down my disappointment with each step. "I'm freezing. Can I have some?" I took one of the cups Sarah had poured from the thermos.

"Everything okay?" she whispered into my ear.

My eyes swept the group, which included Lisa, Casey, JJ and her family, even Darrell. We really did have a wonderful support network. Still, my job was at stake, and it was fucking Harvard. "Couldn't be better."

I was 98.72 percent certain I hadn't convinced Sarah, but she let it go, turning her attention to Ollie, who had made a snow angel. "Great job, Ollie!" I tugged on one of the poufy balls hanging from Fred's beanie. "What about you, Fred? Would you like to make one?"

He looked uncertain.

"What if I did it with you?"

A crooked smile appeared on his lips.

I handed my cup to Sarah and got onto my back. I spread my arms and legs, making a snow angel. Freddie copied me, along with Demi. The two of them giggling, holding hands. Ever since Demi had moved in with us, Fred had taken her under his wing as if he understood she'd need lots of love.

Not to be left out, Ollie collapsed on top of me. "Ollie Mommy's angel," she said.

"You are my angel." I wrapped my arms around her.

Sarah's eyes misted over.

Perhaps the phone call was the best thing to happen for my family. Maybe packing up and getting out of Colorado wasn't the right choice, but a kneejerk reaction to the Petrie mess.

Then again, I was a professor who'd been demoted, making me feel like I was an imposter in my current teaching post.

How would I get past thinking I didn't deserve to teach? Compound that with the need to support a large family and my anxiety reached levels I'd never knew existed. Granted, I had other sources of income, but I couldn't shake the feeling that I was failing. Not simply in my career but letting my family down. Tears started to well in my eyes, but Ollie grabbed a handful of snow and splattered my face, a wicked grin making my daughter adorable, albeit in a scary way. Freddie and Demi, not wanting to be left out, also piled on top of me. I wrapped the three of them into my arms, holding on so I wouldn't lose my shit for everyone to witness.

Sarah tried to come to my rescue and started lifting the little ones off me. "All right, you three. Don't squash Mommy."

This only spurred Ollie to scream, "S-ash, Mommy!"

Sarah laughed and gave me a shrug.

"Is anyone here an organ donor?" I joked.

Not to be outdone, Gabe joined the fun. The kiddos delightfully trampled him, one of them getting a little too close to the family jewels given how quickly Gabe protected the area.

Slowly, I got to my feet, dusting off the snow. "It's getting cold."

Sarah's gaze was on another group, Keri and several of the other moms with their kids sledding. Apparently, Fort Collins didn't have enough space for our rival kid gangs. Keri said something to the group, and every single one turned their back. It was hard not to flip the bird in their direction. Even if they wouldn't see it, it might have made me feel slightly better.

Sarah gave me a sidelong look and then said, "Okay, troops. Let's get loaded into the car. It's lunchtime! The second favorite part of the day."

"Is dinner third?" Allen asked, rubbing his chin.

I put my arm around his neck. "Nothing gets past you, little bro."

* * *

That night, Sarah found me in the library, while I sat at my desk, prepping a lecture for later this week. Or that was my excuse for secreting myself in my space with the hopes of avoiding Sarah's watchful eye.

"There's a serious face."

I stopped absently twirling a pen. "The Nazis bring it out in me."

"Do you ever wonder what it'd be like to study a different time period?"

"You mean one that's less depressing?"

"Yeah."

I squinted an eye. "Can you think of one?"

"Is this when you educate me that all time periods are depressing?"

I smiled. "History is filled with terrible events."

"Who called you earlier?" Sarah perched on the edge of my desk.

"Harvard."

"Hah-vard?" She did her best Massachusetts accent. "Should I start my moving to-do list?"

"Would it really only involve one list?" I teased in my best *everything's fine* voice.

"Oh, no. It'd take at least two." She crossed her arms. "Are you regretting putting out a feeler?"

I laughed, not sounding super happy. "Maybe."

"Is it the new post or city that's making you nervous?"

"Neither. We aren't moving." I started to tap the pen against my thigh.

"You said no?"

God, she believed in me completely. "Uh, no. They did."

"W-what?" The realization of those two words seeped into her face. "Lizzie, I'm so sorry."

I started to say it was okay but stopped myself. "Maybe it was the answer I needed."

"To what question?"

"If I can make it on my own now that Dr. Marcel isn't in my corner. Maybe William was right. Dr. Marcel was playing favorites, and I wasn't the most qualified for teaching."

"William? I haven't heard that name in forever."

"Before leaving the program, he made it clear he thought I was second-tier at best."

"He also tried to ruin our relationship." She folded her arms over her chest protectively.

"Oh, I remember. He's a petty man."

"Then why are you letting anything he said infect you." She peered at me with worried eyes.

"It's not only William's parting shot looping through my head. I'm being sidelined at my current position and can't find another teaching post."

"You've only put feelers out to one other place, which happens to be one of the best universities. It might take time to reach that level." She moved her hand in the air, suggesting climbing the career ladder.

"Or I'm just not that good."

Sarah took the pen from my hand. "Just because there isn't an opening for you at one university, out of hundreds just in the US, doesn't mean you aren't a great teacher. Please, don't go all Lizzie on me and start thinking that way."

"How can I not, Sarah? Everything is piling up in the column of not good enough." I cradled my forehead to shield my eyes.

"You're going through a rough patch. That's all. Not everything is in the wrong column. You're doing great on JJ's show."

"Considering it only involves screaming over other guests, it's not a stellar compliment. You're always telling me I love to think I'm right. This type of work allows me to believe I am."

"But...?"

"I'm having a hard time seeing it these days. The only word I can associate with my career starts with an F."

"Oh really?" She boosted an eyebrow.

"Not that F-word."

"Why not that F-word? I have a thing for hot chicks in sweater vests."

"I'm not wearing one," I said, dumbfounded.

Sarah tapped the side of her head. "True, but I remember the one you were wearing the day we met. I wanted you then."

"You did not!" I protested, laughing it off.

"I did."

I rolled my eyes. "Lying to me isn't going to make me feel better."

Sarah cupped my chin with her palm. "I am not lying. You, Elizabeth Petrie, are an amazing woman. Don't let all this shit that is out of your control make you believe otherwise."

"You only say Elizabeth when you're upset."

"Not true, I said it when we got married."

"I think you had to. Isn't it kinda the law?"

"I'm not sure, but it seemed right at the time." She waved a hand in front of my face. "You're trying to distract me from the point."

"What point?"

Sarah, arms crossed, took a deep breath and glared down at me. She looked kinda hot.

I tugged her arms apart and started to unbutton her shirt.

"What are you doing?"

"Baking a cake. What do you think?"

"You're trying to distract me. Still." Her voice was firm.

"Clearly, I'm not doing a good job. I would like it noted that you said I shouldn't let other stuff get in the way. Really, I'm only following your directions. Setting everything to the side and..." I popped the last button of her shirt, revealing her licorice red bra. Scooting to the edge of my seat, I pulled her head down so I could kiss her on the lips to silence any objections. Her moan gave me the go-ahead I wanted.

I slid the shirt off her shoulders, and Sarah unhooked her bra.

"You're the perfect solution to my problem."

She gazed into my eyes. "Which problem are you referring to?"

"Not being able to get out of my head. But you. Here. Half-naked on my desk, is just what the doctor ordered."

"What doctor?"

"Me. Dr. Petrie. I want to fuck you."

"Shall we go upstairs, then?"

I shook my head. "Nope. I want you on my desk."

"You're acting like we're still in our twenties, without kids."

"Is that a problem?" I started to kiss her stomach, working my way up, knowing I couldn't go where I wanted, not since Sarah was still breastfeeding. "It's just not fair." I stared longingly at her full breasts.

"Says the woman who hasn't given birth to any of our children."

"But you're so good at it."

"Really, that's what you're going with?"

I motioned for her to shut up. "Lift up."

"You know, everyone says I'm the bossy one, but you really can be."

"I thought I made it clear you shouldn't talk." I pulled off her jeans and panties.

She started to speak, but I planted my lips onto hers again. The woman sometimes didn't know what was best. "I want you," I whispered in her ear and nibbled on her earlobe before my tongue dipped in, causing Sarah to lean back on her hands, groaning in her way that gave me the green light to dictate. Finally, I thought. Not that I didn't enjoy her playful banter.

Sometimes, though, I wanted to focus on the physical aspect of our relationship. And since early fall, our time together like this had been so minimal. Then she was out of commission, recovering. I wanted to make up for lost time. Right fucking now.

My mouth trekked down from her lips, my tongue trailing along her collarbone to the hollow of her neck. Then it moved down between her breasts, trying not to focus on both peaks that hardened. Did they miss me like I yearned for them?

I peppered her stomach with hungry kisses, her pungent scent growing stronger the farther south I trekked. Her pubic hair greeted me with the coarseness I craved against my chin. Its abrasiveness was the perfect contrast to Sarah's creamy skin, and I loved the way it left traces as if claiming me. I wanted to be hers. Always.

My mouth reached her wet, swollen lips. Inhaling deeply, I separated her with my tongue.

Sarah moaned.

I inhaled again, pressing my face more fully into her sex. I wanted Sarah all over me.

Given the way her hips moved, Sarah wanted me inside.

I loved knowing her like this. We'd made love hundreds of times, and our need for the other only seemed to grow. I'd always wondered if couples lost the thrill after so many years, when having kids and jobs seemed to suck your energy. But during these moments, I felt like I did the first time I tasted Sarah.

I eased a finger inside, and Sarah lowered her upper body on bent elbows. With one hand, I shoved the desk chair out of the way and got onto my knees, giving me freer access to move in and out of her while my tongue started to lap at her clit.

"Oh, Elizabeth."

I had to suppress a laugh. Even now, she had to make a point. She was such a woman, and God, what a woman. My fingers moved in deeper, my tongue exploring her folds, wandering in her secret areas where only I was allowed. I was the only one who turned her on like this. The sole person on the planet who had the pleasure of tasting her.

She became wetter.

I went in deeper.

My tongue traveled back to her swelling bud, knowing it would continue to grow until Sarah burst. Given she was supporting herself on my desk, not to mention I was on my knees, this wouldn't be a slow, languorous fuck.

I quickened the speed of my fingers and tongue.

Sarah's breathing matched my pace, perhaps kicking my efforts into a higher gear.

My knees started to make it known they didn't like the activity. Not to mention my lower back. I wondered if Sarah's body was also bitching.

Stop thinking, Lizzie.

My three fingers went in deep and curled upward.

My tongue circled her bundle of nerves.

Together we got closer and closer.

Just when I thought my body would call it quits, Sarah started to tremble, and there was no way I could stop. That would be cruel. I pushed aside the shooting pain and continued.

The trembles morphed into full on quaking. Sarah sat up and cradled my head with her hands. This was one of her signs that she was right on the—

Sarah's thighs squeezed my face, cutting off my air supply.

It was do or die now.

AFTER SHE CAME, I YANKED THE CHAIR BACK FOR ME to sit.

"Why do you insist on acting like we're still young?" She sat up, naked and stunning.

"You're beautiful. So beautiful."

"So are you. And a pain in the ass."

I slanted my head. "Is that my thank-you?"

"What type of thank-you were you wanting?"

"Oh, I don't know. What about saying I was the best fuck or something like that?"

"You already know that."

"Do I?" I clutched my shirt over my heart.

"Well, self-doubt is rearing its ugly head again. And so soon after your distraction."

"Maybe you can do something about that." I shrugged.

"Is this your way of saying I should take you upstairs and return the favor?"

"What? I don't get the desk treatment?"

"Nope. Keep it up and you won't get anything."

"That just seems mean." I jutted out my lower lip.

Sarah yawned.

"Now I feel guilty. What about a bath? My back would enjoy the jets."

"I think that can be arranged."

She hopped off the desk and reached for her shirt, but she didn't bother buttoning it. The light from the moon splashed over her skin.

"You really are stunning. How did I get so lucky?" And, how did Sarah get so unlucky tying herself to the Petrie name?

CHAPTER TWENTY-FOUR

JJ HAD TEXTED ME THAT SHE WANTED TO CHAT BUT not on campus or at either of our houses. Intrigued, I agreed to meet her at the diner again. I could go for a cinnamon roll, and my gut said I'd need comfort food to digest the news she was about to deliver.

I arrived at the place early and was relieved to see Ada. Out of all the staff, she was the one I preferred simply because she knew what I wanted without asking and she left me alone. I had a feeling JJ was contacting me about my situation with Dean Spencer. She'd promised to dig into his background to figure out why I was being pushed out. Was it because he was a homophobe? The Petrie taint? A combination of the two? Over the years, I realized people who were uncomfortable with me being a lesbian, but not wanting to outright admit that, were forced to seek out other reasons to hate me so they didn't have to confront their own homophobia.

I sat at my usual table, under the buffalo's head so I wouldn't have to look into his dead eyes, which weren't real but glass. The whole concept of taxidermy freaked me the fuck out, but Colorado had its fair share of places with stuffed animals on display, because how would tourists know they were in the foothills of the Rocky Mountains without at least one dead animal on the wall?

"That's a super serious expression." JJ slid into the booth across from me.

"Everyone keeps telling me that." I circled a finger in front of my noggin.

"Why do you think that is?" JJ wore her typical curious smile. She was the type who found everyday mysteries, like who took an apple from the work fridge, fascinating and worth investigating.

"Some women have resting bitch face, but I have serious face."

"Not all the time. You also convey confusion."

"That's a defense mechanism. If you look confused, people are less likely to strike up a conversation about the weather. I mean how many times can I joke: *if you don't like the weather in Colorado, wait five minutes and it'll change?*"

"It's kinda true here."

Ada set down my tea and a coffee for JJ. We both thanked her, and from JJ's expression, she also appreciated the woman's ability not to intrude too much.

"Two cinnamon rolls?" Ada asked, not bothering to get out her notepad.

We nodded.

"You betcha." She left us alone.

"Back to your weather comment. The day Calvin was born, there was a sixty-four-degree change. What do you think that means?"

"Clearly, your son is the devil, and the world is about to end."

I laughed.

She grinned. "You're unlike a lot of moms. So many would get angry if I said that to them about their baby."

"Oh, I know you're just joking, and damn, it feels good to laugh. I'm so tired of everyone walking on eggshells around me. I know my life is falling apart, but if everyone could stop acting like it, I may handle things better."

"Have you told them that?" JJ used both hands to hold her mug under her mouth, the vapors swirling around her.

"Do I have to?"

"I find people's abilities to read minds is quite limited. Even those closest to us."

"How is it Sarah knows when I'm lying or concealing, except for the one time I need her to know something without telling her because I'm ashamed?"

JJ set down her mug. "That's a good question. But help her help you. She wants to. Let her."

"She's always helping me. She's always having to deal with Lizzie shit. God, I'm so tired of being one of the problems she has to manage all the time." I held my head with my palms. "When is all of my emotional baggage going to disappear? Every time I take a step forward, I get knocked back three steps. I'm tired of my mommy issues. My family issues. My insecurities." I placed a finger in the air. "And don't say I should go back to therapy. I'm tired of that as well."

JJ regarded me as she leaned back for Ada to place our cinnamon rolls on the table. After we again mumbled our thanks, JJ carved a bite with her fork and knife. "You know, you have a lot of expectations from yourself and those around you."

"What does that mean?"

"Nothing. It's simply an observation."

I wasn't buying that. "Out with it, JJ." I popped a bite into my mouth, moaning. "Why can't life be like this? Pure delight from doughy goodness?"

"That would be fantastic, wouldn't it? There'd be a lot less strife on the planet."

I waved for her to finish her other thought.

"One of the things I hate about AA is the whole *one day at a time* shit."

"Oh, my therapist used to say that, and words like that make my brain shut down." I acted like a robot powering down, slouching in my seat.

"I think that's the problem."

I scrunched my forehead.

"As much as I hate the saying, it's also true. Which is why I hate it as well. Every day, I have to tackle my addiction. Fight. It's draining. But if I don't, I drown, risking everything in my life. My wife. Kids. Career. Possibly my freedom."

"Are you saying I'll have to fight my mommy issues every single day of my life? That there won't be a magic moment when it just dissolves into a puff of smoke?" I blew onto my fingertips.

She shrugged. "I'm no expert—"

"I hate you right now." I stabbed my fork in her direction.

"I'm okay with that." She flashed me a grin that made her look truly wicked.

That made me chuckle. "Neither one of us gets hurt feelings."

"I know you don't mean it, but it makes you feel better. More in control. I'm the same. Humor or sarcasm are excellent veils to what's actually going on inside."

"Which is?"

"Sheer panic."

She was right.

We ate in silence for a bit, each letting those words sink in.

After I polished off most of my roll, I said, "What did you want to meet about?"

"Brittany."

"Who?" I ran through the list of troublemakers in my life at the moment, but the name didn't compute.

"Dean Spencer's admin." JJ set down her fork in defeat. It

was nearly impossible to finish one of these cinnamon rolls in one sitting.

"What about her?"

"What do you know about her?"

"She's young. Cocky. Annoying. But she's just an admin." I tossed a hand up in a gesture that conveyed *what am I missing?*

"She's the source of your problem on campus."

"Come again?" I tugged on my earlobe.

"One of your skeletons in the closet."

"Fucking hell. Will you just tell me and not dance around the issue? Or I'll—" I acted out strangling her.

JJ's broad smile proved I reacted the way she'd wanted me to. "Your old grad school buddy, William."

"William!" I smothered my mouth with a palm. "We were never friends."

"I'm gathering that. Brittany is his cousin."

At first, I didn't see what that meant, but as the seconds ticked by, it started to seep in. "This has nothing to do with me being gay or my last name."

JJ shook her head. "It involves good old-fashioned revenge."

"How does Dr. Spencer fit in?"

"Guess who he's canoodling?"

"William?"

JJ shook her head, rubbing one of her eyes. "For someone who studies the Nazis, you can be naïve. Brittany."

"He's sleeping with his admin? She's almost a child!" Once again, I covered my mouth.

"Yes, and she's twenty-seven."

"Brittany is telling him I screwed over her cousin, so I should go?" I hiked a thumb over my shoulder.

"Who knows how she's spinning it? But, a widower in his late fifties sleeping with a woman who's decades younger—how much conniving would it take for her to convince the not-so-good Dean to get rid of you so he can keep screwing her?"

I leaned back in my seat. "William. Wow." I mimed my head was exploding. "He was pissed when Dr. Marcel pushed him out, but it wasn't because of me. William was mediocre at best." At least, that was what I'd always believed. Was I wrong? Had Dr. Marcel protected me because he thought I needed it?

"He's also from a long line of successful east coast types. Not the sort to take personal responsibility. If my gut is right, he was raised thinking he was special and no one should get in his way. But—" She pointed a finger at me.

"I did."

"Yes."

"That was years ago, though. Before I got married and had kids. How long can he hold a grudge?"

"Some people can for the rest of their lives."

I wadded up my paper napkin. "Great. Just what I need on top of everything else."

"There's good news, though."

I perked up in my seat, widening my eyes, ready for JJ to say she had a way to fix it right there and now. She was a pro when it came to these things.

"You know the issue, now."

Was that it? Deflated, my shoulders slumped. "I was hoping for more."

"I know. You're human. Most of us don't like dealing with problems. Avoidance seems so much easier."

"I much prefer ignorance."

"How's that going for you?"

"Again, I have to stress that I hate you."

With a glint in her eye, she said, "Again, I don't care."

CHAPTER TWENTY-FIVE

I PARKED MY CAR ON THE STREET OUT FRONT OF DR. Marcel's house. He'd told me to stop by after I finished my classes. I'd made plans with him right after I learned about William. Now, as I sat in my car, I wished I hadn't bothered the poor man. What could he really do? JJ, though, had suggested I find out what really happened between my mentor and my new nemesis. She babbled on about knowledge being power. The woman could be exasperating sometimes. Mostly because she was usually right.

Come on, Lizzie.

I was almost middle-aged. This wasn't the time to regress to inaction. Thinking that and combating it were entirely different ballgames, though. But this wasn't a game. It was my life. And Sarah's. My children's. Sticking my head in the sand old-Lizzie style wasn't an option.

Opening the SUV door, I got out of the car.

Step one done.

Look at me!

I groaned over my own ineptitude.

Putting one foot in front of the other, I made my way to the front door. It swung open before I had a chance to knock, my fist hanging in the air a beat too long before I let it crash to my side.

"I thought I'd do my part." Dr. Marcel smiled with understanding in his eyes.

I chuckled, tossing my key ring back and forth in my hands. "You know, this whole adulting thing really sucks."

"Preaching to the choir." He stepped aside, waving me in. "Lydia is making tea. She even baked cookies."

My eyes widened with glee, and the house had the delicious scent of chocolate chip cookies.

"I thought you'd like that. No matter what type of adulting you're in the midst of, it's still nice to have people treat you like all your worries can be fixed with fresh cookies."

"I'll have to remember that trick when my kids come running home after they get married and have kids."

He placed a hand on my shoulder. "How is the Petrie brood?"

"Busy little bees."

"Lydia has been filling me in on Sarah's spring birthday bash." His eyes widened.

I rubbed the top of my head.

He motioned for me to take a seat in one of the cozy leather chairs in his front room. He sat on the matching sofa, a knitted afghan on the back. I was willing to bet his wife had made it many years ago, given how sections had been faded from sunlight streaming in through the window.

"Hello, Lizzie dear." Mrs. Marcel entered the room, holding a tray.

I got to my feet. "Let me help."

She relinquished it without complaint.

I set it on the coffee table and took a cup of tea and a chocolate chip cookie fresh from the oven. "Wow, these look scrumptious."

The Marcels exchanged a fond look, and I wondered how much they missed their boys. Now that Dr. Marcel was retired, what did they do with their time together? But how did I say, "So, what in the fuck do you do now that you aren't working?" I'd always been the type to keep my fingers in many pots, and I think that was one of the sources of my panic. When I didn't work myself to the bone, dark thoughts plagued me.

Instead of delving into what Dr. Marcel did with his free time or drowning myself in dark thoughts, I took a bite of the cookie. My blood sugar would be whacked for days given my indulgence earlier and now the cookies. After a sip of my drink, I remembered how much I enjoyed it when Mrs. Marcel made me a cup. Her sugar to tea ratio made it clear there was a reason my mentor was a large man. "Yum," I said.

Dr. Marcel leaned over with effort to swipe two cookies from the platter. "Are you going to tell me the issue?"

"I feel terrible coming to you with my problems."

"I wouldn't have asked you over if I didn't want to help."

"I know. It's just you aren't the dean anymore. I should be able to solve this… thing on my own." I set the half-eaten cookie on the tea saucer.

"That's always been one of your problems. Wanting to take on everything yourself. No one gets ahead without the help of others. Remember your favorite quote—"

"If I have been able to see farther than others, it was because I stood on the shoulders of giants."

"If Newton could accept help, surely you can."

"It's about William."

This took Dr. Marcel by surprise, and his brow knitted with worry. "I really wasn't expecting that."

"I wasn't either when I heard the news this morning."

"You've only found out today, and you already reached out

to me. You *are* learning." His voice was kind and his smile even kinder. "Tell me from the beginning." He supported his chin on steepled fingertips and gave me his full attention.

I did. Every once in a while, he would ask a question, or Mrs. Marcel would tut. It wasn't a secret William wasn't her favorite of Dr. Marcel's students. When I finished, I reached for the rest of the cookie, but it was no longer warm. No matter, I took a massive bite.

"I had no idea any of this was going on. None of the other professors have mentioned it in their emails."

"I'm not surprised. They've been skirting me. I remember when Peter was sentenced, so many of them showed their support. Now, my reputation is worse than Himmler's. People duck into offices to avoid speaking or being seen with me. I can't remember the last time someone in the department said a simple hello or a friendly nod of the head. A handful stare at me menacingly if we cross paths."

He ran a gnarled hand through what hair he had left on his head. "I doubt you've reached Himmler status. Most of them are probably embarrassed about their actions or inaction of coming to your defense."

"I understand." I nodded. "We all have families to support."

"That they do. Still—" He waved a hand as if saying he didn't want to dwell on that part. "Let's brainstorm about William."

"I know he hates me since you gave me the job he wanted."

Dr. Marcel looked to Lydia and then me. "It wasn't that cut and dry."

"What do you mean?"

"William was entirely responsible for having to leave to finish his PhD."

"Yeah, his laziness—"

Dr. Marcel cleared his throat, a trick he always did when he wanted his students to shut up and pay attention. It still worked.

"Yes, that was part of it, but it was more than laziness that got him into trouble."

I waited, trying to figure out what it could be.

Dr. Marcel seemed torn about divulging whatever it was William had done. Slept with a student? The guy thought he was God's gift to the female sex, but that wasn't all that unusual for some guys to believe in their early twenties.

"As you said, William wasn't careful with his research." Dr. Marcel stared over my head, slowly bringing his gaze to meet mine. "He claims it was a simple accident, but he didn't attribute a portion of his dissertation, and I recognized the source right away."

"Are you saying he plagiarized his dissertation?"

"Again, he said it was simply an accident. He meant to footnote it, but somehow that didn't happen."

"B-but, that's w-why you should be extra careful and footnote your footnotes," I sputtered incredulously.

"It's been known to trip up a few academics."

"A couple of well-known names come to mind, but in those instances, they've blamed their research assistants for not being vigilant. It's hard to know the truth. But William didn't have any assistants."

"True. When William argued it was an accident, I had a hard time believing his defense. But he broke down completely in my office. I can still hear his sobs." Dr. Marcel briefly closed his eyes.

"He cried," I said in barely a whisper. "I can't imagine what that would feel like if it really was an accident. To have everything you've worked for go up in smoke over a simple mistake."

He looked at me with sincere understanding.

"When Meg threatened to accuse me of plagiarism, it shook me to the core."

"She what?" Lydia asked, sitting up ramrod straight.

I hadn't meant to say that part aloud, but now that it was hanging out there, I couldn't simply say, "Oh, nothing. So William." Instead, I provided the details of Meg's blackmailing back in the day.

"Lizzie, I had no idea about that. I knew she was difficult and in trouble, but..." Dr. Marcel sniffed. "If I had known everything, I never would have entertained the thought of her getting back in touch with you when she wanted to make amends after finishing rehab."

"It put me in a tough spot. I understood her need to say sorry, but I also knew I wanted nothing to do with her anymore. That was a door I had closed, and I was scared to crack it open again."

There was silence.

"Have you heard anything about William since he left the program?"

"Unfortunately, yes. His indolence got the better of him again. He worked for a senator, and while gathering data for a speech, William didn't triple check a source of a graphic he pulled from the internet. It bit him in the ass when journalists unearthed the truth about the graphic William had inserted in the speech. It was something from one of those alt-right sites, with preposterous claims. The senator was humiliated, and William was unceremoniously chucked off the team."

I was speechless.

"I fear, Lizzie, he hasn't learned the real lesson in all of this."

"Which is?"

"To take a hard look at himself. William has always had a chip on his shoulder, thinking he was smarter than everyone else. It's a curse for some academics." Dr. Marcel swallowed. "When I confronted him about his dissertation, he asked me if you had tipped me off."

"Me?" I placed a hand on my chest. "How would I have known that? I never read his dissertation."

"I don't know, but in the heat of the moment, he said some unpleasant things about you. I had thought, in time, those thoughts would have tempered."

"Instead, they burned hotter."

CHAPTER TWENTY-SIX

AFTER CHATTING WITH THE MARCELS, I CALLED JJ to see if her peeps could dig up some dirt on William and his current predicament. Or at least try to pinpoint why his attack was happening at this particular moment. Was it simply the ideal time, given the Peter chaos, or was I dealing with something more personal? When I went through the mess with Meg blackmailing me, I hadn't taken the time to learn more about her situation until I found her hooking in a hotel. Knowing that ahead of time could have prepared me better for Meg's blackmail. Not that I planned to pay off William, but my historian brain was screaming to learn from my past mistake. Like JJ had said, knowledge was power. Dr. Marcel had also been right about asking those who can to help.

"Can you give me the highlights of what you know so far?" JJ was in investigator mode, and I pictured her with a pen and reporter's notebook.

I supplied the kernels Dr. Marcel had provided.

"Oh, wow. You seem to have made a dangerous enemy."

"Apparently and, all this time, I had no idea. I mean, I knew he didn't like me when we were in the program together, but I had no idea he was holding onto this shit, thinking I was the one who brought him down. It was grad school. Who in the fuck cares now?"

"He's probably like that middle-aged man who can't stop talking about his high school glory days."

"Maybe, but I don't think he ever had any glory except in his own mind."

"That's the part that worries me. Delusions are hard to reason with." JJ truly sounded concerned. "I'll get a guy on this pronto, and I'll be in touch."

"Thanks, JJ. If you need anything from me, just let me know."

She laughed. "We could use a babysitter this weekend."

"Done. Both Mia and Ian?"

"Is that okay?"

"Yeah. I'll see if Casey can come over or plan something with Ethan so the older kids can spend time together. Casey could use time with a friend."

"That's perfect. You're a lifesaver."

I had to laugh. "You're the one saving my bacon. Now, I need to get home and break the news to Sarah."

"I suggest telling her everything. From my experience, wives don't like to find out from other sources there's a crazy out there."

"No, I imagine not. See you soon."

We ended the call, and I aimed the car for home. Might as well get this over with sooner rather than later.

*　*　*

UNFORTUNATELY, THE KIDDOS HAD DIFFERENT plans. All of them, even Freddie, decided to have complete mental breakdowns during different stages from dinnertime to well after bedtime.

Exhausted, Sarah and I sat on the couch in the library, the fire going. Sarah had flipped on the owl wax warmer, the scent of lavender permeating the room.

"Are you as tired as I am?" Sarah went limp noodle on the couch.

I could only grunt in response.

Her body stiffened. "I know there's something troubling you."

I offered another grunt.

"Do you want a five-minute power nap, and then you can spill?"

"I'd love some grappa or a cookie."

"A cookie?"

"Mrs. Marcel made me chocolate chip cookies today. It was really nice." My voice didn't sound happy, though. "When someone motherly is kind to me, it really makes me think just how effed up my own mother was. How many kids had a mother who never baked cookies?"

Sarah returned to the couch, with a grappa for me and bottled water for her. "Probably more than we'd like to think about."

"That's sad." I turned on the couch, sitting with my knees against my chest. "Isn't that depressing? All the unloved kids in this world?"

"Is that what's bothering you tonight?" Sarah's pinched expression said she wasn't buying it.

"No, but it does help me stop my own pity party. It's good to keep it real. Like when I'm drowning with work and mom duties, I like to remind myself that prisoners in Auschwitz had it so much worse."

"Leave it to a German history nerd to make themselves feel better with those types of thoughts."

I offered a guilty grin. "It may not work for everyone, but it works for me." I sipped the grappa. "Are you ready?"

"Should I try imagining myself in a death camp so whatever you're about to say doesn't upset me too much?"

"Give it a go," I said with a little too much glee.

"You're such an oddball."

"You aren't the first person to tell me that. Okay, so I completely misjudged why Dr. Spencer was pushing me out of the department. He's not actually the threat. His admin is. She's not a Lizzie fan."

Sarah's face crumpled with confusion. "An admin hates you?"

"Apparently."

"I'm going to need more. Did you ask for too many handouts to be double-sided?"

"I wish it were that simple. I can only tell you what I know now. It's kinda funny from a historical perspective, because it's my own past wreaking havoc on my life." I mulled this thought over. "No matter what, we can't escape the past."

"Isn't the other part of that thought learning from the past to avoid making the same mistake?" Sarah nudged my foot with her own.

"Indeed. I keep telling my students history is important to surviving life. So, here's what I know."

Sarah listened, her face registering surprise, anger, and more surprise.

I glanced at the ceiling, puzzling out the situation. "My grad school days are now haunting me. If I hadn't studied the Nazis, I wouldn't have met William. Meaning I wouldn't have this problem now."

"I think you're overanalyzing the situation."

"It's kinda something I do."

"I know. It's adorable, really." Her eyes glistened. "But you can't blame yourself for the situation. It wasn't your choice to study the Nazis that's wrecking your career. It's a vindictive man."

"It's so hard for me not to feel that way. I'm well aware that all of my baggage is constantly causing friction in our lives."

"Lizzie." Sarah sat up and placed her hands on my knees. "This is life. Peculiar shit happens. We can't stop it. We can only deal with it together. No matter what, we're bound to run into crazies in this world, because there are so many wandering around." She lowered her head to stare directly into my eyes. "This isn't your fault. Let JJ dig a bit more. When we have a clearer picture, we'll handle it the best we can."

"Speaking of JJ, I said we'd watch their kids one day this weekend. Maybe Casey can come over so Ian's not so bored."

"Saturday or Sunday?"

"Uh, JJ didn't say."

"And you didn't ask." Her snicker made me squirm, even though I knew she wasn't upset. "It always amazes me that a historian is so bad at future dates and planning."

"You try having so many dates crammed into your head. Now we have four kids, and I have to remember four birthdays."

"Technically only three since we have twins."

"Oh, right. That does simplify it some. They were born on December twenty-fifth, right?"

"I'm sure Ollie thinks she has that type of power. Do you know I dated a guy in junior high who once asked me if the Fourth of July falls on the same day every year?"

"You dated in junior high?"

"That's the part you're focused on?" Her eyes widened in confusion.

"Considering I didn't date until college, yeah."

"Why doesn't that surprise me?"

"Because I've told you before."

She laughed. "You delivered that well. Or were you not joking?"

"Not telling." I tried to wink, but it wasn't one of my

strengths, and I'm sure it looked more like I had something in my eye. Rubbing it, I asked, "Can you imagine Casey dating in a few years?"

"Now that's a thought that makes me go cold. What will the world be like in a handful of years? So many countries seem on the fast track to oblivion."

"Don't forget about the environment. As a mom, it scares me. Every news cycle makes me worry. There's just so much bad news all the time it's hard to focus on anything. Pile on all of my own problems, and I'm drowning."

CHAPTER TWENTY-SEVEN

It didn't take JJ's goons too long to get back to her, so when she dropped off the kids on Saturday, she pulled me aside to give me a quick rundown.

"Are you telling me the man who studied the Nazis in grad school is now a white supremacist?" I palmed the top of my head. "Propagating crackpot theories about *white genocide* or the *great replacement* myth."

"He seems to be the perfect candidate. A privileged white male who's been passed over for jobs and fired for incompetence, who still thinks he's entitled to fame and riches."

"Not many historians become famous. I, for one, never thought, *Hey, the best way to become famous is to write history books that less than one percent of the population will ever read.*" I sighed. "What did William expect out of life?"

"I dunno about the last part, but did you pull that stat out of your ass?" She wore her shit-eating grin.

"You can't prove I did." I tucked my hands into the pockets of my jeans.

"I'm disappointed you didn't give a more exact number. And

you're conveniently forgetting that you, in fact, are becoming a known name by being on the show."

"Among other reasons." I rocked back onto my heels.

"Ignore the Peter effect. Have you started getting fan mail, yet?"

"A few emails. Comments on social media." I shrugged it off.

"There's always a dark side to success. Not everyone will be thrilled when you have all you want."

"One: I never asked for any of this. Two: I've worked my ass off." My fingers made a victory sign, which was ironic considering I didn't feel like I was holding a winning hand.

"They don't see that. They see a professor who has a stunning wife, four adorable children, a regular spot on a TV show, and a big house. I'm betting William wants everything you have. His wife divorced him. He barely sees his son. He can't find a decent job. The only shows that will have him on are the ones that can't stream on regular TV or popular social media channels because everyone thinks they're nutjobs sprouting conspiracy theories."

"Naturally then, his best course of action is to try to ruin me instead of looking inward and making changes." I let out a whoosh of air.

"It's much easier tearing others apart to feel better."

***

AFTER JJ AND CLAIRE SKEDADDLED, WHICH I WAS slightly jealous of, I cornered Sarah in the kitchen. "What's the plan today?"

"You don't remember talking about it last night?"

I couldn't determine from her blank face if she was pulling my leg or not. It wouldn't have been the first time I'd tuned out certain details, even more so lately. "Did I not tell you? I'm suffering from temporary amnesia."

"How convenient for you." She waggled her brow, again making me wonder if she had told me or not. "The aquarium in Denver. Maddie, Gabe, and Ethan are helping out."

I counted the adults on my fingers. Five. Considering there were seven kids, not a bad ratio. "Maybe we should buy one of those vans you see day cares use. I think they seat fourteen, including the driver and passenger riding shotgun."

Sarah scrunched her face. "I'd really rather not. As of now, Maddie doesn't mind helping out with her new SUV."

Now that Cambridge was out of the picture, we didn't have to worry about how we'd manage. "Shall we get the process going? Get the older kids into the bathroom, change the little ones, and then fight with Olivia for whatever meltdown she'll have?"

Sarah's phone rang, and from the quick exchange, I figured out the kid-to-adult ratio had evened out with Rose and Troy joining the Petrie family outing. I wondered if Denver was ready for us.

* * *

WE CRAMMED INTO THE NORTH AMERICAN SECTION, the last leg of our visit, listening to one of the staff members, given her khaki pants and blue T-shirt with the aquarium's logo, talk about the otters. She held what looked to be an otter pelt, which disturbed me to no end, and I closed my ears to that portion of the talk. I already knew the creatures had been hunted to near extinction and were now being reintroduced. Did my children and I need to see a pelt as proof as to why they were murdered for decades?

The irony of a Nazi expert unable to stomach listening to certain facts was not lost on me. I'd never been able to handle certain aspects of cruelty, and while many were fascinated by Nazis, I never was. My goal in my studies was to ensure what had happened to millions wouldn't occur again. They weren't mesmerizing to me but proof of how terrible humanity could be when unchecked.

How could William turn his back on history?

The woman said a name that pulled me out of my head.

"Olive is an orphaned otter." The woman's voice was nearly drowned out by the chatter of others in the cave-like space.

I glanced at my daughter, Olivia, smiling.

Another staff member was inside the otter exhibit, standing on some rocks at the water's edge, holding a plastic container, and one of the otters had half its body in the rectangle, gorging on the food.

"So cute," Sarah whispered into my ear.

I smiled at her and Calvin, who was in a baby sling.

"When Olive arrived in Denver, she couldn't be left alone and went home with one of our staff members each night." A small video screen showed the otter in a bathtub, on a leash going for a stroll, and inside a massive dog crate.

Casey and Ian paid attention, but the little ones' interests had waned, and they wandered around the space, squealing and pointing when the otters swam by.

At one point, Olivia gave the woman a curious look when she'd mentioned again Olive the Otter, but even that couldn't hold Ollie's interest for long.

The woman explained that two otter sisters from Alaska arrived shortly after Olive, and they also needed TLC after losing their mother at a young age. "Now the three of them are like sisters, although they do have the occasional spat."

One of the otters came close to the glass, and Freddie and Demi put their tiny hands on the barrier.

Olivia said, "Ollie" to the creature.

I hunched down. "Yes, she's an Ollie, too. You have an otter twin." I tickled my daughter's belly, and my eyes moved to Demi, who also giggled.

While I never envisioned being a mother of four, I couldn't imagine not having one of them in my life now.

Sarah angled Calvin so he could get a better glimpse at the otters, but his eyes didn't seem to register the creatures on the other side of the glass. Instead, he yawned and rested against her shoulder. "I think it's time we head out. Everyone, take your buddy's hand," Sarah instructed.

The adults reached for their assigned children, and Casey reached for Ian's hand. My mind caught a glimpse of the future, where every single member of our family was happy, healthy, and not alone.

I squeezed Demi's hand and vowed right then to do everything possible to ensure that outcome.

CHAPTER TWENTY-EIGHT

When I climbed into bed, Sarah was leafing through a children's book titled *A Terrible Thing Happened*. It confirmed she hadn't given up wanting to write children's stories. This was something she, Rose, Troy, and Maddie had discussed collaborating on when we only had twins and before Peter's arrest and everything that snowballed from the incident. But I hadn't known she wanted to write more hard-hitting kids' books. Not surprising given everything that had happened since she'd been bitten by the writing bug. The teacher inside Sarah always wanted to help in any way, shape, or form.

I squished a pillow behind me. "We don't have any down comforters or pillows, do we?"

She set her book down on her nightstand. "Nope. Too many allergies in this family."

"Good. I heard an advert on one of the podcasts I listen to, and I didn't like what I learned about... the poor geese." My body shook, thinking of feathers being plucked from a live goose. Thousands of them. Geese and feathers.

She placed a hand on mine above the covers and gave it a supportive squeeze.

"I really hate this world. All the hidden nastiness." I adjusted to look into Sarah's eyes. "Did you know the story behind Olive the Otter before setting up today's trip?"

She shook her head. "Why?"

"It seemed like one of your *let's do something fun while teaching Lizzie a lesson* things."

"You don't mean to teach the kids?" She quirked an eyebrow.

"Have you met our children? I've seen hungover college kids with better attention spans." I massaged my eyeballs. Why did it feel so good after a long day?

Sarah chuckled. "Don't be too hard on them. None is older than three."

"I didn't mean it that way. It just seemed like something you'd do to show me how there still is good in the world. Olive was saved and has her otter sisterhood now."

"I did like the story, and I will admit, I used to seek them out for your edification. You drown yourself in the worst aspects of human nature and not solely your studies. What podcast were you listening to with the anti-down advert?"

I puffed out some air from my left cheek. "I can't remember. Maybe one that gives a daily dose of news, dripping with sarcasm and humor to make it somewhat easier to pay attention. It's really the only way I can handle staying informed these days, which doesn't say much for me as a historian."

"I don't blame you. It seems all news is depressing as hell, not to mention overwhelming. It'd be nice if just one day we heard nothing happened."

"My brain keeps telling me it doesn't help hiding, but I don't like hearing about goose abuse first thing in the morning." I shuddered. "Why do people think it's okay to torture animals for luxuries?"

She rested her hand on my forehead. "There's the darkness that's always inside your head."

"In my defense, I didn't seek this knowledge. It was thrust upon me by a woke advertiser." I sighed and squeezed her hand.

"Look at you, using *woke*. Pretty soon, I won't be able to call you stodgy."

"Now that I'm on Twitter for the show, I follow a lot of the memes. As a historian of the Nazis, it's fascinating to watch a term about staying alert to racism and social justice take a turn for the worse this year. Even Obama is warning about woke callout culture." Sarah's eyes clouded over, and it probably wasn't the best trajectory for bedtime chatter. "Thanks for planning today. I think the kids really liked it. Did you see the twins and Demi running back and forth, trying to keep up with the otters?"

She smiled. "I want them to have a normal childhood if that's possible."

"Even Ethan was grinning, and that's rare these days."

Sarah nodded, resting her head on my chest. "Ian and Casey are so cute together."

"That they are. Who gets to give Casey the sex talk?"

She slapped my stomach. "It's too soon for thoughts like that!"

I laughed.

"I'm glad they've become such good friends. I really like JJ and Claire, and their kids are pretty amazing. I know I've been worried about our kids not having friends, but we aren't completely isolated."

"I'll do my best to avoid initiating another Petrie fallout to keep from pushing away our remaining kid-friend options." I tried to sound flippant, but that really wasn't in my wheelhouse.

Not surprisingly, Sarah looked up at me, concern etched into her furrowed brow. "You know none of this is your fault. You can't blame yourself for things that are completely out of your control. Peter got arrested. Tie tragically died in a truly bizarre accident. The public, since the beginning of time, latches on to conspiracy theories."

"Is there evidence of conspiracies in cave paintings? Like one caveman framing another for slaughtering a rainbow unicorn god?"

"Since when did you start believing in unicorns?" She couldn't contain a giggle even if she tried to keep the amusement from her tone.

"When we had kids. It seems depressing to have children in a world that doesn't have magical creatures."

"That's an intriguing side effect of you becoming a parent. Sadly, I don't think cave dwellers had rainbow paint, so they're only monochrome unicorns."

My neck contorted so I could see her, and I had to rub a muscle twitch. "There's actually unicorn cave art?"

"If memory serves, I think so. I mean, there's even naughty pieces?"

"Are you talking about porn?" I asked in a *get outta here* tone.

Sarah nodded.

"That's interesting. I'd like to know more. Maybe I'll ask around in the art history department."

"Perhaps you shouldn't. The conversations might get uncomfortable, fast. With the MeToo movement, we all need to be extra cautious. Besides, that's why Google exists."

I grabbed my phone and typed *porn cave paintings* into the search bar, not expecting anything remotely scholarly, but several articles for erotic cave art instantly popped up. "Wow. I thought you were lying."

"Who lies about porn?" She placed a not-so-innocent hand on her chest.

"Uh, isn't porn based on a lie. At the very least, it's all staged." Not wanting to click on any of the links and scrutinize the merits of the research, I put the phone back onto my side table. "I don't think I'll ever understand people."

"You don't have to. Just the ones in your life." Her hand roamed over my bare stomach. "Can you guess what I'm thinking?" Her hand traveled further down my stomach.

"You want to reenact dirty cave art?"

"Something like that." Her mouth clamped down on my nipple.

"Does this mean you want to stop talking about the darkness in the world?"

"It means not everything is so bleak. There's this." She licked my nipple.

"I do like…" She sucked it into her mouth, making me hitch in a breath before completing the sentence with "that."

Sarah, also naked, climbed on top of me, pinning one of my hands above our heads, while her other hand trailed up and down my side, eliciting goose bumps. *No, Lizzie. Don't go back to thinking about geese.*

"I've needed your touch all day." I pinched my eyes shut to fully enjoy her body on mine.

"I know." She kissed me softly on the mouth. "You've had a faraway look since opening your eyes."

"The kids don't see it, do they?"

Sarah shook her head. "No. You're fine. I doubt anyone else noticed."

We kissed again. Quick, sweet kisses, that turned into more ravenous ones. There were nights when all I wanted to do was kiss Sarah. Having sex could be faked on some levels. But there was no way to hide love and intimacy in a kiss. At least not between the two of us.

Sarah cupped the side of my face and stared deeply into my eyes. "You with me?"

"Yes. Completely."

She wore a sexy grin as her hip started to rub against me,

and we continued kissing. Her mouth started roaming down my body, stopping at the nipple that had been neglected until that point.

Further she went, taking her time kissing the sensitive spots on my stomach that made me squirm with wanting. When she arrived at my pubic hair, which there was little of, she ran her fingers through the strip. "I'm really starting to like this on you."

I had previously shaved it all, but after kids, some things had gone to the wayside.

Sarah's tongue flicked my clit, briefly, before sliding its way between my lips, going inside a moment. Her goal seemed to be savoring the experience. My taste. The way my hips increased their gyrations. My right hand fisted the sheet, and she slid her fingers around mine, holding tightly.

She entered me with a finger. Then another. Easing in and out, while her tongue lapped at my bud. Although the day had been long and tiring, Sarah was proving we still mattered. Our private time shouldn't be rushed, because we both craved each other. Not simply the orgasm. The feelings shared and expressed.

Our intertwined fingers tightened around each other.

I stared down at my stunning wife, watching her enjoy making love to me. There was nothing else in our marriage at this moment. Just the two of us. In love. And being in the moment.

Sarah quickened the pace of her fingers and tongue. My gyrations reached a more frantic level, and my back arched, while my breathing became much more audible.

I was on the brink.

Sarah shoved in deeply.

Lights formed behind my closed eyelids.

"Oh, Sarah…"

* * *

We lay in bed, enjoying the afterglow of making love. Sarah snuggled against my side, her fingers playing with my pubic hair.

"Are you okay, Lizzie?"

I hefted a shoulder. "I really don't know. I've been through the wringer more than a few times, but I'm not really equipped for being treated so poorly by complete strangers. Just by my family. It's odd. It kinda hurts more being treated like a social leper by people I don't know. I guess I always expected Mom and Peter to be assholes and for my father to stay quiet because that's how it was from the moment my childhood memory kicks in."

"Has anyone spit on you lately?"

"No. Just cussed out at the gas station yesterday. It hasn't happened to you at all, has it?"

Sarah shook her head. "No, but you've been handling the majority of the errands. I was slightly nervous about today, but I figured most parents would be too consumed keeping track of their kids to pay you any attention. It is discombobulating seeing you in a baseball hat more often than not."

"Now that I don't have long hair in a ponytail, it's easier to toss one on." She continued stroking my pubic hair, and I glanced down at the narrow strip. "My pussy looks like Hitler."

Sarah's hand stilled. "What?"

"When I was shaving earlier, I wasn't paying close attention and made the strip narrower than normal. From this angle, it looks like his moustache." I started to chuckle, but it quickly turned into quiet sobs.

"Oh, honey. Why are you crying?"

I couldn't answer her right away, and Sarah wrapped me in her arms, giving me time to get it out. But what was it? I sniffled. "I'm sorry, I don't know what's wrong with me."

"I think you do. Deep down."

"It's just... thinking of Hitler made me remember William."

Sarah burst into laughter, but she clamped her lips tightly to stop it. "I'm sorry. I wasn't expecting that. I know William's a worm, but I've never equated him to Adolf."

I scratched my head. After wearing a hat all day, my hair protested by itching way more than normal. "William the Worm. That's a good title for him. Maybe that should be one of the characters in your children's books." I flicked my hand to the book on her nightstand.

"Nice try. Dig deeper about why William caused you to break down."

"JJ's team unearthed some shit about him that's disturbing."

"Go on."

"It seems William has gone all in on white supremacy."

"Oh, the fragile white male ego knows no bounds."

I explained what I knew about William so far. "I swear, Sarah. It seems all of my life decisions are kicking me in the family jewels. If I'd studied something more acceptable, maybe I wouldn't be losing my job or dealing with a psycho."

"You're not the only historian who's focused on the Third Reich."

"True, but I'm pretty sure I'm the only one named Petrie. Have you scanned the posts in that whack job Facebook group? Someone is claiming my studies have stripped me of my moral compass, which is why I turned into a murderer."

"Stop reading that junk. Don't go into that group again." She met my gaze. "Got it?"

I nodded.

"I know you're convinced you're cursed these days, but you aren't. The opposite in fact. You, Lizzie, are one of the luckiest walking this earth."

"How do you figure that?"

Sarah got on top of me and stared down into my eyes. "You have a sexy wife, four kids, great friends, and a family who wants to help you through this."

"I'm tired of having to get through things."

"I have some bad news for you. That's life."

"I just don't see the point to most things these days."

"I know, but you owe it to yourself and to everyone who loves you to seek out the beauty in the world. That's the whole point to life." She placed a hand on my cheek. "Step out of the darkness and into the light. The longer you stay locked away, the more I fear you won't snap out of it."

"Maybe it's best that I'm losing my teaching job."

"No, it's not. I'm not saying you shouldn't pursue your studies. You, my dear, love history. Every chance you get, from the T-shirt you had to buy after spilling lunch to the *History Nerd* hat you rock in public, you proclaim your passion for it. Cutting yourself off from that won't help you find the light."

"But Harvard turned me down."

"It's one school. Keep putting your feelers out to others. Things worth pursuing usually don't happen overnight."

"I haven't heard of any openings in Colorado."

Sarah drilled me with her eyes. "Leaving forty-nine other states."

I placed my hands on the sides of her face. "Is tearing you and the kids away from your support network the right decision?"

"If that's what we have to do to help you, yes. Besides, Mom and Troy will probably follow."

"There's the Peter issue."

She conceded to this with a dip of the head. "After he's out, he may want to leave Colorado as well."

"What about Ethan? It'll hurt him if we leave now. He's outright told me he doesn't want me to move."

"He says that now, but I sincerely doubt the man will hold a grudge. Years ago, he also moved to get away from backward thinking. Lizzie, I need you to hear me. We have to do what is right for you, me, and the kids. Everyone can visit whenever they want. Seeing you like this is killing me. Let's stop thinking there's no escape. There's always a way to do better." She placed her hand on my heart. "You have it in you."

CHAPTER TWENTY-NINE

"You know what you need?" Sarah asked me as she tried coaxing Freddie into another bite of oatmeal.

"Does it start with S?" I wiped banana bits off Demi's hands with a wet washcloth.

Ollie wandered around the table, clapping her hands and singing a song she apparently made up. Or, at least, I thought so since the tempo didn't sound familiar and the words were garbled at best.

Sarah made an airplane sound and tried again to get Freddie to eat one last bite. The oatmeal plane didn't stick the landing, and Sarah gave up. I freed Demi from her chair and got to work cleaning Fred's face and fingers.

"Did you mean sleep or your other favorite S-word?" Sarah sipped her tea. "I can't wait to have coffee again. It'd make this easier to handle."

I surveyed the morning routine madness. The pets were chasing each other around the kitchen island—Hank was the aggressor, but I think Gandhi enjoyed the game. Calvin was in his bouncy chair. The three toddlers wandered toward the front room, where Ethan sat with a book in his hands. Every time I glanced at him, he seemed to be staring at the book, not reading. If simply holding a book helped him relax, whatever. He'd always teased me about loving audiobooks, but maybe I should try getting him to listen to one. Ethan was the type who needed books, but the effort may be too much for him right now.

Perhaps Fred understood Ethan's issue. Freddie grabbed a book from his stash and tottered to Ethan, thrusting the book into his hands. Ethan picked up Fred, and they cuddled while Ethan read the story. Demi soon joined them on Ethan's lap, while Ollie banged away on one of her toys that made god-awful animal noises accompanied by rainbow flashing lights.

"Is silence my other favorite S-word?" I sat at the kitchen table with Sarah, fresh cups of tea for both of us.

"It's quickly becoming mine, but sadly I think it's endangered."

"At least for the next eighteen years."

"Do you think we'll be rid of all of them by then?" Sarah whispered to me.

"With this family, no." I leaned forward in my seat and kissed Cal's head. "What would we do with all our free time?"

"Another S-word comes to mind." She winked at me.

I yawned.

Sarah laughed. "Anyway, as I was saying, I think you need some *friend bonding* time."

I groaned. "When you mentioned Troy was having a boys' night out, I knew it would somehow boomerang to me."

"I'm not suggesting a boys' night out."

"Good."

"Just a night out with Maddie, Gabe, and Ethan."

"JJ wants to join," Ethan chimed in, then resumed reading Freddie's story.

"What about you?" I asked Sarah.

She shook her head. "Mom, Maddie, and I are booking spa days every Saturday."

"Today's Saturday." Just to settle my mind, I glanced at my watch to check the day of the week, and indeed, it was a little after eight in the morning on Saturday.

"Yep. I need to get ready for manis and pedis." She took her mug to the kitchen sink. "We won't be gone long."

"Sweetheart, take all the time you need. You deserve it." I needed a cuddle, so I eased Cal out of his chair.

We settled into the leather chair by the fireplace. I stretched out my legs on the ottoman, while Fred and Demi climbed down from Ethan's lap to sit at the art table to pick up some project that was ready for them.

"Do I want to know what friend time entails?" I asked Ethan.

"Maddie's in charge of the planning, but it starts at six."

"Tonight?"

He nodded. "I need more coffee. How's your tea situation?"

"You don't have to wait on me. You've really been pitching in around here with the kids."

"I'm not waiting on you. It's common practice for the person going to the kitchen to ask others if they need anything. So, do you?" There was a tiny smirk on his lips.

"I always need more tea."

He smiled and took my mug with him.

Demi watched our interaction with a curious expression.

"How's my little Demitasse?"

She treated me with a brilliant smile that made my blood run cold. Every day she looked more and more like Peter. What was I going to tell her when she started asking questions about "her uncle" when he got released from jail in a handful of years? Maybe I should read the children's book Sarah had been flipping through last night. How soon could a child start therapy? If we got all four kids involved, would there be a group discount?

Ethan returned, his eyes following mine to Demi before settling back on me. "I see it, too."

"Did Peter make a mistake? With…" I mimed signing a signature, hoping Ethan would understand I meant giving up his parental rights.

Ethan sat down and took a heavy slug of coffee. "That's the thing about being an adult that no one prepares you for. You have to make decisions that impact others, without knowing if they'll be the right ones or not. I can tell you this: she's happy here. The twins have taken her into their gang. She's like the otter from yesterday. If only the rest of us were so lucky."

Freddie offered Demi his blue crayon, and she gave him her orange one.

Rose and Maddie walked into the family room, chattering to each other.

"Well, isn't this a picture? You two minding the children, not looking stressed at all." Rose hunched down to sweep Ollie into her arms.

"We're the new Norman Rockwell prototypes," I joked.

"You know, that's not a bad comparison. It gives me an idea for a photography project." Maddie had that lost expression she got when her creative juices flowed into action.

Again, my blood turned to frigid sludge. Whenever a lightbulb went off over her head, it usually involved something pushing me out of my comfort zone, something I really didn't need at the moment, which oftentimes was overlooked by Maddie.

Sarah swept into the room, looking refreshed from her shower. "I don't think we'll be back after you leave around five-thirty, but just in case we're delayed, Bailey and Jorie will be here at three for the kids' private music lesson, and if I'm late, they agreed to stay until I get home. Like I said, though, I don't plan on being late, but—"

"You like to have contingency plans for your backup plans." I grinned at Sarah.

"We won't be late. Our last treatment is at three. We'll be out of there by four, I promise." Maddie started to leave, but she wheeled about. "Oh, that reminds me; Court is joining us tonight."

"Great," I muttered, but I wasn't upset by this news. The first time I'd met Courtney, I didn't take to her. That was part of my MO, though. It took me time to warm up to people because my first instinct was not to trust a soul. Courtney made it hard for me to like her since she spent the first night hitting on my pregnant wife. My eyes landed on Sarah, who looked stunning in jeans and a cream sweater. No wonder Courtney had hit on Sarah. Some women didn't age well. Sarah was more like Audrey Hepburn. More beautiful with each passing year.

She noticed me watching her and mouthed, "I love you."

I kissed my fingertips and blew it in her direction, which she caught in a ham-fashioned way and pressed to her lips.

"You two are so obnoxiously in love," Maddie said in a teasing voice, but I detected jealousy.

"It's what kids do to you," Sarah defended.

"I've read enough online polls to know kids usually strain a marriage. Which makes you two even more of a mystery." Maddie looked to Rose and Sarah. "Let's roll. My feet need some serious love."

CHAPTER THIRTY

LATE THAT SATURDAY AFTERNOON, WHILE JORIE AND Bailey watched the kids, I was sitting at my desk in the library when Maddie burst through the door.

"You ready for dyke night?"

I peered up from the journal article I'd been reading. "I thought Gabe and Ethan were going."

"They're honorary dykes for the night."

"Are they aware of that?"

"They will be when I put their badges on them. Come on. It's time to cut loose." She did a little dance.

"That's what I was doing." I pointed to my reading material. "It was relaxing me."

"Tonight isn't about relaxation, Lizzie. It's about having fun with other humans. Just give it a try. I promised Sarah I'd take you out."

I sat back in my chair. "Is this a pity thing, then?"

Maddie shook her hands in the air. "Why do you have to do that?"

"What?"

She pointed a finger at me. "That."

Still not getting it, I asked *what* again.

"Question everything."

"It's how I've survived. Collecting data and indications from behavior patterns. I've learned from my childhood and this"—I lifted the corner of the article on the Nazis—"that most people have ulterior motives and not to blindly follow. Not ever."

"You got me." She stuck her hands in the air like she was under arrest. "I do have ulterior motives tonight. To get drunk and have fun. If you don't get out of your chair at the count of ten, something really bad will happen to you."

"Are you threatening me?" I asked, floored. "Forcing me to go out to get drunk so tomorrow morning will start off badly?" Like the panic attacks weren't enough. Why not add a hangover?

"You don't have to drink. But I want to. One. Two. Three." As she progressed to ten, her voice took a serious tone, and I knew her well enough not to test her.

"Fine. I'm out of my chair."

"Are you wearing that?"

"If the night requires anything other than jeans and a sweater, I'll sit my butt back down, thank you very much." I looked longingly at my chair.

"Can you at least wear a sweater that isn't so boring?"

"You really don't know when to quit, do you?" I crossed my arms.

I left her in the library to see if Sarah would take my side.

"See you on Monday," Jorie said, and Bailey waved goodbye on their way to the front door.

Sarah was in the front room with the kids and Rose. "Hey, is this sweater boring?" I held out the hem of the navy V-neck.

Sarah slanted her head. "I feel like this is a trick question."

"Maddie said I'm too boring to go out with her tonight."

"I said your sweater was boring, not you."

I flipped around to Maddie. "How do you separate the two?"

"You look fine, Lizzie. Comfortable. And that's what tonight is all about. You getting out and relaxing." Sarah's eyes zeroed in on our friend. "Right, Maddie?"

"Whatever. We did purchase a sweater for the occasion, if you remember, Sarah."

"Funny. I remember you saying you were buying Lizzie a sweater, and I said she'd never wear it."

It was a relief to hear the three of them went shopping recently. Before kids, Sarah and her mom used to go shopping on a regular basis. I wanted Sarah to enjoy the things she'd always had.

Maddie rummaged through a bag next to Sarah's chair and pulled out a grape-colored sweater that had deer on it with the words: *Queens of the Stone Age*. "I know it's a Christmas sweater, and it was dirt cheap, but I thought it was perfect for the first dykes' night out. It's sort of historical. You love history."

"Barely historical and not even close to my time period." I had to admit I didn't hate it. "Hand it over."

"Really?" Maddie, Sarah, and Rose chorused.

"Might as well. Do you promise not to chastise me all night?"

"No," Maddie said.

"Points for being real."

After she gave me the sweater, I stripped off the so-called boring one, which was the usual type worn in Colorado, and yanked on the grape one. "Better now?" I made a ta-da motion with my hands.

"You have no idea how much." Maddie pressed her hands together. "Let's roll. Everyone is meeting us there."

***

ON THE OUTSKIRTS OF TOWN, THERE WAS A NEW BAR

that wasn't exactly new. But the owners had done a significant amount of work to the old factory-like building to make it look like a quaint pub you'd stumble upon in the English countryside, not in the foothills of the Rocky Mountains. Fingers crossed there weren't any animal heads adorning the walls inside.

It was only six on a Saturday, and the place was already buzzing with people ready to get their drink on for the night. A quick glance assured me there weren't any taxidermy atrocities, but the number of taps behind the bar made this place *oh so American*. There had to be at least fifty different types of beer. Some of them had plastic cups over the handles, and I took that to mean they were tapped out. Was that the way to put it? I squinted one eye, looking upward at the ceiling. Run dry? Who knew not cruising frat parties when an undergrad would seriously impede my beer vocabulary?

Maddie nudged my side. "They have over seventy beers on tap."

"Really? I guessed fifty." I started to count them, feeling foolish for keeping track with my fingers, but my math skills ranked down there with beer terminology.

She looked around. "We're the first to arrive. Let's get our drinks and snag that table in the corner."

The bartender raised his brow in a way that said, "What will you have?"

Maddie requested a pale ale I'd never heard of, which really wasn't that shocking. I'd be hard pressed to name five beer types or brands.

He looked to me, expectantly.

"Uh, got any root beer?"

His smile was kind. "The best from a local brewery."

Before Maddie could take a swipe at me, I said to her, "I'm wearing the sweater, which means you can't pick on me about my drink selection." Not that I planned on telling her, but I'd learned the hard way, my nightmares increased when I drank alcohol.

"I wasn't going to say a word." She wore an expressionless face, which must have been hard for her.

Ethan and Gabe strolled through the door.

"Check out the sweater." Gabe hugged me and seemed to second-guess doing the same with Maddie before finally embracing her more like they were guy friends. His awkwardness wasn't surprising considering he'd ditched the latest couple's therapy with Maddie, not giving her the heads-up before pulling a no-show.

It was hard to hold the power move against Gabe. Their dynamic was toxic. Maddie was still in love with Peter, and Gabe had always wanted to be a full-fledged member of the family. He was like the dude in *Little Women* who married the youngest sister, saying he knew he was meant to marry a March girl. And, Maddie had issues with ending things. She'd waited until her wedding day to ditch Peter at the altar. Apparently, neither could make a clean break.

Ethan wore a quizzical look and motioned to my sweater, so I explained, "Maddie made me."

"I wondered." He turned to the bartender. "What's good here?"

I took my drink to the table to secure seats. I was well past the age of wanting to stand in a bar, pretending to drink, to hang with the cool kids. My lower back ached, and a tension headache was nibbling at the edges of my forehead. I really had to wonder why Sarah thought this was what I needed, when I had been content in my office, researching. The thought, I guess, was nice, so here I sat with my fizzy kid drink, waiting for my friends to do their best to cheer me up so they could feel like they were helping.

Geez, Lizzie. Take a fucking chill pill.

It wasn't like Sarah had insisted I try one of those retreats where you had to eat food only suitable for rabbits and chant about channeling power from your coochie or something. What was the movie with women holding mirrors to see their vags? Sarah, Maddie, and Ethan had recently watched it.

JJ and Courtney were the last to arrive about thirty seconds apart, and like me, JJ had ordered root beer. After taking a sip, she said, "Not bad."

"I kinda wish I could make a root beer float out of it." I took another sip.

Maddie took it from me. "Yum."

Courtney helped herself as well. "I wonder who does their ads." She looked over her shoulder for adverts or whatever.

"It's the little things in life that offer the biggest rewards." I reclaimed my glass.

"Hear, hear," JJ raised her glass.

The group joined in.

"So, what are we supposed to do?" I asked, looking around at the mostly youngish crowd. "It's possible we're the oldest ones in this establishment."

"Hey now, the forties are the new twenties," Gabe said.

"Says the man who isn't in his forties." Ethan jabbed Gabe in the side with an elbow. "I'm starting to make those sounds old men make when getting out of a chair."

I nodded. "Yesterday, when climbing a staircase in the history building, I uttered *Oh boy* when I took the first step. My knees and back were not enthused. I remember the days when I bounded up them two steps at a time."

JJ and Ethan bobbed their heads like they understood completely.

"Why not take the elevator?" Gabe slugged his beer.

"It's faster to take the stairs. Getting out of the house on time is a challenge these days." I gave an *I have four kids* shrug.

There was a ruckus in the back of the place, and we watched two guys bump chests, screaming something unintelligible. It probably had something to do with the playoff game on television, but I hadn't been following the NFL at all. I did know the Broncos were out of the playoffs before the season really got off the ground.

JJ and I exchanged a look that could only be interpreted as *why are straight men so kooky?* To his credit, Ethan also wore a questioning expression, and I tried imagining the high school English teacher going to a football game for fun, not as a school official to keep the students in line.

"Well, well, well. Look who it is, girls."

I glanced over my shoulder to see Keri and her mom-followers.

A mom-bully. Just what my day was missing.

Keri had a *gotcha* glint in her eyes, and she did her best to look formidable. What I saw, though, was something different. A woman in her early forties, wearing too much makeup, sporting an orange fake-tan glow, and exhaustion in the creases in her face.

"Hi," I said.

She seemed taken aback that I greeted her.

"I didn't know your wife let you out of her sight." Keri laughed, but the other moms didn't join in until she gave them a *laugh now or you're dead to me* smile. At least, that was how I took it, and well, it made me laugh.

Keri probably didn't mean for me to join in, but I couldn't help it. She was so pathetic. All bark and zero bite, because I didn't give a damn if she did attack me. Did she really think her words would land as hard as the barbs the Scotch-lady had dished out? While I didn't appreciate the way my mother had raised me, in this regard, it had toughened me up some. For weeks, I'd forgotten that. No more. I was tired of being a doormat.

"Oh, she lets me off my leash every once in a while," I joked and started to turn back to my friends.

"I didn't know it was still Christmas." She circled a finger in the air, indicating my sweater. Again, there was the aggressive laughter, the others joining in a tick too late for Keri's liking, given her death stare.

"I didn't know we were still in high school. Spoiler alert. I wasn't one of the cool kids then, and I don't deign to think I'm one now. I just don't give a flying fuck." I took a sip of my drink, feeling so much better saying this aloud.

It took Keri a second or two to process what I'd said, and her false smile turned into a sneer. "Such naughty language for a college professor. If I were in your shoes, I'd be careful."

I leaned over on my stool and kicked out my sneakers. "My feet seem okay, but thanks for the concern."

Everyone at my table seemed to be enjoying my performance, and Keri's gang wasn't sure how to react, so they chose the classic *stare off in the distance*, pretending nothing was happening.

"For someone who's about to go to jail—"

I nearly spat out my drink over the absurdity. "For what? Not allowing you to bully me?"

"For aiding and abetting a murderer and not to mention for being a Petrie! Your family is rotten to the core with cheaters."

I burst into laughter. "The first charge is ridiculous given Tie wasn't murdered and the police aren't investigating at all." I wasn't sure how she meant the cheaters comment. Actual infidelity or breaking rules? I opted not to pursue that thread. "I'll have to consult my lawyer if you're committing slander. As for the second, yes, I am a Petrie. Is there a new law in Colorado I'm not familiar with?"

"I hear you're being pushed out of the history department," Keri countered, and it was difficult to determine if my threat of seeking legal advice rattled her or not.

"Because of a white supremist with an axe to grind. Is that the side you want to be on?"

There was a gasp by those at my table and the other moms.

"N-now that's slander," she spluttered.

"Which part? That an old colleague who now writes for a Nazi-loving online publication has installed his cousin in my department to sleep with the history chair to convince him to boot me out? Or that you're siding with my female-hating nemesis?" I joggled two palms in the air.

"I'm doing no such thing. I don't hate females. I just hate you."

I placed a hand on my chest. "Why? You don't even know me."

"Because... you're a Petrie!"

I inclined my head. "I'm betting before my brother went to prison, you didn't know anything about the Petries. And don't feed me that cockamamie story that Peter had his wife killed. She died in a tragic accident. If there was anyone who wanted her out of the picture, talk to the man she was sleeping with. The one who helped set up Peter to get arrested. There's so much to the story that you don't know. But you aren't the type to want to know the truth, and again I have to stress, her death isn't under official investigation. It's only being questioned by crazies who have nothing better to do."

Keri gasped.

I continued to press. "You just want to sit in your ivory tower to be praised by all because you have this need to feel like you matter. I've got news for you; you don't. None of us does aside from those close to us. It's our wives, husbands, kids, family, and friends that are important in this world. Chasing more than that is a fool's errand." I gave her a once-over. "But given your Botox-loving self, you won't understand anything I've said. I feel sorry for you."

"Sorry for *me*?" Keri cackled, but I sensed my words had cut her deeply.

"I do. I don't know what it's like for you in your life, but I imagine it's not satisfying, and for that, I am truly sorry. If you need someone to talk to, I know a good therapist, but I'm betting you're the type who wouldn't seek help to get your head on straight. You prefer to cast blame on everyone else in the periphery. My brother may be in prison, but at least he's taken responsibility for his wrongdoings and is paying restitution. When he gets out, I'll be there for him. Who'll be there for you when you need them?"

I looked to the gaggle of women and noticed many of them had taken a step or two back from Keri.

I spoke to them. "In case you hadn't heard, Sarah is planning a big party at our house in March for our youngest daughter's birthday. We'd like all the kids from the music class to go, because that's what matters. Making our kids happy. There'll be tents, stuffed animals, lots of food, and even a kangaroo. I'm betting your kiddos will love it." I met each mother's eyes, finally landing on Keri's. "Even yours."

"Like I'd step one foot into Satan's house."

"Suit yourself, but your child will always be welcome." I turned my back on Keri.

I didn't hear any movement behind me until I reached the count of six. At first, it was the sound of one moving away after letting out an angry huff, so I assumed that was Keri. Slowly, the rest followed, but their foot falls were much quieter. What did that mean?

JJ clamped a hand on my shoulder. "That was either brilliant or extremely stupid."

Courtney nodded, and I noticed she held her phone in her hand.

"It seems there's always a fine line between the two, depending on the outcome." I sipped my drink, but there was only ice left. "I'm getting another. Anyone else need a second round?"

"Check you out, Miss Living Dangerously." Maddie hopped off her stool. "I'll help at the bar."

After we ordered the drinks, Maddie pulled her phone out of the back pocket of her jeans. "I better tell Sarah about this and the mention of the party."

I sipped a fresh serving of root beer, the bubbles refreshing on my parched throat. "Are you ratting on me while standing next to me?"

"Just giving her the heads-up. That's all." After her finger flew over the screen in dizzying speed, she said, "I am proud of you for speaking your mind to Keri."

"It made me feel better, but I doubt it helped. It's nearly impossible to get through to people like her." I thanked the bartender as he placed two beers with the rest of the order, my mind processing how Keri knew anything about my current job. As far as I knew, none of the moms in the music group had a connection to the university.

"You're right about Keri, but I think your words are sinking in with some of the others. While we've been standing here, two of them have left. And... yep, there goes a third, but don't look. She has her head tucked into the collar of her jacket."

That depressed me even more than the moms siding with Keri. Shame was a powerful emotion, and it was too easy to inflict on people these days. I wish I could tell the ones who left that I supported them for standing up, even if they took the least resistive road. Over my decades on this earth, I'd learned baby steps led to great change and happiness. I may have forgotten that as of late, but that was changing right here and now.

CHAPTER THIRTY-ONE

By Wednesday morning, the reckoning of my standing up to Keri came into fuller view.

"Everyone, aside from Keri, has RSVP'd to the Birthday Bash."

I stared over my mug at Sarah. "Is that the actual name of the party?"

"It is. Do you hate it?"

"I wouldn't say that. It's kinda tame for you; that's all." I took another hit from my tea. "I'm so not in the mood to teach today."

"Trade you. I have about twenty diaper changes in my future."

I looked down at Calvin, sitting contentedly in my lap. "Are you a pee and poo machine, Cali Pali?"

He didn't stoop to reacting.

"How is he even more serious than Fred? We used your egg for Cal."

"Are you saying no one in my family can be taken seriously?"

I hadn't meant to get myself into this pickle and was unsure how to yank both feet from my mouth, so I simply gaped at Sarah.

"Mom says he takes after my father." Sarah's eyes reddened with sadness, and I had to wonder about the frequency of this happening to her. Was it a byproduct of being middle-aged or the stress of our lives?

"He would love both boys, then."

"Not the girls?" Sarah dabbed the corners of her eyes with the sleeve of her robe.

I smiled at Olivia and Demi at the art table. "I can't imagine anyone not loving all of our children." I sighed. "I better hop into the shower and hit the road. Might as well get this day officially started so I can come home as soon as my evening class is done." I handed Calvin off to Sarah before heading to the staircase, still not wanting to teach. Was that a sign that maybe it was time to accept my days as a teacher were over?

***

AFTER MY TWO-O'CLOCK CLASS, I SAT AT MY DESK IN my office on campus, fine-tuning my evening lecture. The semester had barely started, but my lack of excitement was more like how I typically felt closer to final exam time. My work computer dinged. The vast majority of the emails that arrived via my university address were the definition of mundane. Students pleading for last-minute extensions on papers. Boring announcements from the administrative offices. And junk mail about buying basketball tickets or something.

Needless to say, I didn't pounce on my mouse when the email arrived, too focused on my lecture. It wasn't until an hour later, after fixing another cup of tea, that I decided to clean out my inbox so I could leave right from class to head home to Sarah and the sleeping babes.

That was when I saw the email from Wellesley College,

inviting me to fill a speaker's spot in a symposium the first week of March, which wasn't all that far away. Intrigued, I skimmed the email, then fixed another cup of tea to read it with an eye for details.

When I arrived home in record time, Sarah was reading in bed. She set her book down on the comforter. "Everything okay?"

"What? Yeah." I ran my right hand through my hair, realizing I was still clutching my messenger bag with my left hand. Setting it on the bench at the foot of the bed, I said, "Sorry. It's just been a long day." That was when I remembered while I'd taught all day, my lovely wife had been kid wrangling all on her own. As it turned out, Wednesday was the one day of the week neither of our nannies could work, and Ethan was also at his home. Today, Rose had her annual physical. "I'm sure yours was even more stressful. How'd you manage without any help today?"

"It wasn't as bad as I thought. There were brief moments of wondering why we had four kids, but they passed quickly. Usually when Ollie stopped having a meltdown, followed by one or more of her siblings."

I sat on the edge of the bed, leaning over to kiss Sarah on the cheek. "You really are amazing."

"Anything happen in your exciting academic life?"

"Three students need more time on their research proposals that are due by midnight. One week into the semester and it's just like all the others." I waved to imply *la di da*.

"It's astounding how quickly the world changes, and yet it doesn't on some levels."

I chuckled. "Tell me about it. Oh, I did receive a last-minute request to speak at Wellesley. Get this, the woman who asked is a sister of one of the moms from music class."

"Which one?"

"If I remember the email correctly, Gayle."

Sarah stared off into the distance for several ticks, before saying, "That has to be a good sign."

"Too bad it's so last minute. I'll have to say no."

Sarah's eyes tapered. "Why?"

"How can we arrange for me to leave without reinforcements for you? You just said there were moments today you regretted having four kids."

"That's just something stay-at-home-moms say sometimes. Your use of reinforcements—it's not like I'm waging war with the kids. This is the gig I signed up for when I got pregnant. Not every day is paradise, but it's what I want and love." She stared into my eyes. "Do you really think this is the time to turn down offers like this? You're unhappy at your current situation. Get out there and network. You've never spoken at Wellesley, if my memory serves."

"But—"

She held up a hand. "Say yes. What's the worst that can happen?"

"I'll come home to an irate wife."

"That's a risk every day." Her honest expression made me smile. "Say yes, please."

"I don't have anything prepared. Usually, I know my speaking gigs ages before now."

"You love research. One of the things worrying you has been the thought of only teaching Western Civ. We both know it won't be challenging and won't allow you the opportunity to dig into aspects of your specialty, denying you the chance to run ideas by students before presenting the information in a journal article. You know what they say. You don't know something until you have to teach it. This offer fell into your lap. Sometimes, things happen for a reason, and I feel it in my bones that this has materialized right now for the best reason possible."

"Which is?"

"You need a tick in the win column." She made a check mark in the air. "If you even think of declining, no sex until summer."

I laughed. "You're such a strange wife."

"I know how to motivate you."

"Any chance I can sample the bill of goods?" I waggled my brows.

"You do have a way with words."

"Me writer." I thumped my chest, cavewoman style.

"About Nazis. Not sure you're selling this." She crossed her arms, putting her girls on display, which I was certain had been her intent.

"You are." I moved to bury my face in her cleavage, but she redirected my landing to her lips. "Just so you know, this isn't punishment."

"Just so you know, I wasn't trying to punish you. Trust me, Lizzie, if I wanted you to know I was mad, you would." She kissed me again.

"Are we a weird couple?" I asked in between kisses.

She pulled her face away from mine, a quizzical look in her eyes. "You ask outlandish things at the oddest times."

"Is that your answer? I'm the weirdo, and you put up with me?"

"No, honey. We're not a weird couple. Why'd you even ask?"

"We went from talking about Nazis to... hopefully..." I waved for her to fill in the blanks. I didn't want to bring up my crying from the other day when I said my pussy looked like Hitler.

"I'm pretty sure many people have unusual conversations in private. That's why they're private."

I glanced at the Echo Dot on my bedside. "Not sure they're private anymore."

Sarah followed my eyes. "What do you say? Should we give

Alexa a show?" She mouthed the name to avoid triggering the device, all the while lifting my sweater and shirt off my head. "This is new." She ran a finger over the top of my bra.

"Maddie took me shopping yesterday, saying I needed to find my mojo again. I think she's convinced herself my wearing the Christmas sweater she got me sparked my inner warrior or something."

She made a show of checking out the purple bra. "Is it helping?"

"Not sure. Does it cup my boobs right?"

Sarah grinned but obligingly placed a hand over my right boob. "It seems to."

"And the other?" I looked down at my left breast. "No playing favorites."

"I would never." Sarah now had her hands on both. "I do like the softness."

"Of the fabric or the fact they're getting bigger?"

"They are bigger." She nodded her head in an approving way.

"I need to start riding my bike again."

"Right now?" she teased. "I'll make sure you get enough exercise to burn some calories." She leaned in for round two of kissing, pulling me down on top of her.

"Hold your horses, missy." I stood up and shucked off my trousers, panties, and socks.

"And, you're accusing *me* of being in a rush." Her smile was sexy as hell, but the love in her eyes was the part that spoke volumes.

I undid the tie of her robe, not surprised but still excited she had nothing underneath. Getting back on top, we continued kissing, while one of my hands explored her milky skin. "I love that you still get goose bumps when I touch you."

"It's chilly in here."

"It's not, and you know it."

"Don't be getting a big head just because you got a speaking gig."

"Don't forget my television appearances. I'm da history bomb these days."

Sarah rolled me onto my back. "Let's see if I can detonate you."

I dug my head into the pillow, laughing. "I really hope no one is listening to this, or they'll think we're the cheesiest—"

Her mouth clamped down on my nipple, and her hip separated my legs, her rocking movement doing wonders for my libido. She moved to the other nipple, biting it before sucking it into her mouth. I let out a mouthful of air and dug my head farther into the pillow. "That feels so fucking good."

Sarah reached for my face, but I took one of her fingers and sucked it into my mouth. She let out a moan, her tongue licking its way down my stomach, not stopping on any patch of skin for long. Not that I minded. My southern region was reaching the point that needed all of her attention, and she removed her finger from my mouth, to insert two fingers inside me.

"Yes," I said, releasing a shudder, which intensified when her tongue flicked my clit. "You do know what I need."

"I've had plenty of practice." She glanced up at me.

To see her gaze into my eyes while she was going down on me, it was off the *scorching hot* charts. The word magical wasn't the right one to describe how well we fit. Perfection. Not even the past few months could destroy the bond we had. The connection that continued to cement with each day. Sometimes it seemed the more obstacles the world threw in our path, the closer we became. Because of moments like this. We weren't simply making love. Or just getting our jollies. We were proclaiming our love in the most intimate way possible. Sarah took my right hand into her left, entwining our fingers. I loved how in tune she was with me the majority of the time.

Her fingers pumped harder inside me, and her tongue sensually lapped my sex in that way of hers to get me to come hard. The closer I got to the edge, the deeper her fingers went, until they curled up, triggering my orgasm with such magnificence I ended up coming twice.

When the tremors subsided, Sarah was pressed onto me, her weight making me feel content. She yawned.

"Does this mean it's bedtime?"

"It is after eleven, and some of us need our beauty sleep."

"Way to cut me down after taking me to the pinnacle of heights," I teased, kissing the top of her head.

"Yes, that's me. The one who destroys after showing you how much I love you."

"It's mean."

Sarah rested her chin on my chest. "I love you, Lizzie."

"You know, I'm starting to believe you."

She laughed. "You can be so thickheaded."

"I'm game for you showing me again."

She yawned, and I could practically see her back molars.

"Fine. I'll have to wait until next time."

"There'll be many." From her voice, I knew she was already drifting off to sleep, so I wrapped my arms around her and let her stay on top of me, our heartbeats in tune with each other.

CHAPTER THIRTY-TWO

While I sat at the table, with a screaming Ollie, who didn't want any banana slices on her tray, Sarah consulted the schedule on the desk. I'd never understand why we needed a desk in the kitchen, but I assumed it was there from the old days when landline phones were still a necessity.

"What's this Wells thing during spring break?" she asked.

"I couldn't remember how to spell Wellesley. Is it just *ly* or is there an *e*?" I handed Demi one of the banana slices Ollie didn't want. "I thought banana was Ollie's favorite fruit."

"You're going to Massachusetts over spring break?"

"Apparently." I gave Fred a banana slice, but he only eyed it with curiosity.

Sarah swiveled her upper body around and held onto the back of the chair. "What do you mean, apparently?"

"Do you not remember telling me to accept the speaking gig? When I woke early this morning, I emailed them and then added it to the calendar." Not doing so had caused problems in the past, and I, for one, tried to learn from my personal history.

"I didn't know it was over spring break."

"That's why I'm able to go. Otherwise, I'd have to cancel a

class. Given I'm being pushed out, that didn't seem like a smart move. Or does it matter anymore?"

Sarah tapped a pen against the side of her head. "Do you know what's happening over spring break?"

"In general or here? I'm assuming most of my students will be drunk on some beach."

"Here."

"Ollie will scream about something. Fred will refuse to eat. Demi will be a sweetheart, and Calvin will give everyone some serious not-so-subtle shade."

"How do you not remember?" The knuckles on her right hand whitened as her grip on the back of the chair intensified like she wanted to snap the wood into two.

"Uh, can you give me a hint? You know I'm terrible with future dates. They break all types of rules for historians."

"I imagine other historians are able to keep better track of things. You just use it as an excuse." Her voice was becoming testier and testier.

Demi polished off the rest of the banana slices.

"Good job, baby girl."

She lifted two hands in the air, Freddie joining her.

Sarah cleared her throat.

"Oh, yes. You were about to yell at me. Please recommence." I hoped making light of the situation would soften her up some. Not to mention remind her our children were witnessing her performance.

Instead, her eyes flashed red.

Maddie, with fresh cinnamon rolls, strolled into the kitchen. "Who's the best person on the planet?"

"Not Lizzie," Sarah growled.

Maddie looked to me and then back to Sarah. "What'd she do?"

"She said yes."

"You told me to say yes. You said it many times. *Just say yes,*

Lizzie," I mimicked her to the best of my ability, trying to siphon the tension from the situation. From the fire now shooting out of her eyes, my jokes were crash-landing like the Hindenburg.

"I'm not following. You told Lizzie to say yes to whom?" Maddie asked.

"Wellesley," I said.

"That's an unconventional name. Boy or girl?"

"Neither."

Maddie gave me a quizzical look. "Are you trying to be obtuse?"

"That's her personality. Wellesley is a school Lizzie is visiting to shoot the s-shitake about the Nazis." Sarah slammed the day planner shut and stormed out of the kitchen."

"Too bad Gandhi doesn't have a doghouse because you're not going to enjoy living in the elements until she thaws." Maddie filled the coffee maker.

I finished feeding the kids. "I don't understand why she's so upset. I only did what she wanted."

"Maybe she's having second thoughts about you leaving her alone with your demon brood."

"Why are they *my* demon brood during these situations? I only contributed DNA to half."

Ollie let out a howl.

"The demon half." Maddie freed Ollie from the high chair. "What's the matter, Ollie Dollie?"

"Nanna." Ollie pointed to Demi. "Want."

"I don't get the women in this family. I really don't." I stopped myself from flicking my hands up in the air. Instead, I asked in a somewhat steady voice, "Would you like some banana, Olivia?"

She nodded, her eyes and face red.

"Okay, baby girl. Let me slice another."

"I got it. I'm thinking you holding a knife right now may not be the best thing. Girls like it when you keep all your fingers. Especially lesbians." Maddie put Olivia back into her chair. "Try explaining the Sarah situation."

I wiped Freddie's face and fingers. "He ends up with more food *on* him than *in* him."

"You're stalling." She pointed the knife at me.

"What happened to keeping sharp objects from me?"

Maddie didn't blink.

"Tough crowd. I'm sure it's just a simple misunderstanding. We didn't get much sleep last night."

"Really, Lizzie. I don't need to know the details about that part of your life." She resumed slicing the fruit.

I released a frustrated sigh. "Calvin was the reason." He wasn't, but I didn't want Maddie to know those details either.

Calvin eyed me like he understood I'd tossed him under the bus. Great, not only were the Petrie women mad at me, so was my youngest son. I just couldn't win.

Maddie gave Olivia some more banana and a few grape halves, which Ollie smashed with her fingers. Maybe this would be a good day for finger painting. To help all of us get our aggression out with an art therapy session.

"When's the speaking thing?" Maddie asked.

"Over spring break."

Maddie stopped pouring a cup of coffee and glared at me.

Now, I knew I was really in the doghouse. I looked out the window at the backyard to find the best patch of level leftover snow for sleeping.

"How could you forget about spring break?"

"We're not going anywhere. Only students get a break. Professors usually have speaking gigs. But I didn't add one to my schedule until late in the game. Which Sarah approved of. Have I mentioned that part?" It seemed important to keep reminding everyone of that detail.

"Did you tell her the date?"

"No, I just said it was coming up soon."

"That's when the birthday party is happening."

My heartbeat thudded behind my temples. "It is not." I spoke slowly and enunciated each word with conviction. "Demi's birthday is the week after."

"Oh, it is."

"Did she change the date? Of the party? Not Demi's birth certificate."

"No. It's always been over spring break because you would be home to help out with the wingding. It really is amazing how much you suck at dates, considering."

"It's a Petrie trait. Or have you forgotten your ex-fiancé planning his wedding on my birthday?"

"Not sure that's the best defense right now. Saying you can't help it because you're just like your convict brother. Something tells me Sarah won't take kindly to that defense."

After we got the kids settled in the front room, I cuddled Calvin in my lap. "Okay. How do I get myself out of this jam?"

"I'd say flowers, but your stepmom and stepbrother own a shop, so that's too easy." Maddie tapped her fingers to her chin. "I really don't know, but I'd prepare for a dirt nap."

"You think she's going to—?" I made a slicing motion over my throat.

"Oh no. If she hasn't killed you yet, she won't. But she may tackle you to the ground and rub your face in dog dirt."

A shudder zigzagged through my body, and I looked at Gandhi sleeping on his dog bed in front of the fire. "It doesn't seem fair that the dog will have a cozier place to sleep than I will."

"Sarah can be somewhat unreasonable when it comes to throwing off her party plans." Maddie's pinched expression didn't match her words.

"Tell me about it." I rubbed my right eye with the heel of my palm. "I should have waited before sending the acceptance email this morning. This isn't the first time I've messed up planning a speaking gig. You'd think I'd have learned my lesson by now."

Maddie laughed. "Oh, I don't think you will. It's probably one of the things Sarah secretly adores about you. How you can be so intelligent and clueless at the same time."

Rose appeared, all smiles, but after taking the pulse of the room, said, "What's wrong?"

Maddie extended a long finger at me.

I'm sure I looked like I was being asked to walk the plank with a frenzy of sharks below. "I messed up the birthday party."

Rose blinked. "How?"

"I said yes." I waved a hand for Maddie to fill in the blank since I still wasn't entirely sure about all the details. Perhaps, I was in denial.

Rose rounded to Maddie for more, but Sarah chose that moment to stride in, all eyes zeroing on her, even the kiddos'.

"Good morning, Mom. Would you like a cup of coffee?" Sarah was freshly showered but still wore her robe, and there wasn't a trace of anger in her.

This wasn't a good sign, and I knew I had to do something quick to get back onto her good side. I absolutely detested her perfect Stepford Wife impression, and I suspected she knew that.

"Sarah, honey, what if I send you to the... woman who rubs you?"

All three of them turned to me. Rose and Maddie's jaws dangled, but there was a twinkle in Sarah's eyes.

"What exactly are you offering, because I might want to join Sarah for some female rubbing?" Maddie asked.

"I didn't mean... not that..." I looked to Sarah.

"What Miss Vocab is trying to say is she'll send me for a massage." Sarah treated me to one of her beaming smiles. "Lizzie, it's okay. I had some time to think in the shower.

You're right. I absolutely told you to say yes. And I still think that's the right decision. It'll be fine." I could tell she was doing her best to sound breezy.

"Can someone please tell me what Lizzie saying yes means?" Rose eyed me with suspicion, and I hoped this wouldn't cause the old Rose to return. The one who made car revving sounds, her threat of mowing me down with her Caddie.

"Lizzie's been asked to speak at Wellesley." Sarah tightened her robe. "I could use some tea. Anyone else?"

"Can we still sign up for the woman rubbing? I could use some… relaxation." Maddie spoke to Sarah, not me.

"Don't ever get married, Calvin. Women will eat you whole." I raised my son into the air, and he giggled.

Everyone turned to us.

"It giggles," Maddie said.

I stuck my tongue out at her. "One more dig at any of my children and no rubbing for you." As my words sunk in, I said, "That didn't come out exactly like I intended."

* * *

AFTER GETTING THE KIDDOS READY FOR MUSIC class, there was a quiet moment when Maddie and Rose, who were taking the kids, finally said their goodbyes.

Sarah, feeding Calvin with a bottle, sat in one of the leather chairs in the family room.

I took a seat on the ottoman, our knees pressed against each other. "Are you sure everything is okay between us?"

She looked up from Calvin. "I am. This is a good thing for you. I can't explain, but something is telling me this is exactly what you need right now. The timing is unfortunate, but Troy has already volunteered to step into your shoes. He's much better at leading the kids in songs than you."

"Do you remember the days when you hated him?"

"I didn't hate him." Her tone was laced with guilt. "It was an adjustment. The older I get, the more I'm coming to terms with the fact that things like this are adjustments. Not to be feared or despised. Just something to get used to. I know you're the parent who works outside of the house. Sometimes, I get jealous about that. Then, when I hear about the office politics you have to put up with, I remember how lucky I am to spend all this time with the kids. We're truly fortunate that we can afford to have only one of us work. So many can't, and the thought of dropping the kids off at day care..." Sarah ran a hand over Calvin's bald head.

"If it makes you feel better, I also get jealous when I'm hunched over my desk grading papers or when I spy students bored out of their gourds when I'm lecturing. But when I get through to one student, it's like magic." I made a fist and then opened it like a mind expanding.

"I know that feeling."

"Do you think you'll go back to teaching once the kids are in school?"

Sarah gazed at Calvin. "I don't know. I've been considering doing something else."

"Writing children's stories?"

"I'm still thinking of that, but I feel like there's something else I should do. With all this stuff about Peter and Tie and adopting Demi, I'd like to help kids more."

"In what capacity if not teaching?"

"What would you say if I went back to school?"

Sarah had never mentioned anything of the sort, and I was surprised. "For?"

"Law school."

I'd heard the words, but they didn't align correctly in my brain right away.

"I want to fight for kids' rights."

"You want to go into family law?" I shook a finger in my ear, still not sure I was hearing everything correctly.

"Do you think I'm too old?"

"What? No, that's not what I meant at all. Like you said earlier, it'll be an adjustment, but... wow, I'll be married to a lawyer. My mom may have been proud of that."

"If I had a Y chromosome."

I bobbed my head. "Can't win them all."

CHAPTER THIRTY-THREE

"There you have it. The political atmosphere is ripe for authoritarian leaders and governments to shove democratic institutions to the side for their own personal gain. The question is: have we as a whole learned enough from the horrors of the twentieth century to stop history from repeating, or will millions of lives have to be sacrificed once more?" I glanced around the room, making eye contact with some of the members of the Wellesley audience, before finishing. "Thank you for allowing me to speak at your university. Madeline Albright, one of your alums, has written a thought-provoking book on this very subject. I implore all of you to read or listen to *Fascism: A Warning*."

There was a splattering of applause, but this wasn't the type of talk that spurred many happy feelings. No wonder Sarah worried about my deep dives into the darkest layers of history.

"Wow, Lizzie. That was amazing." Dr. Arden shook my hand. "Thanks so much for coming out here."

"It was my pleasure." I dipped my head as a way of showing my esteem for the world-renowned scholar and dean of the department. "On my flight here, I listened to your latest tome. It's excellent in a sobering way."

There was a twinkle in her eye. "I have to take care of some business, attend the rest of the lectures this afternoon, shake the right hands, but would you like to do dinner tonight? Eightish?"

"It'd be an honor."

We said goodbye for the moment, and after some of the students and professors chatted with me, one surprising me by asking me to sign a copy of my book on the Hitler Youth, I was able to make a clean break. These speaking gigs were such a roller coaster. All the anxious hours prepping, the high of speaking, and then coming back down. I always needed a few hours to myself after everything. I'd never been in this area before, but I'd looked up walking trails and decided on the Lake Waban path, a three-mile loop on the campus.

The path started behind an admin building. I was a little confused by which direction to take but went to the right. Soon enough, I ended up on a dirt trail covered with pine needles, fallen leaves, and gnarled tree roots that would trip up even the more cautious runners. I'd never taken to the sport, and I think it was because I'd always felt like prey in my family. Running would only reinforce this feeling.

The wind kicked up, nearly ripping my hat off. The water lapped the shoreline. The temperature was bone-chilling cold, but the brilliant lapis blue sky made the bare tree branches really pop against the horizon. Part of me was sad the talk had been scheduled so early in the spring. In a month or thereabouts, I imagined the new green leaves would be quite the sight to see. There was something special about the newness of the leaves that for the first week or so glowed with green, as if they were thrilled to be back. I was willing to bet the fall colors would more than put Colorado autumns to shame.

Ice covered parts of the lake's edges, but that didn't deter a lone swan from skimming along the water. I stood on the path, taking it all in. This was the perfect spot to bring the little ones for weekend adventures. Ollie would love getting as close to the water as possible, giving me heart palpitations. Fred would probably collect pine needles for some construction project. Demi would cling to my hand, peering up at me with her beautiful smile. And Cal, more than likely would grumpily trudge along. I could picture it all. A twitch of disappointment of the Harvard job falling through settled deeply in my chest.

Maybe Sarah was right. I should keep putting out feelers. More than likely, I wouldn't find a new teaching gig for a year or two, but I promised myself right then and there I wouldn't stop until I did. I enjoyed writing historical books and journal articles along with being on JJ's show, but teaching was what I was born to do. There was no greater feeling than connecting with one student and sparking a passion for a subject I believed deep in my heart to be vital to protect not only democracy but human rights for generations to come.

The trail led to a wooden path through a marsh area, and a sign about keeping dogs on leashes caught my attention. The fines kept increasing up to three hundred smackaroos.

On the far side of the lake, I sat on a bench, contemplating my next steps, once again spying the swan all alone. I didn't want to end up that way. Was the universe telling me to get the heck out of my teaching position?

Another whip of wind propelled me to finish the walk, but not too much farther down the path, there was a private property notice and a sign that read, *End of Wellesley Property*. I'd grown up in the West, where trespassing could get you shot. I wheeled about and headed the way I came.

I returned to my hotel room with enough time to hop in the shower before dinner with Dr. Arden.

* * *

After getting out of the car, I took care of the tip for my driver on the app on my phone. Sarah had installed it before I'd left town and had me do a couple of practice runs so I'd get the hang of it. She made it clear I had to tip and rate the experience because the drivers were rating me as well. If I got a bad score, I'd have a harder time finding rides.

When I glanced up from my phone, I was relieved the place wasn't super fancy. I always appreciated nice places that didn't go out of their way to make it known they were the cream of the crop. Being good was all that was needed. Screaming "Look how great we are" put me off.

Dr. Arden waved when I entered, and I made my way to the table. "Did you have any trouble finding the place?"

"Nope. My wife made me promise I'd use my ride app at every possible chance. We have four kids. She doesn't want to have to worry about my inability to find my way out of a wet paper bag."

She chuckled and took a seat after I sat. "My wife is that way. Way back when GPS first became a thing, I got her one for the car. Before then, she'd call me in tears. Even going to places she'd been going to once a year always caused her stress."

"I can relate, but I didn't call anyone. And, I won't confirm or deny there were any tears. My father's the same way, but he hides it better by having a driver."

A waitress brought over a bottle of red.

"I hope you don't mind. I ordered my favorite wine."

"Sounds great." I hadn't had much alcohol since Christmas, so I was relieved when the waitress barely filled my glass, and there was a decent-sized water glass already at my place setting. I raised my wine. "Cheers."

She clinked mine. After a sip, she said, "I was really impressed with your talk today." Fortunately for me, she plowed on because it was always a bit awkward trying to come up with a comment. "My sister was right about you."

"Is that right? May I fish?"

"She said you had a way of getting your point across."

This puzzled me some since her sister was one of the moms who'd been part of Keri's mom-bully gang. Truth be told, I couldn't pick out the professor's sibling in a lineup. "It's kind of her to say that."

"It takes guts to stand up to people like Keri."

"She told you about Keri?" To say I was flabbergasted would be putting it mildly.

"We have a good relationship. She hated toeing Keri's line and would call to bitch."

"That's interesting, given you study fascism."

"Oh, she probably got tired of me citing historical facts or acts of bravery during the Third Reich."

I grinned. "I'm sure those in my inner circle think the same thing. Recently, I told my wife I remind myself about death camps when going through stressful times as a way to cheer myself up."

She tilted her head back and laughed. "It does put things into perspective." Dr. Arden threaded her fingers on the table. "It's my understanding this is your first time to the university and city."

"It is."

"What do you think?"

"It's a beautiful place, and I admired the students at the talk. The questions they asked were insightful and spot-on."

"We're proud of our girls." She opened her menu. "Now, I hear you aren't a seafood fan, so may I recommend the grass-fed burger?"

How did she hear that? And, why had she bothered to inquire? "Done. I prefer not making many decisions when it comes to meals."

"I had a feeling."

She caught the waitress's eye and placed the order. It was

odd having another woman order for me, but I sensed she was the type who liked to take charge in all situations. Given her role at the university, she probably had to wine and dine all the time, and it was kind of her to fit me into her schedule so I wouldn't be lonely.

"Now that that's taken care of, tell me what I need to do to convince you to consider Wellesley." She folded her hands on the table.

I held my water glass in the air. "For?"

"I have a teaching position to fill this fall, and I want you."

Everything started to click into place, and I was kicking myself for not seeing how this dinner would play out. Jesus, why had I mentioned being directionally challenged and stubborn? Did I insinuate I cry when lost? "Uh—"

"I know you've lived in Colorado all your life and that you have four kids and a wife. So, packing up your life won't be an easy feat. We're prepared to help you every step of the way. Fort Collins is a great place, and I may be biased, but this is a better place to raise a family. The schools are fantastic. For a historian, there's so much here for endless teaching opportunities with your kids. Within an hour, you can be in another state. Four hours from New York City if you time the traffic right."

"We're only forty-five minutes from Cheyenne, Wyoming—"
Jesus fucking Christ, Lizzie! Comparing the capital of Wyoming to the Big Apple.

Her smile was kind. "To sweeten the pot, I'd like to toss in I'm not having an affair with a young admin. Nor do I know anyone who's related to William Connor Abernathy Thornhill the Fifth."

I blinked.

She gave me time for everything to sink in.

I forced some water down to lubricate my throat. "How did you know about my current situation?"

"Dr. Marcel and I go way back. I'm also friends with Cora Matthews, and she reached out to JJ for me for some intel. You've been handed a rotten deal, but it hasn't broken you." She pointed a finger at me. "You're the type of person we want around our students. One who stands up for what's right, like when you told off Keri. One who stands with those she loves, like your brother and adopting his daughter. And, you're a damn good historian. While I don't agree with the politics going on at your school, I'm kinda glad they're fucking up in such an unbelievable way, because their loss will be our gain."

"I haven't said yes."

"That's right. You haven't. I would be disappointed in you if you did without consulting your lovely wife."

"I'd be dead."

There was the professor's smile, the one that was kind, conniving, and controlling. It should have terrified me, but I liked being around intelligent, strong, and confident individuals. They pushed me to be better.

"How can I help convince Sarah?" she asked.

I chuckled. "Geez, I really didn't prepare well for this trip. You even know Sarah's name." I twisted the linen napkin around one of my hands under the table.

"On the contrary, your lecture was well researched, and your delivery was perfect. That was your job, and you knocked it out of the park. Are you a baseball fan?"

I shook my head.

"If you do move to Massachusetts, it'd behoove you to pretend to be a Red Sox fan. I learned the hard way, being from New York."

"Are you a Yankees fan?"

"Not anymore." She boosted her eyebrows. "It does relieve me some that you know a little about baseball. It's a religion here."

"Coloradoans do like their sports, but fans have to be

diehard because trophies are hard won and few and far between."

"The Rockies made it to the World Series in 2007. They were swept by the Red Sox." She flourished her wine glass before taking a swig.

"Naturally." I hadn't remembered this fact, but I tucked it into my *need to know* sports trivia folder. While I didn't personally know many sports nuts, I knew it was best to stay semi-informed for awkward conversations around the so-called water cooler or when chatting at parties. Not everyone wanted to hear about the Nazis, which confused me. Especially given the rise of nationalism around the globe. This was the time to dissect the Nazis. Not literally because that was more in tune with Dr. Mengele.

"I have to hand it to you about the video of you telling off Keri." She took a sip of her wine.

"Uh, that video was never posted." If it had been, I was going to ream Courtney.

"I know."

I tapped my fingertips against my forehead doing my best to hammer all these details into my brain. "Then how do you know about it?"

"JJ told me you flipped your lid when Courtney suggested putting it online. You didn't want Keri, who tormented you, to be dogged by the video the rest of her life."

"Not just Keri. Her family and friends. She has a son. I know what it's like to have everyone hate you and to worry about how it'll impact your children. I couldn't take part in something like that."

She regarded me. "You're a good person. I want people like you on my team. You're flying back tomorrow?"

"Yes."

"Good. I'm hoping to hear good news a week from today."

CHAPTER THIRTY-FOUR

I ARRIVED AT DENVER INTERNATIONAL AIRPORT A minute before ten-thirty on Saturday night. By the time I found my car in the parking garage and hit the road, it would be after midnight before I got home. I had a feeling my Monday classes were going to be torture for me, even with one day to recover.

Much to my surprise, Sarah was in the kitchen, pouring hot water into two mugs. "How was your trip?"

I yawned.

"Thrilling, I see."

Setting my laptop bag on one of the stools, I took a seat on the other. "It was, actually."

"Let's go in the library and chat."

"How do you know?"

She gave me a puzzled look.

I backpedaled. "Okay, I guess you don't."

"You're always wired after flying. I thought a cup of chamomile would help you relax." She picked up the mugs. "However, I may need the tea's power more than you, judging by your worried expression." She circled a finger in the air.

We settled on the couch, the fireplace going, Gandhi asleep on the bed in front.

I sipped my tea much too soon, scalding my tongue.

Sarah cradled hers right below her chin. "Can you just tell me?"

"I got a job offer."

Sarah slanted her head. "That's what has you worried?"

"In Massachusetts."

"I'd guessed that much considering that's where you returned from. Do you want the job?"

"I think I'd be a perfect fit." Since my dinner with Dr. Arden, I'd dug into the backgrounds of all the professors in the department, something I foolishly hadn't done before my talk, not having enough time.

Sarah set down her mug and took my hand into hers. "You're scaring me. What aren't you telling me?"

"I have one week, well, six days now, to say yes or no."

"Why would you say no? It's Wellesley that offered, right?"

"Yes."

"So…?" She waved for me to fill in the blank.

"It's all the way across the country." I made an arching movement in the air with one hand.

"Someone told me it's really only two-thirds of the way." She squeezed my hand.

"But, when I first told you about looking in Massachusetts, you balked."

"I wasn't prepared for the topic when you first dropped the bomb. Not to mention I didn't know a lot of what was going on with you. Now, I know. This is a great opportunity. Wellesley is one of the best universities in the United States."

"According to the *U.S. News and World Report*, it's ranked third in liberal arts." I'd done a lot of research in the past twenty-four hours, not to mention I'd spent a good portion of the morning wandering the campus, once again exploring the area around the lake. "How long is Gandhi's leash?"

"I have no idea. Why?"

"It can't be longer than seven feet, or we'll get fined."

"Lizzie..." Sarah seemed to change her mind about probing the dog leash thread. "You can't say no to the offer."

"It's all happening so fast." I drank my tea, luckily without burning myself this time.

"I told you when you first got the offer to speak there that it was meant to be." She leaned back into the couch. "I just knew."

"That I'd get a job offer? I wish you told me so I could have been prepared. I looked like an idiot when I thought I just had to carry on normal dinner chitchat. I had no idea it was a job interview, or whatever it was."

Sarah grinned. "You look so cute when you're taken by surprise. She probably found it charming."

"She's not interested in dating me. She's interested in my mind." I tapped a finger to my forehead.

"You don't think I am?" Sarah spoke in her sexy tone.

"You know what I mean."

"Do you know what else Massachusetts has?"

"The Red Sox."

"Yes, but I was thinking of something else."

"It's colder there. That took me by surprise. And, I hear the humidity is brutal in the summer. We're used to a dry heat."

"Still not where I was going."

"Can you please just tell me? I'm wiped out on every level." I slouched and yawned again.

She cupped my cheek. "You do look more exhausted than normal, so I'll be nice. Law schools. Colorado has two. Massachusetts has more than triple. Four in Boston, one in Newton, and one in Cambridge. Newton is pretty close to Wellesley, if I'm remembering correctly."

"Which one is in Newton?"

"Boston College."

"I guess I'm not the only one who's been doing research." I googled the school on my phone. "It's ranked number twenty-seventh. Hey, if you study tax law, the number is fourteen."

"Who studies tax law?"

"Only the most exciting people, I imagine." I ducked to miss her hand swat. "You really want to go to law school?"

"I do. If we stayed in Fort Collins, I'd have to commute to Denver or Boulder."

"Not ideal in the winter."

"Nope."

"Can we sleep on this? I'm of the mind no major life decisions should be made at one in the morning."

"Just think of all the babies conceived at this hour."

"Not for lesbians. Not without precise planning." I rose to my feet and put out my hand. "Tuck me in, please."

She eyed me, not taking my hand yet. "Can I say one final thing?"

"You usually do." I offered her my *don't kill me* grin.

"I'm proud of you. Always have been. Always will be."

* * *

THE ROOM LOOKED LIKE A MIDDLE SCHOOL cafeteria, with picnic style tables and plastic benches scattered throughout. I sat at one in the corner, a cement wall behind me and gray linoleum underfoot. In the beginning, the flooring had probably been white, but years of being mopped with dirty water had permanently stained it.

The metal door opened, and I offered a wave to Peter, who was wearing a matching khaki shirt and pants. I missed the days of seeing him in his ridiculous golf outfits, and I never thought that would be the case. I also never thought I'd spend one day a month visiting him in prison. However, this wasn't my regular visiting day.

He didn't wave back, but his eyes shone with relief. Did he know beforehand who was waiting in the visiting area?

"Hey," he said, sitting across from me.

"How are you?"

He nodded, making it hard for me to guess if he was good or bad.

"Do you have enough funds for the commissary?"

"Yeah. Dad takes care of it. Or his assistant does." His hand wave made me wonder if he resented the ways of our father. Dad got shit done by telling others to do it.

When I first heard we had to go through Western Union to get money into Peter's account, I had to laugh. I didn't even know Western Union, which came into being in the nineteenth century and monopolized the telegraph industry, still existed. Peter's max monthly spending was three hundred and twenty bucks. More than likely that was what he usually spent on one business lunch for two.

"How's your job?" I asked.

He looked away.

It was a relief when we learned Peter was going to a prison located in between Englewood and Littleton, about an hour and a half from Fort Collins. When I found it on the fifty most comfortable prisons in the world list, I heaved a sigh of relief. The mid-forties rank was unsettling, and I wondered if that made it forty times more unbearable than the number one slot, Halden Prison in Norway. Their cells are furnished along with TVs and fridges.

"I'm sorry. I never know what to say when I come." With a wave of my hand, I offered him a bottle of Coke and a Snickers bar I'd purchased in the hallway outside the room.

He wore a lopsided grin, unwrapping the candy. "That sums it up for everyone. How's Demi?"

"She's great. Freddie adores her, and Sarah threw Demi a birthday bash." The prison didn't allow me to bring anything into the visitation area, except drinks and food purchased from their vending machines, so I couldn't show Peter the most recent photo of his daughter.

"I can't believe she's two." He swallowed, his Adam's apple moving up and down cartoon-like. "She'll be five when I get out."

It was my turn not to speak, because how could I appease him by saying the time would fly? It would, but he'd miss three years of his daughter's childhood. Kids grew up fast, and he was missing many of her milestones.

"She's liking music class. Unlike you, though, she doesn't hit anyone with her maracas."

He laughed. "Does Fred still like the drums?"

"Yep. I honestly don't know where he gets that gene from. My idea of being musical is bobbing my head two steps behind the beat."

"Do you even have a favorite song?"

"I do."

"Care to share?" He held his palm in an attempt to get me to tell him.

"You'll just poke fun." I briefly crossed my arms in a teasing fashion so the guards wouldn't react, but I put my hands back on the table in clear view like the signs instructed.

"That's my job as older brother."

I could see in his eyes he really needed to hold onto his older brother status. "'Monster Mash.'"

His neck made a whiplash movement. "It is not."

"It is. If you don't believe me, ask Maddie the next time she's here."

Again, he looked away.

I glanced at the clock on the wall. We didn't have much time left. "Peter... I need to tell you something."

He slowly turned his head back to look me in the eye.

"I've had a job offer I'm seriously considering."

His face went blank but then morphed into relief. "I was expecting terrible news."

"It's good news, but… it's far from here. I won't be able to visit once a month." Legally, Peter was allowed four visiting hours per month. Luckily, he was in a minimum-security prison, so the warden was more lenient, but Dad and I tried to stick with one visit each within thirty days. I suspected Maddie filled the other times so Peter didn't have any weeks alone.

"Where?" he asked, seeming genuinely interested.

"Massachusetts. Wellesley to be exact."

"Are you going to be a professor at Wellesley?"

"It's possible."

He whistled softly. "Look at you, little sis. That's great. You'll be surrounded by your kind." His laughter sounded good. "I'm proud of you, Lizzie. I really am."

My eyes became watery, but I did my best to staunch the flow. "They have some great schools for the kids there. Even Sarah is looking into law schools."

"Really?"

I nodded.

"She does love to argue and to be—"

"Right. I know." I blew out a breath.

We laughed, but his expression darkened. "Can you do me a favor?"

"Sure. What?"

"Take Maddie with you."

I hadn't expected that request. "Why?"

"She needs to move on. I know she and Gabe broke up. I think she's hoping for what she can't have."

"Are you sure she can't?"

He rubbed the stubble on his chin. "What can I offer? She deserves better. She always did."

"You know Maddie. She won't listen to me."

"She'll listen to me if I say I want her to be there for Demi. You getting this job—it's a godsend for all of us. I know things have been hard for you, even though you've never told me. Don't worry; I get it. You're a good person, which is why I want more for you as well. Get yourself and your family out of Colorado. The East Coast is filled with criminals. No one will give two shits about you there." He reached for my hand and spoke earnestly. "Leave. Promise me you'll leave. I want the best for Demi. Not for her to be hounded by my shadow."

CHAPTER THIRTY-FIVE

Returning to Fort Collins after my visit with Peter, I found Ethan in the front room with the kids, and while I didn't want to tell him the news, I knew I had to because, with the Petrie grapevine, he'd hear sooner or later. If he hadn't already.

I met Sarah's eye, and she gave me a swift nod.

"Ethan, want to have a drink with me in the office?" I asked as breezily as possible.

Ethan closed his paperback, a finger holding his spot. "Are you kicking me out?"

"Not at all! Do you really think I would do such a thing?"

Ethan checked out Sarah and then faced me again. "I don't know what to think these days. Something's going on. All the whispering and surreptitious glances."

I hated how observant he was when I didn't want him to be, and yet, he hadn't picked up on the clues about his wife stepping out of their marriage. "Come on. I could use some grappa." I didn't want any, but I knew Ethan had taken to the stuff lately and wouldn't turn it down.

The offer worked, and I tailed Ethan to the library, glancing over my shoulder to Sarah, who gave me her good luck, tight-lipped smile.

At the bar, I poured two drinks, the memory of my first sampling way back when Sarah and I dated tugging at my memories. So much had happened since that night.

"Everything okay?" Ethan asked when I handed him a glass. "You have a guilty look."

I settled on the opposite couch so I could look him in the eyes. "I do feel guilty. I just got back from visiting Peter."

"It always does a number on you." He sipped his drink, his shoulders still tense.

"It does. This time was more difficult than usual."

"Why? Is Peter okay? He wasn't—"

"No. Nothing like that." I shook my head, not wanting to think of all the things that could happen to Peter in prison, even if it wasn't full of hardened criminals. "I had to deliver some news."

Ethan seemed to brace for the next part.

I inhaled a fortifying breath. "It looks like Sarah, the kids, and I will be moving."

"Where?"

"The East Coast."

"Care to whittle that down?" He sounded a little more relaxed.

"The home of the Red Sox."

Ethan's face twisted up. "You know I hate sports."

"I do. I love that I know more about sports than you," I gloated.

"You're the dyke. I'm the scholar." He delicately splayed his fingers over his chest.

I chuckled. "Yeah, I'm the first picked for softball teams. Little do they know I suck." I looked deeply into his eyes. "Wellesley."

"That's wonderful." His smile was heartfelt.

Since he was reacting well, I launched into the thorny part of the conversation. "Sarah and I would like you to help us out."

"Please don't ask me to carry boxes or drive a U-Haul or something."

"Oh, no. I learned on Christmas Eve that you and manual labor are not friends." I sipped my drink. "We don't want to sell the house, but we'll need someone to stay here to keep it up."

Ethan glanced around the room like he'd never been in it before. "Why do you want to keep it?"

"To be close to the ski slopes."

"You don't ski, and we're two hours away from any decent runs."

"You don't know the Red Sox, but you know how close we are to the slopes? You're a maddening man when you want to be." I prepared for the next argument Sarah and I had plotted. "Sarah fell in love with this house the minute she crossed the threshold. I can't ask her to sell it because of the Petrie mess." I clutched a handful of my sweater, like Sarah had shown me. "I'm being real with you."

"What about Maddie?"

"Uh… we're hoping she comes with us." Sarah didn't know about this turn, but I doubted she'd fight it, and more than likely she would agree with Peter.

"And leave Peter."

Even Ethan had guessed the reason behind Maddie drifting away from Gabe. Ethan and Maddie had been spending more time together, and it was possible they'd had many heart-to-hearts.

"Peter asked me to take Maddie with us."

Ethan's mouth fell open. "That's going to hurt her."

"Yes, it is." I took another pull of grappa. "It really is."

Ethan stared off into the distance for many seconds. "It might be the best thing for her."

"That's Peter's hope. Besides, I think he wants Maddie to be in Demi's life. He never wanted a child with Tie, but he did with Maddie. Maybe keeping Maddie and Demi together gives some life to that dream."

Ethan nodded thoughtfully. "Are you the one who gets to tell her?"

"I think Peter will, but..."

"You get to pick up the pieces. That's your role in the Petrie family."

The words sunk in. "It is, isn't it?"

Ethan leaned forward. "Be honest with me. Are you lying about wanting to keep the house for Sarah? Are you doing this for me?"

"I'm not lying," I fibbed to the best of my ability.

His gaze didn't leave mine. After several heartbeats, he said, "Can I think about it?"

"Of course. There's always Darrell. JJ and I have joked about the two of you rooming together."

"He has a house."

"So do you."

"Only every other day."

"This place is big enough for you, Lisa, Casey, and Minnie, your cat. Hank and Gandhi will be coming with us."

Ethan stared at me.

I returned it.

"Would she go for it?" he whispered, maybe afraid of wrecking the chance before it could take root.

I knew he meant Lisa, since Sarah and I had already agreed to the house plan. "You won't know until you ask. Casey loves it here. I checked out the student to teacher ratio, and it's slightly better in Fort Collins. If you don't have a mortgage, you can send her to a private school. I know you've been wanting to do that for years."

"That would—do you think you could convince Lisa?"

"Me?" I covered my heart.

"People listen to you."

This is a turn of events we hadn't planned out. "Why can't you talk to Lisa? She's your wife. I have to deal with my own."

"I can, but she doesn't really like me these days."

"She'll always love you, ya numbskull. I've seen you together since the separation and you're still a great team. Just the dynamic has changed."

"I know that deep down, but I sincerely doubt she'd listen to me about this. Can you try? For Casey?"

"Oh, geez. Using your daughter?"

"You have a soft spot for kids and doing what's best for them." He tapped his fingertips together, not even hiding his plotting.

I let out a huff of air. "I can try, but don't think this gets you off the hook from acting like an adult."

"What if she wants De-lor-ass to spend the night?" His butchering of the woman's name made it clear I should be the one to talk to Lisa.

"I don't think that's an immediate concern."

"Have you heard anything? Have they broken up?" He perked up in his seat.

"Haven't heard a thing. I know Lisa, though, and she wouldn't do anything to hurt Casey or you."

"She had an affair."

"Okay. Let me rephrase. I don't think she's the type to throw it in your face."

We chatted for a bit longer, before Ethan exaggerated a yawn. It was nearing seven at night, the time I was learning he liked to take a soak in the tub and then read in bed. "Are we still on for pizza tomorrow night?" I asked.

"Yeppers. I'm glad dyke night isn't at a bar anymore. I'm just too old for that scene."

"You aren't alone in that. Enjoy your bath."

***

IN BED, I FILLED SARAH IN ON MY VISIT WITH PETER and talk with Ethan.

"What do you plan to tell Lisa?" She scooted farther down on the bed so the covers came to her chin.

"Can I pay you to do it?"

"Nope."

I sighed. "I feel like I'm on some type of apology tour. I'm sorry your life sucks, but mine is looking up. So best of luck, sucker!" I stuck two thumbs up in the air.

Sarah laughed. "I don't recommend saying that to Lisa."

"I won't, but can I put it into my resignation letter."

"Absolutely. Don't forget to mention you know about his admin and that he's siding with William the Worm."

"Does that make Dr. Spencer a worm?"

"He's a sad old man who's risking his legacy for pussy."

"Another great line to include in my letter." I sighed. "It's a shame, really, because before this, I held him in high esteem for his achievements. But you're right. If word gets out about his relationship with Brittany, it'd ruin everything he's worked so hard for."

"You know, you've been in possession of the rock that could bring his life crashing down. All you've had to do is expose his relationship. Did you ever consider it?"

"For a hot second." I had mentioned it when confronting Keri, but I hadn't pursued proper channels to file a complaint at the university.

"What stopped you?"

"One: I'd need hard proof." I raised a finger. "I don't really want photos of him with Brittany or love letters—" I wiggled about like I'd walked into an enclosed space filled with cockroaches.

"More likely texts. People don't pen letters anymore."

"A true shame from a historian's perspective, but you're trying to distract me. The second reason for not outing his relationship: what type of person would that make me? He's an asshole for trying to destroy me so he can keep a young woman in his bed. He's really not worth the effort to bring down, because I believe his time is coming. Karma is a bitch, and it springs obstacles into your way when you least expect it. I'll let the universe do its job." I held my palms up, my thumb joining my fingers, and made a chanting sound, like I was truly enlightened.

Sarah grinned broadly.

"Besides," I continued, "I have more important things to worry about."

"Such as?"

"Holding you while we drift off into a blissful sleep."

"Will you sleep?"

"I'm exhausted."

"You know what I mean. Will you sleep through the night and not have nightmares?"

I jerked toward her. "You know about those?"

"Yes."

"How?"

"Sometimes, you cry in your sleep. Other times, I just know they're happening. Your breathing changes, and you reach out for me before you wake. Then you try to hide it from me, so I've been letting you. No more, though. If you have a nightmare, talk to me about it."

"I'll try. I don't always understand them or—" I cut myself off.

"Or what?"

"Do you really want to hear about dreams where my own mother is trying to kill me?"

"If that's what they're about, yes, I do want you to talk about them. Have you thought about going back to therapy?"

I checked out my fitbit. "Look at the time. I need to get some shut-eye. Big day tomorrow." I rolled onto my side, pulling the covers over me.

"Tomorrow's Sunday." Sarah wrapped an arm around me. "I'll take your evasion as a yes because I know you want to be the best parent on the planet and you need to address these issues."

"I really hate it when you use emotional blackmail to get your way."

"I don't like it when you refuse to do what's best for you. Until tonight, I didn't know how bad the dreams were, but I've heard you struggle to breathe, watched you thrash out, and don't try to tell me you don't force yourself to stay awake after a nightmare until an acceptable time to get out of bed in hopes I don't notice. You're not getting any younger. You need sleep. Peaceful sleep." Her arm tightened around me. "I want you to put as much of this behind you as possible. You can't do that on your own. And I'm done hiding the fact that I know about them. I know you pride yourself on being strong. You need to learn that you are. These dreams don't make you weak. Not facing them does."

CHAPTER THIRTY-SIX

"Dr. Petrie, Dean Spencer would like to meet with you this afternoon." Brittany's snobby voice coming through the phone grated on me.

"My schedule is tight. Does he have time on Monday?"

There was a gasp on the other side. "I don't think you understand. He wants to talk to you today. Not wait an entire weekend."

"I don't think *you* understand. I have two classes, a podcast interview, and a TV segment to record. I don't have any wiggle room in my schedule."

"Is that right? You're too busy doing non-university things?" Her snobbishness kicked into screeching mode.

I laughed. "Oh, please. I noticed the department's website lists that I'm a regular on JJ's show. All of my podcast interviews get linked as well. You can't have it both ways. And, honestly, who do you think you—?"

"Who do you think you are?"

"Not William's cousin. Nor am I the one fucking Dean Spencer." So much for my taking the higher ground, but I couldn't stop. "Why don't you connect me to your boyfriend so

I can share all the things my team is unearthing about William, a former student of this university, who's been caught on camera carrying a tiki torch and chanting about white power. He's the model alum, considering he used to study the rise of Nazis and how that was terrible for human history. Now, he's using tactics straight out of *Mein Kampf* to recruit white supremacists into his delusional fold. Do you think Dean Spencer would like to learn about that? Or the president of the university? Would they like to know about your connection to William? And your role in squeezing me out because poor William can't cut it in the real world and wants to blame me for all his failings?" I took in a breath. "I've been playing nice, not wanting to stoop to your level. But sometimes people don't know when to stop. I'm done biting my lip. By all means, keep pushing me with your snotty tone, nasty looks in the hallway, smearing my reputation, and I'll make you regret it. From what I know, William is barely surviving. Living in a friend's basement, bashing out batshit crazy vitriol about *white genocide* or the *great replacement* myth. Do you want to join him? Does Dean Spencer?"

When I finally finished my rant, I realized there was a dial tone ringing in my ear, and I wondered when she'd stopped listening. Hopefully, well before my threat, because I really didn't want to go down that path. I also didn't want to be bullied anymore, so if that's what it took, maybe I had no choice. Fight fire with fire. Just to be safe, I emailed my father, briefly outlining the situation and asking for a recommendation for a lawyer.

My father rang me within seconds of sending the email. "Why didn't you tell me everything?"

"I thought I could handle it." I stuffed my laptop into my bag.

"Are you?"

"Somewhat, but I won't turn down legal guidance. Know

anyone?" I scanned my desk to ensure I had everything I needed for class.

"Leave this part to me. No one attacks my daughter. Not like this. Let's do dinner tomorrow night. Helen's been saying she needs time with the grandkids."

"Come up for the day. We've got kids galore this weekend, including Casey. Allen's staying the weekend as well."

We quickly made plans, and I texted Sarah before heading for my lecture. The fifty minutes flew by, and after addressing a handful of issues from students, I dashed back to my office, gobbling a bagel with cream cheese on the way. I had fifteen minutes before my podcast interview, and I wanted to glance at the questions and my notes again.

Sitting behind my desk, I guzzled water from my Nalgene bottle to force down a much too large bagel bite. There was a knock on my door. I suppressed a groan since I had a note on my door saying, "Recording. Do not disturb."

"Yes?" I said with annoyance in my tone.

The door swung open to reveal Dean Spencer.

Uh-oh.

"Yes?" I repeated but with trepidation, wiping cream cheese off my chin.

"Do you have a minute?"

I really didn't, but biting Brittany's head off seemed easier than battling a Pulitzer-Prize winning historian. "Sure, but I have an interview in seven minutes." I lied about the starting time, but knowing professors and their penchant for droning on, I didn't feel too terrible about it.

"There's an issue with the fall schedule. Students are petitioning to include a class on the rise of fascism."

"Okay." Did students want a class on how to become a fascist? Or how to recognize the warning signs?

"I know you're slated for Western Civ, but can you also take on a history of fascism?"

"Uh—" I'd been meaning to submit my resignation but hadn't been able to squeeze it in or curb the desire to simply write, "Fuck off!"

He waited expectantly, but I sensed some nervousness in the way his eyes flickered about not wanting to look me in the eye.

"I've been meaning to tell you." No time like the present. "I've been offered a job back East, and I've accepted."

His eyelids closed. Opened. Closed. It was hard not to equate it to a lizard. The only part missing was his tongue whipping out to grab an insect for a snack.

"Are you unhappy here?"

I nearly laughed in his face. "This opportunity fell into my lap. I'd be foolish to turn it down. I'll have my formal resignation on your desk by Monday." My eyes slid to the clock in the corner of my laptop. "I'm sorry, but my interview is about to start ."

He stood in the doorway for a tick too long. Would I have to shoo him away with a flick of the hand? That didn't seem like a wise choice.

Finally, he said, "Let's chat on Monday. I'm sure something can be worked out."

It already has, you pathetic mother fucker. "Sounds great. Have a fab weekend!"

He closed the door, and I slumped in my chair, completely drained.

CHAPTER THIRTY-SEVEN

On Saturday morning, Lisa dropped off Casey so Allen could take her to their Russian lesson, and then the two planned to come back to our house to tackle another puzzle.

"Ethan mentioned you wanted to talk to me," Lisa said.

I glared at Ethan, who sat in his chair in the front room, pretending to read a novel. He had the nerve to say that, but not to have the house tête-à-tête with his wife. Sure, they were heading to divorce court, but did that really mean I had to step in? Apparently.

"Oh, right." I snapped my fingers. "Let's go into the library."

Maddie made a *mwahahaha* sound, but Sarah's stink eye forced Maddie to stop.

In the library, I motioned for Lisa to take a seat and asked, "Would you like a drink?"

"Do I need one?" She crossed her legs.

"Depends on your definition."

"Do you have water?"

"Yep." I grabbed a bottled water from the fridge.

"I hear congrats are in order." She twisted the cap off her drink.

"Thanks." So Ethan had enough nerve to tell her I was moving but not the other tidbit. Or had she heard from Gabe? "I know you're worried about me leaving and Ethan's living situation."

"It's crossed my mind." Her nervous smile was like a dagger.

"I feel terrible the way it's worked out. I—"

"It's okay, Lizzie. You're not responsible for Ethan. Or me. Or Casey."

"I disagree. All of you are part of my family. You three have been by my side during some of my roughest moments. I won't forget that. Now that we're moving this summer, I need to ask you for more."

Her eyebrows shot up.

"Don't worry. I'm not going to ask you to pack any boxes. Everyone has made it clear our friendship ends there." I chuckled at my lame attempt to lighten the mood. "It's the house. Sarah doesn't want to sell our first home together. I've asked Ethan to hold down the fort."

The relief on her face was evident, and her shoulders returned to their normal tension.

"There's more."

Her face crumpled into confusion.

"I'm not sure how to propose this, but this is a big house. Plenty of room for my family of six and two friends."

Her bewilderment didn't clear. It'd be great during awkward times if people could read my mind.

"What I'm trying to say is you and Casey are welcome to live here as well."

Her upper body stiffened. "Did Ethan put you up to this?"

"Partly. I'm not suggesting this as a way to repair your marriage. I have no say in that—"

"Do you hate me?" She hid behind her water bottle.

"Uh... how do you mean?" Did she think my asking her to stay in the house was my way to punish her?

"For the affair?"

"Oh, that." I tugged at a string on my sweater. "As far as I'm concerned, it's none of my business. It's been hard to watch how it's affecting Ethan, but if you're asking if I hold it against you, I don't. Maybe when I was in my early twenties, before I learned how hard and lonely life can be, I would have thought differently. As I approach middle age, I'm more of a *live and let live* type."

"How would you react if Sarah cheated on you?"

"I'd probably crumble at first."

She nodded, her bottom lip quivering. "I do love her."

I really hoped so, because tearing a marriage apart for a bit of fun still seemed reprehensible to me, no matter my *live and let live* line. I didn't think I should say that, though. "Does she love you?"

"Yes. This hasn't been easy. Not to sound overly selfish, but after my mom died, I realized my time on this planet would be short, and I wanted happiness. She makes me happy."

By the giddiness in her eyes, I could see it was true. "Are you two planning on... living together?"

"Not anytime soon. Casey doesn't know about Lola, and I really don't know how to tell her. This will play out over time."

I didn't envy Lisa on that front. "Speaking of Casey and circling back to the house. We wouldn't charge any of you rent. I know you and Ethan wanted to put Casey into private school. I don't know the particulars of your finances, but if you didn't have a mortgage... perhaps... private school would be feasible."

"You'd do that?"

I would have paid for Casey's schooling, but I knew neither Lisa nor Ethan would accept that. This was a possible solution to a couple of thorny issues. "I'm not saying it would be easy for the two of you to live under the same roof, but if you can manage cohabitating, it might behoove your daughter. It's no secret she's smarter than all of us put together. I'd like for her to be given the opportunity to flourish."

Lisa seemed to mull over my words. "I just don't know how it would work."

I had no fucking idea. "Yeah, it's not something to agree to on the spot. Think it over. Discuss it with Lola. With Ethan. Because I'm done with this part. I'll always be there for the three of you, but you and Ethan are adults and parents to a wonderful daughter. Time to step up." I chuckled. "Really, I never thought I'd be the rational one out of all of us. When did this happen to me?"

She offered me a beguiling smile. "You've always sold yourself short. Ethan has told me on many occasions he admires your inner strength. He looks up to you, Lizzie. I do, too. You and Sarah are amazing parents, with enough love for everyone in your life. I have no idea how you hold it together. Maybe you should teach a class on how to juggle everything when the world is crumbling around you."

The last thing I needed was adding more people with problems expecting me to guide them through rough seas, but I didn't say that to her. Instead I said, "Please. Talk to Ethan. He's hurting and terrified about ending up all alone."

"I'd never let that happen." There was defiance in her eyes.

"I know. You need to convince him of that. Relationships evolve, but when you have a kid together, you have to do what's best for the child. Maybe start family therapy and figure out a way for everyone to be as happy as possible. You can end a marriage, but you can't end a family."

"How'd it go?" Sarah whispered in my ear.

"Why does everyone expect me to clean up their messes?" I reached into the fridge for a bottle of sparkling water, wanting bubbles to help settle my stomach.

"That good, huh?"

"It was fine. Uncomfortable but fine, I guess." I drank heavily from the bottle, making me burp. "Excuse me."

"Your dad and Helen are here."

"Oh, shit. I completely forgot they were coming. Did I even tell you about it?"

"You sent me a text yesterday."

"I did?"

She felt my forehead with her hand. "Are you getting sick? You're long overdue since you didn't over the holidays."

"Nope. I just can't remember sh-shitake these days."

Sarah kissed my cheek. "Breathe, Lizzie. Everything's going to be okay. Do you need some alone time?"

"Can we get away with that?"

She gave me a *don't be crazy* look. "Not suggesting whatever you're hoping for. Gandhi needs to go for a walk before I kill him."

"Yes. I can do that. Really, I'm surprised I didn't figure out dogs are the best way to escape a house full of family and friends. Maybe we can get more, and I can walk them all separately."

"That's just what we need. More creatures to take care of."

Before I could escape the house with the demented yorkie, my father found me. "I'll join you two."

Sarah gave me a *you can't win them all* shrug.

It was a beautiful spring day, the temperature hovering in the upper fifties. Snow was predicted by Monday, so wearing a T-shirt with a puffer vest felt like a luxury.

"How are you hanging in?" Dad walked beside me, his hands in his trouser pockets.

"Getting everything and everyone in line so I can skedaddle." Gandhi sniffed a patch of the sidewalk with such intensity, and for the life of me, I couldn't figure out what was so interesting about the spot. "How's the planning for your move?"

"Fine." His voice was gruffer than normal.

"How are you doing?" I laid a hand on his shoulder.

"Retirement is going to take some getting used to."

"I imagine. One of my prevalent memories of you from my childhood is your nose always buried in the *Financial Times*. Is retirement what you want?"

"I don't think I have a choice if I want to save the company. Trust is important. No one trusts a CEO whose own son is in prison for cheating the system. If I don't leave, the board will vote me out. This way I get to leave with some dignity." He grunted. "I envy you and Allen. Both of you are getting fresh starts at a young age."

"Has Allen heard from BU?"

"Not yet, but I imagine it'll work out."

Translation, Dad still had enough pull to get his youngest into school. "You're getting a fresh start in Santa Fe. You won't be working, but you get to travel with Helen. Set up a house together. Have visits from your grandkids. Is Ollie too young to fly by herself?" I nudged his side.

He chuckled. "She has a mind of her own."

We crossed the street to head back toward the house on the other side so Gandhi could sniff more random patches of concrete. Dogs were goofy, but this made him happy, so who was I to judge.

"What's weighing on your mind?" he asked.

I chewed on the meaty part of my left cheek. "I'm worried about leaving. Ethan is a mess. Peter's in prison. We've become good friends with JJ and her family. Gabe will be on his own all the while taking over the shops. And…" I glanced up at the brilliant sky over the front range. "I've never lived outside of Colorado. Not even for college. What if I'm nothing more than a Rocky Mountain rube?" One who compares Cheyenne to New York City.

My father tugged on my arm to get me to stop. "Elizabeth, you're an amazing woman. No matter what you put your mind to, you succeed. You've beaten Graves' disease and overcome a difficult childhood. You're landing on your feet after the Peter mess. I know leaving your friends will be rough, but in today's world, it's easy to stay in touch. You've been there for everyone through so much. Don't think it's selfish to take care of yourself. You owe it to Sarah and your children. This move will be the best thing for all of you. I just know it."

CHAPTER THIRTY-EIGHT

Monday night, I walked into the kitchen with a fat legal-sized envelope tucked under my arm.

"What's that?" Sarah asked.

"My life."

"It fits into an envelope. Aren't you lucky?"

"Very funny. It's all the paperwork for the new job and move." I tossed it onto the counter with a thud.

"So it contains all of our lives." Sarah eyed it with awe. "It's kinda petrifying how that"—she pointed at the yellow envelope—"has all the details about our future."

"It is. And I need to sign and initial the papers by midnight."

Sarah checked the time on the microwave. "Five hours."

"Yep."

"Are you getting cold feet?"

"Yep."

"Luckily for you, I've prepared for this." She pulled a pen out of her pocket.

"You knew I had to sign the papers today?"

"Nope. But I knew it was soon. I've been carrying this for

days now." She pulled the papers out of the envelope and clicked the pen. "Get signing."

"Shouldn't we take a moment to discuss this further?"

"If you don't start signing, I will do it for you. I've been doing it for years on credit card slips because you can't figure out a twenty-percent tip."

"You can't forge my signature on our future."

"I can, and I will. This is the right thing for our family."

"But i-it's not legal," I stuttered, unable to think of anything clever to stall for more time.

"Are you going to have me arrested?"

"You aren't playing fairly." I sat on a barstool and cradled my chin. "It's a big decision."

"It was when we made it weeks ago. You've already given your word, which to you is more important. This is just an annoying formality."

"But we'll have to box up our lives." I looked at the stuff just in the kitchen.

"Not everything. We're leaving some stuff behind for Ethan's family."

"Not my books."

"No one will take your swastika books."

"But—"

Sarah took the pen and placed the nub on the first line. "Are you going to make me commit a crime, or will you be woman enough to put your own John Hancock on this?"

"You're cheating. Using a historical reference."

"I'm terrible that way." She put the pen in my hand and wrapped her fingers around mine. "Let's do it together."

I fought her when she tried to move the pen. "I don't know if I can do it."

"I know you can. Let's start with a section where you only have to initial. That's not a big commitment, right?"

"Baby steps."

"Baby steps," she repeated in the sweetest and most supportive voice.

When it came to the last signature, Sarah let go of my hand.

"I thought we were doing this together."

She smiled at me. "I know you can do it."

"Fine." I signed the last page. "But you get to scan and email everything."

Sarah swept the pages into her hand. "Already planned on it."

***

That night, both of us had tablets in our hands, checking out houses on Zillow. "Holy shit. This three-bedroom, two bath is seven hundred thousand." I squinted. "It's cute. Yellow. That says home, right?" I showed Sarah the screen.

"Why are you looking at three-bedrooms?"

"I put seven hundred and fifty as the ceiling for the price."

"That amount works for Colorado. Not Massachusetts. Look at this place."

"Four million!"

"Don't look at the price." She tried to cover that part of the screen with a finger.

"How can I not when you're being completely unreasonable?"

"Me?" She shook my iPad. "How do you figure our family will squeeze into a house that's only thirteen hundred square feet?"

"I can commute. We don't need to live in Wellesley. Let me look." I tapped the screen. "Here's a nine bedroom with three baths for half a million."

She grabbed the device from me, bringing it close to her face. "It's in Worcester."

"Yes. That's in Massachusetts." On my phone, I looked up the distance. "There's a train from Worcester to Wellesley. Boom!" I mimed dropping a mic.

Sarah typed something into the search bar of her tablet. After a couple of minutes, she said, "Want to hear how much private school is in Worcester? Thirty thousand per kid."

"Why private school?"

"Because after just a cursory glance at reviews online, the public options are a hard no. Then there's your house. Look at the photos. It needs a new roof. There's no yard. The siding is falling off. To make it habitable, we're talking easily another hundred thousand. So, thirty thousand per kid for seventeen years is over one million."

"Why seventeen years? Kindergarten to grade twelve is thirteen years, isn't it?" On my phone, I pulled up the calculator and subtracted five from eighteen.

"You're conveniently forgetting preschool. Not to mention college."

"Is preschool that much?"

"It's not cheap," she said in all seriousness.

"You're a teacher. You can homeschool the kids all the way through high school."

Her head whipped around, and she gave me a look that conveyed that was never happening, and if I pressed my luck, we'd never have sex again.

I didn't say a word or move a muscle.

She returned her attention to her tablet. "The commute by train is one hour. Not to mention the distance to and from train stations on both ends. The winters are brutal. Do you really want to commute two to three hours a day?"

"I don't want to fork over four million for a house," I pouted.

"It's a beautiful house," she defended.

"It's four million dollars. Do I look like a woman who would pay that for a house?"

"Do I look like a woman who'll take care of your brood and homeschool them so we can live in a shitty neighborhood where I couldn't let the kids play in the front yard because there is no front yard?" Again, her finger pounded on her iPad. "According to the FBI, the crime rate in Worcester is ninety-eight percent higher than all the cities and towns of the same size in Massachusetts. And in Wellesley…" More finger tapping. "It's eighty-two percent lower than the national average. National. Not state."

"Because no one can afford to live there!"

Sarah sucked in a breath and steepled her fingers. "Can you just put the dollar amount aside?"

"You've met me, right?" I picked up her tablet and pulled up the house screen. "The estimated monthly payment for your house is twenty-thousand. Who pays that a month? That's what some people make in a year."

"We'll have to put down a chunk."

"Not happening."

Sarah stared at me.

I returned the glare.

"Fine." She continued looking through the Wellesley options. "What about this house?"

I scanned the screen. "Three mill is still a bazillion miles from my comfort zone."

Sarah continued to scroll through the options. "Here's one."

"No," I said without looking.

"If you keep this up, you can live in Worcester in your nine-bedrooms all by yourself, and the kids and I will stay here."

I grumbled.

"It's a five-bedroom for one point five." Sarah shoved her tablet in front of me. "It has an office for you. Look at all the space for your swastika books."

"You've tricked me before with books."

"What?"

"When you wanted to buy this house. You kept taking me shopping for used books and said, *Now, we have to buy a house.*" I spoke in a shrill voice.

"I sound nothing like that."

"Have you listened to yourself when screaming?"

"Look at the fucking house. Now!"

"There's the shrill."

She gave me the death glare.

"It's yellow."

"You seem to like yellow houses. Who knew?"

I scrolled through the photos. "The yard is really nice."

She cuddled up to me. "It is."

I looked back at the dingy house in Worcester. "Thirty thousand per kid for school?"

"Yes. Add up what it would cost us over the years, and it works out to be more than the price of this house."

"That's not possible." I used the calculator again to multiply thirty thousand by four and then by seventeen years. "Over two million," I said in a defeated tone. "Why are houses so expensive?" I sulked.

"We got ours during a buyer's market. You need to get this price out of your head. You also need to get Colorado prices out of your head. And you are not moving our kids to a place with such a terrible crime rate. What if Freddie got shot?"

"Don't you ever say such a thing."

"I know you love being in the top two percent, but not when it comes to crime."

"It's probably not all violent crime. I'm sure it includes people breaking into cars."

"Still not okay to play Russian roulette with our children."

She was right, and I closed the screen on my tablet. "I'm not looking forward to our house-hunting trip."

"I can go with Maddie."

"And buy a four-million-dollar home. Nope."

"You don't trust me to be reasonable."

"You started at four."

"Because I knew if I started at one point five you'd freak out."

I glared at her, the pieces slotting into my brain. "You already looked at houses and planned this. Did you also have all the stats for private schools and the crime rate?"

"For the most part. I didn't know you'd suggest Worcester, though. Have you even been there?"

"No."

"You really do amaze me sometimes. We have an appointment on Saturday at the one-point-five house you secretly want but are too stubborn to admit." She patted my cheek.

"You're conniving!" I wagged my finger in her face.

"You're really going to hate the next part."

I waved for her to spit it out.

"Your father overheard me talking with Maddie about the house. He's putting down half."

"No... I can't allow that." I shook my head back and forth, unable to stop.

"He paid for Peter's house."

"Look how that worked out for Peter."

"Your father buying Peter a house didn't put him in prison. Peter put Peter in prison."

"I promised myself never to take money like Peter did." I flicked my hands up in the air. "I want to succeed on my own."

"You have, and you'll continue to do so."

"But half of the house will belong to Dad."

"No, it won't."

"It will in my head."

"Fine. Legally it won't. Can you, for once, set your stupid

pride aside and do what's right without fighting? I'm tired of arguing with you."

"Do you mean tonight or forever?"

"Keep pushing and it'll be forever."

"Can I see the house again?"

Sarah handed me the tablet, saying, "I can see our family in this house. Grilling in the backyard on the Fourth. It has a gourmet kitchen. You can't go in there, ever. Do they still have Easy Bake ovens? I might trust you with one of those. Might."

Curious, I looked them up on my phone. "Yes, but they're on a list of toys that should never have been released." I continued reading. "Oh, one girl had to have part of a finger amputated."

"That's a no, then. You can't have one. I like your fingers."

"Did the finger end up in the cake, you think?" I looked back at the webpage, but it was silent on this issue.

"Sometimes, I really don't understand the way your brain works." She laughed. "Please, keep an open mind."

"About the house or cake mishaps?" I joked.

She treated me to a death stare.

"Tough crowd. Shall I use all ten of my fingers to convince you to lighten up?" I wiggled them in the air.

Sarah rolled onto her stomach. "I'd love a massage."

"Nicely played."

She glanced over her shoulder, her expression hitting all the right buttons. "One step at a time."

CHAPTER THIRTY-NINE

It was a stunning July day, and basically everyone I knew, aside from Peter, was over for a going-away bash.

Dr. and Mrs. Marcel arrived, the kindly professor with a six-pack tucked under one of his arms.

"Whatcha drinking?" I asked.

"Not sure. One of our boys left it." He held it out and read, "Voodoo Ranger IPA. Would you like one?"

"Oh, I have enough trouble in my life. No need to add voodoo. But let me get you some chilled glasses. It's boiling, and the hottest part of the afternoon hasn't hit yet."

"Are you another one?" Mrs. Marcel asked and jerked a thumb to Dr. Marcel. "He's always checking the temperature."

I raised my arm. "My fitbit has a weather app." I showed Dr. Marcel and then took the beer from him, unable to stand watching him hold it another second.

"I never wanted one before, but that is handy. What other apps does it have?"

"We're breaking Lizzie in slowly." Sarah looped an arm

around my waist. "It came preloaded with others, but she only uses the weather app."

"Why do I need a Starbucks app? You don't let me have sugary drinks anymore. Would both of you like some Voodoo?"

Dr. Marcel nodded, and Mrs. Marcel requested a chilled white wine.

While I was in the kitchen, Ethan came from the dining room. "She's here."

"Who?" I located a chilled pint glass for Dr. Marcel. "Would you like a Voodoo?"

"Do you have a doll of De-lor-ass I can poke pins into?" He demonstrated this with too much demented glee in his expression.

I sucked my lips into my mouth. "You promised you wouldn't cause a scene."

"I'm not."

I made a circle in the air with my fingers. "This behavior doesn't elicit much confidence you'll be able to hold it together. Do I need to lock you in the basement?"

Ethan shoved his hands in his pockets. "No. I'll... try."

I sighed. "Please try really hard. If you start to crack, come to me. You can rant and rave all you want to me and only me." I gripped each of his shoulders, being reminded how tall he is, and stared through his coke-bottle thick glasses. "This is for your daughter. She needs to know her parents will always be friends and a cohesive parental unit."

"I know," he said, his head hanging low. "It's hard."

"I'm not saying it isn't." After spying the groupings of people in the yard, I said, "Can you take these drinks to Dr. and Mrs. Marcel? Keep talking to peeps who are on the other side of the party."

After dispatching Ethan, I took a moment to center myself. When I turned around I bumped into Lisa and Lola. "Hey there. I'm Lizzie. Welcome to the party."

Lola, a short brunette with nerdy glasses, a Great Gatsby T-shirt, much like the one Ethan used to have, and linen shorts was a bit of a shock to my system. I'd been expecting a demure and confident woman who turned heads because she'd brought Lisa to the lezzie side. I felt like an ass for making so many assumptions.

"Thanks for the invite."

"What can I get you?" I pressed my palms together, but Sarah came into the kitchen with a screaming Ollie and an upset Fred.

"I got this part." Lisa shooed me away to help.

I went to Sarah and the twins. Getting to their level, I asked, "What's the matter, you two?"

Freddie, in his pink T-shirt with a rainbow unicorn, hugged his stuffed animal. "Monk-ee."

I squinted up at Sarah, since Freddie usually appeased his sister and gave her his toy, but we'd been working on both of them. Was he following our direction to stand up for himself, or was the heat making him cranky?

I tugged on Ollie's Wonder Woman shirt and said in a firm voice, "Olivia, we've talked about this. You can't steal Fred's monkey. You have your own."

"Want!" Ollie screamed, tears streaming down her reddened cheeks.

"I think they both need a nap," Sarah said. "I'm going to take them upstairs."

"Do you want help?" I stood, shaking out the tightness in my right knee.

"Oh, this is just another day for me. I got it." Sarah kissed my cheek and herded the twins upstairs.

"She really is an amazing woman." Gabe grinned and slugged some beer straight from the bottle.

I nodded and flipped to face him. "Speaking of women, I hear you're dating someone."

He shuffled in his flip-flops and puffed out his chest. "You heard right."

"Did you bring her?"

Gabe shook his head. "I think introducing Lola is enough for one Petrie party."

We looked at Ethan, who was at Maddie's side, the two of them in conversation with the Marcels. It was going to be hard on Ethan since Maddie, like Peter had predicted, wanted to come with us to be close to Demi.

"Will you keep an eye on him for me? He can be annoying, but he's my best friend and..." My nose started to burn, and I couldn't finish the sentence.

"I will, and I'm asking you to take care of our baby brother. He's a lot like Ethan. Sensitive."

Again, the two of us found the man in question standing next to Bailey and Janice, who had flown out for the party and for some time in the Rocky Mountains with her husband and kids.

"Has Allen said what he and Bailey plan to do about their relationship?" I asked Gabe.

"They're going to try long-distance dating," Gabe said without any confidence.

"With all of us heading to Massachusetts and Helen and my dad moving to Santa Fe, you're going to be alone. Are you going to be okay?"

"I'm not alone. There's Ethan, Lisa, and Casey. And, Peter's here."

I flinched. "Have you seen him?"

"I went last week. We had a good talk."

Did they commiserate about Maddie or being left by everyone? Both? It wasn't my business, so I didn't ask.

Gabe drifted to Lisa and Lola, the three at ease with each other.

Sarah came back downstairs and put an arm around my shoulders. "How are you doing?"

I surveyed our friends and family outside. "It's such an unnerving feeling."

"What?"

"Saying goodbye."

She pulled me closer. "Don't think of it as saying goodbye. Everyone out there is part of this family. They'll always be in our lives."

By five in the evening, the party was starting to run out of steam. My father, maybe sensing people would start to leave, got to his feet and said, "If you don't mind, I'd like to say a few words." He met my eyes. "You constantly amaze me. The past few years have included a lot of shocks, family secrets, and worse. You've been a pillar of strength for everyone, and you always have room in your heart for more family members. You, Lizzie, are such a special woman. I'm proud of you, and I wish you and your brood the best of luck in Wellesley." He raised his beer glass, and the other guests joined.

"Speech!" Maddie cupped her mouth and chanted the word, with Ethan joining her.

I snorted, but Sarah raised her brow, implying I should say something, and she tugged on her tank top in a way of giving me a glimpse of the girls, which were no longer off-limits. I got the message. If I behaved, I'd be rewarded. "You don't play fair," I whispered in her ear.

"You're just noticing?" She treated me to her *I want you* expression, and my knees wobbled.

I stood in the center of everyone, not a place I ever relished, but it seemed to be my new role in the Petrie family. As Sarah told me, I was the glue. It was stressful, but looking around at all the faces, I knew I didn't want to have it any other way.

I coughed to get rid of the lump in my throat. "I have no idea what to say, really. Some of you I've known for years—" I looked to the Marcels, Ethan, Janice, and Maddie. "Others, I'm just getting to know." I met Helen's and my brothers' eyes. Then JJ and her family. "Even a new person who I just met today." I tipped my glass in Lola's direction. "Poor thing. You already have to listen to me lecture." Most chuckled. I felt my eyes start to water, and I cleared my throat again.

There was silence, but I still had everyone's attention.

"Sorry. I think being a parent is making me soft." I wiped away a tear, and much to my shock, no one cracked a joke. I think everyone was in the same boat, and I saw Maddie rest her head on Ethan's shoulder. "A wise woman told me earlier that this party isn't about saying goodbye. Because it's not." I took the time to look around. "It's about until we see each other next time. I can't live without any of you. Even the pain in the asses. You know who you are." There was more crying than laughing. "I love all of you, and I'm lucky to have such an amazing family. All of us may not have the same last name, but I consider each and every one of you an integral part of who I am. To the Petries!" I raised my glass.

EPILOGUE

Sunlight streamed into the bedroom, and I rolled onto my side, pulling a pillow over my head to blunt out the intrusion.

There was a shushing sound, followed by the pitter-patter of feet. And then little bodies climbing on top of me.

"Wake, Mommy!" Ollie commanded.

There were giggles.

Carefully, so I wouldn't squash any of the kids, I rolled onto my back, cracking one eye open.

Demi stared at me and then said, "Mommy, wake!"

She'd never called me that before. My gaze found Sarah in the room, and I quirked an eyebrow, while I pulled Demi into my arms and kissed her forehead. "Mommy's awake now, baby girl."

Sarah grinned, but I could see in the crinkles around her eyes the emotions of Demi calling me mommy.

"Hungry?" Fred asked.

"Famished. Did you eat, Freddie?" I tweaked his nose.

He nodded.

"At least three full bites of oatmeal." Sarah settled on the edge of the bed, Fred climbing into her lap so she could tickle his stomach.

I fluffed a pillow behind me and put my arms out for the girls to snuggle with me. "What's the plan today?"

Sarah eyed me. "Are you sure you're up for anything? You didn't get home until late."

"It's Saturday. Family day." I stifled a yawn. "After two cups of tea."

"Maddie has that covered. She's even making you pancakes."

"Is that right? What'd she do?"

Sarah laughed. "I don't think she's in trouble. She's just being nice."

"I'll believe it when I see it."

"Okay, kids. Let Mommy get up." Sarah set Fred on the floor, and he toddled toward the doorway, followed by the girls.

When it was just the two of us, Sarah asked, "How was the trip?"

I covered a yawn and stretched my arms overhead. "Good. You'll be happy to hear Ethan, Lisa, and Casey have the house decked out for Christmas. Casey wants a dog from Santa, and she's wearing down Ethan."

"How's Peter?" Sarah rested her hand on my stomach.

"As well as can be expected. His lawyers are hopeful his continuing cooperation into a case the feds are working on will help him get an early release."

"That would be great." Sarah didn't sound too excited, and I understood why.

"He's talking about going back to California. A small beach town to enjoy the surf and sun. I think he just wants to disappear, but not in a city. He kept saying he'd suffocate here or anywhere with too many people."

"What about Demi?" she whispered.

"He's looking forward to getting reacquainted with his

niece in small doses. Besides, he still has two years if he doesn't get out early. It's strange hearing him being completely rational about the reality of his life. He's nothing like the Peter I grew up with. The braggart has been replaced by a calm and thoughtful man. His hair is nearly all gray now."

Sarah nodded with heavy sadness. "Did you sleep?"

"I did. Really well, actually."

She regarded me for a few seconds. "When's the last time you had a nightmare?"

I closed one eye and looked at the ceiling. "I don't know. It's been ages."

"I can tell. You don't have that haunted look in your eyes. Come on. Let's get tea in you. It's almost noon."

DOWNSTAIRS, ROSE AND MADDIE WERE IN THE kitchen chatting and making a breakfast feast. Calvin was in his bouncy chair, grinning ear to ear when he saw me. I freed him and held him close. "How's my youngest?"

He cooed.

"It lives," Maddie declared, flipping a pancake over on the griddle.

"Not fully. Tea." I held out my free hand, Frankenstein-like.

"With sugar." Maddie presented me a mug. "How's Ethan?"

"Doing well, but you'll see him in a couple of days. We can't have a Petrie Christmas without all our family members. Dad, Helen, and Gabe will be here on the twenty-third." I sipped my drink, heaving a satisfying smile. "Lots of sugar. What's the deal?"

"I know how much you like it." Maddie opened the oven door. "You ready for pancakes?"

"Always, but what's the occasion?" I fixed a cautious stare on Maddie.

She chuckled. "I see your paranoia hasn't disappeared. Not entirely."

"When you start acting like the perfect roommate, it sets off alarm bells."

"Hello, Lizzie. Welcome home." Troy kissed Rose's cheek and then swiped a crispy bacon slice from the baking sheet. "Breakfast for lunch. I like it."

"Someone just got out of bed," Maddie teased.

"Someone didn't get to bed until after six in the morning." I had an overnight flight from Denver and arrived in Boston at five in the morning.

"It'll be good to see everyone. Is Lola coming?" Maddie placed a serving platter on the table and removed her oven mitts.

"Nope. Ethan hasn't reached that level of acceptance yet. But she does come over to the house for meals a couple times a week." I took a seat at the table with Calvin on my lap, bobbing him up and down on my knee.

Rose and Sarah rounded up the toddlers, placing them in their high chairs.

Troy poured a tumbler of OJ. "Anyone else?"

I shook my head, but Rose and Sarah took him up on the offer.

With everyone seated, I asked again, "So, what's the plan today?"

"We're taking the kids to Old Sturbridge Village this evening. There'll be caroling, a Christmas tree lighting, and the kids can get their photos with Santa." Sarah poured syrup over a pancake.

"They also have hot chocolate and apple cider donuts." Maddie munched on a slice of bacon. "That's the only reason I'm going to a living nineteenth century village that's stuck in the past at night in December."

The village, which consisted of antique buildings and a

farm, had been a hit with the kids when we took them during the summer. Those who worked there wore costumes, and it was like stepping back in time.

"And, here I thought you were the best aunt on the planet." I placed a maple-syrup-soaked bite of pancake into my mouth.

"I am," she said.

"Then no complaining." I handed Fred half a grape, and he put it on his fingertip like a helmet. "Oh, wait." I shook my head to get rid of the exhaustion behind my eyelids. "Didn't you have a date while I was in Colorado?"

Maddie's cheeks reddened. "I did."

"And...?" I motioned for her to fill in the blanks.

Maddie shoved pancake into her mouth.

"They've had dinner twice now," Sarah filled me in. "And, she's coming with us tonight."

I sat back in my seat. "Is that right?"

Maddie met my eyes. "She also likes hot chocolate and donuts."

"Does she have a name?"

"Alex. She owns a photography studio, and she adores Maddie's modern version of Norman Rockwell subjects." Sarah smiled at me. "There's going to be an exhibit of the photos Maddie has taken, including a few of us in the spring."

"Isn't that something?" I said to the kids, who paid me zero attention. "At least the fame isn't going to their heads."

Ollie, perhaps sensing this was her moment, started to cry.

Fred gave her a banana slice.

Demi handed her a piece of bacon.

Ollie, like a queen, took the offerings with a nod of her head.

"It's good to be home," I said.

"It's good to have you home. I want to work on the basement before we leave this afternoon. There are still a ton of boxes that have to be dealt with. How did we accumulate so much stuff?" Sarah spoke more to Maddie and her mom.

I envisioned taping up boxes with kid stuff we wouldn't need until Calvin was a bit older, unpacking other boxes, and sorting through kid clothes, determining which should be saved or donated.

"You know, if we had to make all of our clothes and furniture, we wouldn't have nearly as much junk," I said.

"Says the woman who takes twenty-minute hot showers." Sarah finished her pancake.

"Please, I haven't been able to do that in years." I gazed at our children and then met Sarah's eyes. "Let's get cracking on the basement project."

"You don't seem upset about it," Maddie observed. "I thought you'd kick up a fuss."

"What can I say? I'm happy." I half covered my mouth. "Besides, I started a new audiobook, and I'm looking forward to slipping on my headphones so I don't have to listen to you moan."

"Some things don't change." Sarah rose to her feet, smiling.

I got up, with Calvin on my hip. "Isn't that a good thing?"

"It's much better than when you went into full-on meltdown over the mere suggestion we should move in together way back in the day."

"I never did such a thing."

Everyone laughed.

"We have four children. A beautiful house. Our entire extended family is coming for Christmas. What proof do you have that I'm a commitment-phobe?" I asked with a smug smile.

"For a historian, you like to conveniently forget certain things." Sarah placed a hand on her hip.

"For a woman, you like to keep reminding me." I preempted a nasty retort by kissing her on the lips. "I'm looking forward to the next fifty years with you. All the good, the bad, and the ugly times."

"Can we focus on the good?" Sarah took Calvin from my arms.

"Every day with my family is perfect." I surveyed the room. "Absolutely perfect."

AUTHOR'S NOTE

Thank you for reading *A Woman Complete*. If you enjoyed the novel, please consider leaving a review on Goodreads or Amazon. No matter how long or short, I would very much appreciate your feedback. You can follow me, T. B. Markinson, on Twitter at @IHeartLesfic or email me at tbm@tbmarkinson.com. I would love to know your thoughts.

ABOUT THE AUTHOR

TB Markinson is an American who's recently returned to the US after a seven-year stint in the UK and Ireland. When she isn't writing, she's traveling the world, watching sports on the telly, visiting pubs in New England, or reading. Not necessarily in that order.

Her novels have hit Amazon bestseller lists for lesbian fiction and lesbian romance.

Feel free to visit TB's website (lesbianromancesbytbm.com) to say hello. On the *Lesbians Who Write* weekly podcast, she and Clare Lydon dish about the good, the bad, and the ugly of writing. TB also runs I Heart Lesfic, a place for authors and fans of lesfic to come together to celebrate and chat about lesbian fiction.

Want to learn more about TB. Hop over to her *About* page on her website for the juicy bits. Okay, it won't be all that titillating, but you'll find out more.

Printed in Poland
by Amazon Fulfillment
Poland Sp. z o.o., Wrocław